Turnabout

Turnabout

Jeremiah Healy

Five Star • Waterville, Maine

Five Star First Edition Mystery Series.

First Edition, Second Printing.

Published in 2001 in conjunction with Tekno Books and Ed Gorman.

Set in 11 pt. Plantin by Minnie B. Raven.

Printed in the United States on permanent paper.

Library of Congress Cataloging-in-Publication Data

Healy, J. F. (Jeremiah F.), 1948–
    Turnabout / Jeremiah Healy.
       p. cm.—(Five Star first edition mystery series)
    ISBN 0-7862-3561-6 (hc : alk. paper)
    1. Security consultants—Fiction. 2. Kidnapping—
Fiction. 3. Grandchildren—Fiction. 4. Generals—
Fiction. I. Title. II. Series.
PS3558.E2347 T87 2001
813'.54—dc21   2001050177

Turnabout

Chapter One

Propped up is better than lying flat, I think. With the pillows behind me, at least I can see the room. Out of the corner of my eye, the late afternoon sun rations cones of light through the window. Dust motes float like fireflies, flickering off when they reach the shaded areas. It's not so bad when the music is playing, but the disk jockey's FM voice and weak patter and constant reminders of the time make me . . . Jesus. But with just the music, I can think, think back to what happened . . .

General Alexander Van Horne telephoned me at Fred Dooley's and my office in Somerville. 9:03 a.m. on a Monday morning in October, 1988. His words said, "Langway, we have a security problem. Could you be here within the hour?"

Those were only his words, though. His voice said, "Jump, Langway!" When a man like Van Horne says jump, you don't ask why, and you don't even ask how high. You just jump as high as you can and pray to God it's high enough.

The General had spent his military career riding tanks in our army and his subsequent civilian career selling tanks to a lot of armies. He'd done well by both, well enough to have his own estate in Beacon Harbor, twenty miles north of Boston on the coast. The previous April, he'd wanted a check run on the estate's security system. Given a twenty-seven room house on forty acres with perimeter fence, no small task. The General contacted my former supervisor at the FBI's Boston office, who said he'd been sorry to lose Fred and me and vouched for us as qualified private security consultants. It seemed a hell of a good assignment, especially given our cash flow needs at the time. The head of security at the estate, an automaton named Turgeon, got his nose out of joint over being second-guessed. But the fact was Turgeon had missed some things, so the General got his money's worth and we got a solid, satisfied customer.

Until that Monday morning.

I got off Route 128 at the Beacon Harbor exit, the Chevy S-10 Blazer complaining on the ramp's tight curve. With all the gear we had to haul around, however, some kind of utility vehicle made sense, and Fred's then brother-in-law got us a deal.

Beacon Harbor itself was a small New England center, carefully maintained. A gazebo for band concerts sat in the middle of the town green. Opposite the four sides of the grass were an Episcopal church with steeple, a red-brick town hall, a summer-stock theater, and a block of renovated stores selling things only tourists ever bought. The glorified alley next to the theater angled down toward the harbor.

Just off the green, the main drag renewed itself. Large, white clapboard houses with front lawns that were disproportionately shallow because the houses were built before the road was widened. Shutters in black or green, the porches wrap-around style with empty brass flag holders nailed into the railing. The kind of upper-middle-class community that produced well-mannered kids with high college board scores.

Farther along, the lots got bigger, the sidewalk reverting to only one side of the street before disappearing altogether as the road stretched closer to deeper pockets. Dappled shade trees, mainly maple and elm, lined the shoulders, with generous stands of pine and spruce hugging the hills above them. Within a country mile, I saw the General's driveway, flanked by granite monuments of eagles.

Turning, I passed between the eagles. The perimeter fence began a discreet fifty feet into the trees. I saw the vehicle gate, and the guard box behind it, any underbrush cut away from the intersection of the drive and the fence. My twin, interlocking video cameras were mounted in the gateposts and fitted with automatic irises to adjust for changes in the available light.

A guy in a uniform you could mistake for an MP held up his hand in a stop sign from the other side of the fence as I approached it. I honked my horn so he'd open the gate. He shook his head and beckoned me out of the car.

I unsnapped the seat belt. As it retracted, I could see the strip of soaked shirt that ran diagonally from my left shoulder to my right hip, shadowing the impression of the seat harness. The air wasn't warm enough to merit so much sweat. I shrugged into my suit jacket as I left the car so the guard wouldn't see the stain.

"Name, sir?"

As I got closer, I recognized the guard from the security work last spring. At six-feet and a muscle-bound two-twenty, he had one inch and forty pounds on me. His red hair was clipped the way the General would like it. He also wore a headpiece earphone and mike, like a technician in a television studio.

"O'Meara, right?"

"I meant *your* name, sir."

I was close enough now so that he could see me clearly. The look in his eyes said he recognized me, too.

"Matthew Langway. The General called this morning. Wouldn't do to keep him waiting."

"May I see your ID, sir." It wasn't phrased as a question.

I handed him the identification I had made up for my private investigator's license. He scrutinized it. If I hadn't already known the General had a security problem, O'Meara's belt-and-suspenders approach would have tipped me.

O'Meara returned my laminated card. "Please go back to your car, sir. I'll open the gate, and this driveway will take you to the fountain in front of the main house. Chief Turgeon will meet you at the fountain."

"There are only four of you counting Turgeon himself. He makes you call him 'chief'?"

O'Meara grinned but put his finger to his mouth in a *shush* sign. He walked back to the guard box, stuck his hand in, and the gate swung open. I got back in the Blazer. Just as I cleared the gate, O'Meara pantomimed that I should stop and lower my window. I did.

Into his mouthpiece he said, "Coming up. Gate, out," then clicked a button atop the transmitter on his belt.

O'Meara said to me, "Sorry about all the procedure, Mr. Langway, but the Chief was monitoring me on his." He tapped the headset. "You need any information on anything, you just ask me."

"You always this helpful?"

Again the grin. "After what happened last night, I figure a good word from somebody like you might get me another job in the business."

Insider dope on current job as springboard to next job. Whatever happened to loyalty?

Leaving the window down, I said, "Thanks, I'll keep that in mind," and stepped on the gas.

The driveway rose gently through a meadow, with free-

10

standing stone fences perfectly aligned as horizons. Beyond the meadow at the top of the rise, the main house was visible. Even from a quarter mile away, you could see it was built to last. Fieldstone walls, granite pillars, and the kind of beams they haven't hewn much since the Vikings plundered England.

Turgeon was waiting for me at the fountain, all right. Wearing aviator sunglasses and camouflage fatigues, a black baseball cap and headset riding low on a head I remembered was shaved. He stood hip-cocked, the butt of an M-16 resting just below his web-belt, hand on the pistol grip and a taped banana clip in the weapon.

I stopped. "Locked and loaded, Turgeon?"

"Cut the shit. The General's waiting. Get out and let's go."

"How bad is it?"

"They're on the patio. Move."

I made a ceremony of activating the alarm system on the Blazer, Turgeon champing, before I followed him through the front door. A second guard was immediately inside. Moon-faced and stolid, he wore regular khakis and another headset, but also carried an M-16, slung muzzle down under his arm. I recalled his accent but not his name.

Turgeon said to him, "Zoubek, you're here till I get back. Then take the video room again."

"Right, Chief."

Turgeon and I walked through the vaulted entry hall toward the kitchen and scullery areas. Somewhere upstairs, a woman's voice yelled "The fuck do I care?" and a door slammed. Turgeon pretended not to notice.

There was no one in the kitchen. We went outside again through the mudroom at the back of the house. Apparently we approached the patio from a different direction than the two men seated there expected, because both had to twist their necks forty-five degrees to see us. Each man stood and re-angled his chair. There was a leather attaché case on the table between them. Peeking around the case were a portable telephone and an expensive mini-tape recorder with a multi-directional mike.

General Van Horne, in L.L. Bean corduroys and a raglan sweater, looked two days older than dirt. He had a short crewcut over white sidewalls at the ears and a beak for a nose. His ramrod straight back hadn't bent often in his eighty-some years, but the flinty spark I remembered in his eyes had been replaced by a tic under the left one. The pouches of his cheeks receded, as though he were sucking on a tooth. The freckled, bony hand trembled as he gestured to his companion.

"Langway, this is my attorney, Sumner Kerstein. I believe you've talked over the phone, but never in person. Sumner, Matthew Langway."

Kerstein, about my size, offered his palm and I took it. The strong, manly shake of a fifty-year-old who brags at the health club about weighing the same as he did at Harvard. Charcoal gray pinstripe, white oxford shirt, red silk tie with white pindots. He had curly, wheat-colored hair razored in a way that didn't look like it ever grew unfashionably. His haircuts probably cost more than the clothes I was wearing.

Making no attempt to shake hands, Van Horne eased himself back into the chair. "Sit, Langway. Turgeon, why don't you stay for a while."

"Yessir."

Kerstein said, "Mr. Langway, I understand you are a licensed private investigator?"

"We talking for the tape machine?"

"No. That is, it's not on."

I said, "Yes, I still have my license, just as I did last spring when I sent you a photocopy of it."

"You are aware, then, of the requirement of confidentiality between client and investigator which your licensing statute imposes?"

"I am."

Kerstein reached a hand into the attaché case and pulled out a check. "The General would like to retain you. And your confidentiality."

"Maybe I ought to hear a little more before I agree to that."

Van Horne said, "Read the amount on the check, Langway."

I did. "$10,000" appeared just to the right of "Langway and Dooley, Security Services," with "Ten thousand and no/00" just below it.

I said, "I accept this retainer against future efforts by our firm on the General's behalf."

Kerstein said, "I also recall you were the firm that certified the security system here."

I shifted in my seat and reached into my inside jacket pocket. "After the General phoned me, I reviewed the contract. Also the diagrams and report I submitted last April." I took out a folded document of four pages with a staple through the upper left-hand corner. "This is a copy of the contract, the one you drafted for us to sign, Mr. Kerstein. I think it speaks for itself."

Lawyers don't like laymen making legal noises at them, but Kerstein made an effort not to show it. "We have a subsequent security problem, Mr. Langway."

"So I gathered from the siege mentality. What—"

The General's fist came down like a wrecking ball on the table. Everything in sight jumped, including me.

Van Horne said, "Goddammit, Sumner! You can't get to the point, I will." The General fixed me with an inspection stare. "Somebody's stolen Kenny, Langway."

"Kenny?"

Kerstein said, "The General's great-grandson."

Van Horne loomed forward in the chair. "Some scorpions have taken my blood, and I want you to fix it. Understood?"

Reflexively, I said, "Understood, sir."

The General teetered to his feet and turned away, breathing heavily and leaning on the back of his chair for support.

Chapter Two

As Van Horne composed himself, Kerstein said, "There was a note."

The attorney reached into the attaché case again. He came out with a plastic Baggie, which he held by a corner. Inside was a five-by-eight piece of paper with purple Magic Marker writing on it.

Kerstein passed the bag to me. "By the time I thought about fingerprints, everyone—including me, I'm afraid—handled this, but I thought protecting it was still possibly a good idea."

I held the bag by the corner, too. In block printing, the note read:

$1,000,000

NO POLICE

WE WILL CALL

I gave it back to Kerstein. "Why would they use purple?"

"I'm sorry?"

"Why purple, rather than black or red?"

"I expect because there was a purple marker near Kenny's bed. We found the note on the pillow, you see."

"Who's we?"

"Well, the child's mother, actually. Janine."

"She was alone when she found the note?"

Kerstein said, "As I understand it."

I said, "You figure the note was written in the boy's room itself?"

"Well, we can't know that, I imagine, can we? A marker was there, together with a pad the same size as the paper in the note."

"And the police. You haven't called them?"

"No."

"Why me?"

"I'm sorry?" said Kerstein.

"Why call me into this instead of the cops or the Bureau?"

Van Horne turned around at that point, breathing slowly, rhythmically. "Two reasons for now, Langway. First, you know the security system here. If you can determine how the kidnappers got in, perhaps we can determine who they are. Second, you used to work for the FBI, so you know how a kidnapping investigation should be conducted."

I shook my head. "Take your second reason first, General. I was a special agent, but I had only two kidnappings the whole time I was in. Mostly I dealt with security systems, fugitive warrants, and forgery scams."

"Your former supervisor thinks highly of you. I've trusted commander's assessments of their line officers before. I'll trust this one now."

I thought about Paul Iannelli, how he'd sound to the General. Like a guy who knew his men.

"All right, then. Take your first reason. You have any evidence the security system failed?"

Turgeon said, "No."

I looked first at Turgeon, then at Van Horne. "General, it's going to be tough for me if Turgeon here answers my questions instead of you."

Turgeon started to say something, but Van Horne cut him off. "Please be quiet, Turgeon. Go on, Langway."

"I'll say it again. Anybody have any reason to think the system failed here?"

The General kept looking at me. Kerstein glanced at him once, then said, "Mr. Langway, there is no intention of pursuing you or your firm for any malfeasance at this time. Of course, should—"

"Sumner," said Van Horne, "Why don't you be quiet, too."

Kerstein dipped his head. The General always spoke in reasonable requests, but his crispness turned them into orders.

Van Horne said, "I think Langway here is bright enough to realize that if we intended to sue him, we wouldn't be retaining him now. To answer your question, Langway, we have no reason to believe that the system failed. That is one of the things I want checked."

"One of the things."

"Correct."

I let my shoulders rest against the back of the chair. Turgeon's jaws were clenched so tight the muscles were throbbing. Kerstein didn't intend to talk again until the General pulled the string on his back.

Van Horne just stood there, watching me. He knew how to wait for a decision.

I said, "If the system checks out, that means it would have been pretty hard for an outsider to pull this off without inside help."

Nobody said that's what they thought, but from their faces, nobody had to.

I gestured toward the house. "And we're sitting out here because you're afraid the rooms might be bugged."

Van Horne nodded.

"General, you want me to look into the kidnapping itself."

"That's correct, Langway."

"If there's an insider involved, then the kidnappers will know you've brought me in."

"The note said no police. You're not official."

"I may not be official, but I am professional help."

"So are Turgeon and his men, who the kidnappers must know are on the estate, even without an insider advising them."

Van Horne's arguments really didn't answer mine, but I wasn't trying to win a debate with him.

I said, "The Bureau's policy is to dialogue with kidnappers, emphasizing the return of the hostage unharmed. They're very good at that. For the record, my advice is to call them in."

"No," said the General in a "next-question" tone.

Closing my eyes, I took a breath. "I'm going to need some lists. The number of every phone line into this place. Everybody who's been here over the last week. Residents, guests, service people, florists, whatever. Even those beyond reproach, if you get me."

Van Horne said, "See to it, would you, Turgeon?"

"Yessir." With a last look at me, Turgeon marched back inside the house.

"I'd like some sense of motives, here. Who needs money, who benefits from Kenny's disappearance, that kind of thing."

The old man seemed to double just a bit, the way you do from a stitch in your side when you run. The knuckles on the chair back turned pale. "Some of the things you . . . should know are . . . painful for me to hear, Langway. Sumner . . . perhaps the two of you could . . . walk and talk."

Kerstein said, "Certainly, General," and indicated to me the path toward the sea.

18

* * * * *

The only parameter of the General's property not enclosed by fence was the waterside. As the lawyer and I walked, a rabbit and a squirrel darted for the treeline. Two gulls dove in low before wheeling and soaring back out to sea.

The land sloped upward again as we approached the cliff overlooking the ocean. The grass was still dewy, so Kerstein and I stayed on the flagstone path. I could hear the waves pounding the rocks below long before I could see them.

"I imagine you've covered this part of the property before, Mr. Langway?"

"When I reviewed the General's security system. Just a minute."

I risked soaking my shoes to move to the edge of the cliff. Squatting and using my hands as supports, I peered over and around the face of the cliff. It was as sheer and unforgiving as I remembered, with boulders the size of Buicks chop-blocking the surf in the dull thud of lackadaisical linemen.

Kerstein decided to stay dry behind me. "Do you seriously believe the kidnappers came by sea?"

I stood, whisking the caked sand from my palms. "Not without remaking 'The Guns of Navarone.' But just because they didn't come in this way doesn't mean they didn't go out this way."

I rejoined Kerstein on the path. He directed me toward some Adirondack chairs arranged with a view of the distant shipping lanes.

The lawyer said, "Persons unknown got in somehow, then climbed down that cliff with Kenny on their shoulders?"

"If they planned it well enough, they could thrash

through the surf to an anchored rubber dinghy and motor out."

"Yes, but what about climbing down with Kenny?"

"A strong man could do it. Or they could have lowered Kenny. Or they could have just dropped him."

Kerstein said, "I see," in that funereal way people use when they're sorry they asked.

We sat on the chairs, set just far enough from the edge to enjoy the breeze but miss the spray.

The lawyer said, "You should know the estate has a rubber dinghy."

"Where?"

"At the yacht club. It's the access for the General's *Cheoy Lee.*"

"What's a *Cheoy Lee?*"

"A sailboat."

I thought a moment. "A longshot, but I may want to see it."

"That can probably be arranged."

A tanker was visible on the horizon. "Just how much do you and Van Horne suspect Turgeon in all this?"

Kerstein replied immediately, as though he'd already considered it. "The General has instructed me to be completely open with you, including conferences between him and myself that would otherwise be privileged. Do you understand how the attorney-client privilege works?"

"Enough to know I don't care about it."

Kerstein paused, probably politely counting to ten.

I said, "What about Turgeon?"

"The General doesn't see him as likely. 'The man's too damned narrow and anal for this, Sumner.' I'm inclined to agree, but as a lawyer I must, of course, keep an open mind. Why?"

"Somebody had to beat the security system. Turgeon's in charge of the team that monitors it from central station in the basement. You wouldn't have brought an independent like me back into all this if you didn't feel a lack of trust somewhere."

"I will concede Turgeon had opportunity and ability, Mr. Langway. But then, many of us have enough knowledge of the system not to bump into it, so to speak, while we're on the grounds."

"Turgeon's list ought to take care of opportunity. How about motives for the insiders?"

"Fine, but before we turn to motive, I must advise you: I will be on Turgeon's list. I dined here last night and stayed over."

"All right, you'll be on the list." I took out a pad and pen. "Now, motives?"

"I'm glad you came prepared to take notes. A million dollars is probably an independently sufficient motive for most people one might know. However, you might wish to begin with a family tree."

"Go ahead."

"The General and his wife had two children, Quentin and Lila. Quentin was an early child, Lila quite late, so late in fact that the General's wife died giving birth to her. Quentin and his own wife were killed in an auto accident, leaving the General to raise their two toddler sons just as Lila, the child of autumn, so to speak, was feeling her oats."

"I'm really going to need all this?"

"I don't know. I intend merely to see that you have it. Now, where . . . yes, Quentin's sons, or the General's grandsons. Their names are Ethan and Allen."

"You're kidding, right?"

"No. Quentin had an exquisite sense of humor, quite the

21

best in the family. In any case, Ethan has, as the saying went, turned on, tuned in, and dropped out."

"Drugs?"

"Oh, possibly, I suppose. I really meant more lifestyle."

"Where does Ethan live?"

"In Maine. Quite humbly, which is just as well."

"Why just as well?"

"The General doesn't care for Ethan's attitude and has instructed me to use every estate planning device I know, and believe me, I know them all, to functionally disinherit him."

"What about Allen?"

"Allen and his wife Janine are the parents of Kenny. Did you meet them last year?"

"Allen just in passing. The wife, Janine, I remember as too attractive for him."

Kerstein watched me write for a minute. "Just so. Do you remember Kenny at all?"

I decided to be honest. "I didn't pay much attention to him. No real sense of the boy at all."

Kerstein looked uncomfortable. "Kenny is . . . in another age, we would have called him retarded. His tutor can elaborate, if a clinical diagnosis is important to you."

"The tutor live here?"

"Yes. Casper Binns. He helps Kenny with . . . well, the basics. Coaching him on things like speaking with audiotapes, drawing in workbooks, that sort of thing. We can arrange a meeting, too, if you'd like."

"Probably. Back to grandson Ethan for a minute. How pissed off is he about being out of the will?"

"An estate plan of the complexity required here is more than a 'will,' Mr. Langway, but I believe you would say he doesn't give a flying fuck about it."

I laughed. It felt good to laugh, and I had to clamp down not to laugh too long about it. "I'll try to curb my language, Mr. Kerstein."

The lawyer made a noise between a sigh and a grunt. "Forget it. It's just that—" Kerstein seemed to catch himself sounding human. "Frankly, the General hasn't had much luck raising any of the people he came in contact with as children. His son Quentin was a good egg, but died young. His daughter Lila is, well, have you ever known someone who confused getting older with growing up?"

"Sure."

"Well, when Lila decided for vanity reasons not to get older, and she's nudging forty-five, she decided not to grow up, either. She's living here now, and she takes advantage of the General in a lot of ways."

"What about the other grandson, Allen?"

"Allen is . . . a pale imitation of his grandfather. It's as though the General's genes were passed down only as a matter of form, not substance. A line drawing instead of a painting, so to speak."

"Any of these lovely folks have motives?"

"That's why I suggested the family tree approach, Mr. Langway. When the General passes away, everything goes in trust for the benefit of Kenny."

"Everything?"

"Some token bequests to the others, including even Ethan, just to cement the fact that the General was intentionally depriving them."

I chose my words carefully. "How far off is the General's passing likely to be?"

Kerstein wrinkled his nose. Talking about estate planning is one thing; talking about real death is another. "The

23

General is very sick, Mr. Langway. I think that is all you need to know."

"All right. You must have a provision for what happens if Kenny dies first."

Kerstein seemed pleased to return to his lawyerly expertise. "If Kenny predeceases the General, most of the estate goes to Lila."

"Most to the General's daughter, skipping the grandsons entirely?"

"Basically."

"What sense does that make?"

Kerstein pursed his lips. "The General's kind of sense, I'm afraid. Ethan is a pariah, and Allen will forever be paid a salary from the Foundation."

"The Foundation?"

"The Quentin Van Horne Foundation. The General established it in memory of his son. Medical research, mainly. Allen is a doctor, and the nominal head of the Foundation."

"Who really runs it?"

"Competent administrators."

"Yeah, but ultimately, who?"

"Me, Mr. Langway. I'm a trustee for life."

"Save me asking the General an embarrassing question while you're around."

"How much do I benefit from Kenny's death or disappearance?"

"That's the question."

Kerstein folded his arms and crossed his legs. "Some. My fees as trustee would increase."

"Why?"

"Because—and understand, I am grossly simplifying the situation for you—because the smallish part of the estate that Lila would not get would pour over into the Foundation."

24

"What's smallish here?"

"Three million."

"Dollars?"

A smallish smile. "Of the General's approximately one hundred million, yes."

"Your law firm happen to represent the Foundation, too?"

"Mr. Langway, my father and the General soldiered together. They were best friends long before they became attorney and client."

"And you inherited the General and the Foundation?"

"Only in the vaguest sense of the word."

"Back to the Van Hornes themselves. Is the General's 'estate plan' common knowledge within the family?"

"Yes."

"Aside from Ethan who couldn't care less, any bitterness?"

"Of course."

"Specifics?"

Kerstein unfolded his arms and hunched forward, clasping his hands on the top knee. "Mr. Langway, whenever the pie is large, people naturally will be bitter when the pie is divided to their detriment. Everyone has potential reason to be bitter."

I re-read my notes. "Is there anyone I'll see on Turgeon's list that will surprise me?"

"There is an au pair for Kenny. He needs rather more . . . care than his mother Janine tends to provide. The au pair's name is Gloria Rivas."

"Rivas?"

"Yes. You might remember her from last spring, been with the family for years. South American, rather a peasant-faced woman?"

"Isn't Rivas the name of one of Turgeon's men?"

"Past tense. Jaime Rivas was, I believe, the name. A cousin of Gloria, from the old country."

"Why past tense?"

"Turgeon will have to help you there."

I stood up, putting away my pad. "I'm not looking forward to it, but I need to talk with the General again. I could also use some photos of Kenny, recent ones if you've got them."

"Not a problem. The General has a virtual gallery on Kenny." Kerstein didn't rise. "Aren't you forgetting something, Mr. Langway?"

"I don't think so."

"It may not be obvious to the layman, but there is another permutation on the estate plan you haven't asked about."

I took the pad back out. "What is it?"

"I told you about the consequences of Kenny predeceasing the General. What if the reverse occurs?"

"I thought you said everything, or basically everything, went into trust for Kenny?"

"Yes. But where does it go if *Kenny* then dies?"

"I give up."

"To Allen and Janine, with some spill-over to the Foundation."

"So you win either way, counselor."

"That's not what I meant."

"Let's go see the General."

The old man was still in his chair on the patio, Turgeon nowhere in sight. A cut crystal tumbler was on the table at his right hand, filled with ice and an amber liquid I didn't think was tea. Van Horne played with the glass, using its bottom to make little circles of moisture on the tabletop, like a child with a sand pail at the beach.

"General?" said Kerstein.

Van Horne looked up. "Are you finished, Langway?"

I said, "No. A few more things. First, ten thousand isn't going to do it."

Kerstein started to say something, but the General said, "How does fifty sound?"

"Just right. In cash, up front. Fifties and hundreds would be fine."

"Sumner, you can have that within the hour, can't you?"

Kerstein buried the words in his mouth and instead said, "Yes, General."

I said, "Second, I want everyone in the house out of their rooms."

The lawyer said, "Where do you want them?"

"I don't care. I've got some equipment in my truck, probably enough to check through the system here for holes or failed components. I want everybody out of their rooms so I can work in peace."

Van Horne said, "Done."

"I'm going to need Turgeon's crew to help me on that. I'll also want full cooperation from Turgeon himself."

"You've got it."

"Let me be clear about what I mean. I don't want to waste my time or your money playing cock of the roost with him. As long as I'm on the job for you, he follows my orders or I'm gone, with the fifty."

"I'll see that he understands."

"Third, I want everybody who was in the house last night to give me his or her version of what happened. Where they were, who they saw, and so on. Then I'm going to want to talk to each of them."

27

Kerstein said, "To save time, I can have some secretaries from the firm come out to type their statements."

"No. I want their own statements in their own words and handwriting. Fourth, I'm going to need some time to clear my calendar so I can work on this around the clock if necessary."

Kerstein said, "Why can't you just stay here and do that by phone?"

"Because I don't have a law firm behind me with probably fifty associates I couldn't identify in a line-up. I've got one partner, and I have to make sure he can cover his work and mine for an indefinite period of time."

Very evenly, the lawyer said, "Anything else, Mr. Langway?"

"I take it you haven't gotten a call yet?"

Van Horne managed not to look at the portable phone. "No."

"I'm going to install a cross-frame trap on your phone. How many different numbers do you have here?"

"Four."

"Any place that all four lines are on one phone?"

"My library and my bedroom."

"I rig it in the library for all of them, so that we can be in the same room when they call, regardless of which line they use."

Kerstein said, "My field is not criminal law, Mr. Langway. What is a cross-frame trap?"

"It's the opposite of a pen register. A pen register records all telephone numbers dialed from a particular phone. The trap picks up calls to a particular phone or phones, here yours."

Kerstein said, "And you'll record the calls for voiceprint purposes?"

"Yes, but I doubt that will do us much good."

"Why?" asked the General.

"Whoever was smart enough to set this us up will probably dial from a payphone somewhere and use a scrambler box to disguise the voice."

The lawyer said, "Why is it you want handwriting from all of us?"

I looked at him. "Because even smart kidnappers foul up. I don't understand why they used materials on hand to do the note. They planned everything else so well, why didn't they bring their own note? I don't know, but since we have some handwriting, even block printing, and some use of the language, let's see what people come up with."

Van Horne turned to Kerstein. "What about Ethan?"

Kerstein said, "The General raises a good point, Mr. Langway. Should I try to contact Ethan and ask him to write out his version?"

I said, "Ethan? The grandson from Maine, you mean?"

"Yes."

"Why do that?"

The lawyer said, "Because Ethan was here last night, Mr. Langway. We attempted a . . . reconciliation you might say, but unsuccessfully, so he stormed out, oh, around nine, nine-thirty?"

I said, "Whose idea was this reconciliation?"

Van Horne snorted. "Sumner's."

Kerstein said, "I had hoped to smooth the waters, even after all this time. That's how I came to be at dinner last night myself."

"And stayed over till this morning."

Kerstein stiffened. "As I mentioned earlier."

I said to the General, "I'm also going to need a recent photo of Kenny."

Van Horne looked down at the phone this time, then nodded. "I'll go up to the viewing room, see if I have any duplicates that would be suitable. Stop up there before you leave in any case, would you?"

"I will. Can Turgeon's list and the individuals' statements be done by early tomorrow morning?"

Using the arms of his chair, Van Horne levered himself to his feet. "Sumner, find Turgeon. Tell him about Langway's requirements, including the 'cooperation' issue. Be sure he's moving on the list and the statements, too."

"Yes, General."

The old man moved toward the door, shuffling rather than striding.

Kerstein waited until Van Horne was in the house. "I'll just call Turgeon from here." He picked up the portable, smiling, "If they get a busy signal, I'm sure they'll call back." He pressed one button. "Turgeon? Sumner Kerstein. How's that list coming? . . . Good, good. Listen, Langway is going to be on this matter for us . . . You're to provide full cooperation . . . The General's own words were 'Tell Turgeon he is working for Mr. Langway and he'd damned well better act like it.' Are we clear on that? . . . Good, good."

Kerstein outlined the room-to-room and lifted his eyebrows at me.

I said, "I'll need some kind of internal communicator and one of his men staring at the panels in central station while I work on the detector units."

The lawyer repeated it into the phone, then said, "Fine, fine. I'll tell him you'll meet him in the front foyer, then. Good-bye."

Kerstein put the recorder into his attaché case. "Since you'll now be receiving your retainer in cash, may

I have that check back, please?"

"Sure."

He took the check and put it next to the recorder. Closing and holding the case by the handle, he wedged the phone under his arm like an umbrella. "Quickest way is back through the house."

I turned for the door, and Kerstein fell in beside me. "Mr. Langway, tell you what."

"What?"

"Let's not you and I play cock of the roost, either, shall we?"

"Fine with me."

"That's good. That's very good. Because you see, I've been cock of this roost for quite some time now, and I'm not at all ready to yield the position. Do I make myself clear?"

"Tell you what, counselor. You and I have any problems, why don't we let our mutual client decide them? Generals are good at that."

The lawyer opened the door for me, but he wasn't smiling anymore.

Chapter Three

As soon as Kerstein and I stepped into the house, I could hear angry voices.

He whispered to me. "The bereaved parents, Allen and Janine."

Allen and Janine Van Horne were arguing at the end of the corridor. Allen was as tall as the General, but gawky instead of spare. He wore a tweed jacket and twill pants under a blank patrician expression that made you think he chewed every bite twenty times before swallowing. Janine, long auburn hair pulled straight back, stood statuesque in high-heel sandals, designer jeans and a loose-knit, cowl-neck sweater that showed off her figure, especially in profile.

Suddenly aware of Kerstein and me, Janine broke off the argument. She stamped over to us, ignoring the lawyer and saying to me, "I remember you. You're the one who did the security system, right?"

Her voice was husky, as though she'd just snuck a cigarette. She leaned close into me, uncomfortably so. Hazel eyes, small curls of hair framing her face like the curved spikes of an exotic plant. She gave off a musky fragrance that came only partly from a perfume bottle.

It was five seconds before I remembered to say, "Yes, Mrs. Van Horne. My name is—"

At which point she swung her open right hand and clouted me across the face. I'd say "slapped" instead of "clouted," but the truth is she nearly knocked me off my feet.

"Bastard! You fucking, incompetent bastard! If you'd

done your job right, Kenny would still be here!"

Janine spun on her heel and strutted away like an insulted showgirl, slamming her gaping husband into the wall as she blew by him and broke into a run for the staircase.

I rubbed the left side of my face, tears stinging my left eye. Kerstein said neutrally, "A high-strung woman, Janine."

Allen haltingly approached us. "I . . . I'm terribly sorry, Mr. . . . ah?"

"Langway, Mr. Van Horne. Matthew Langway." I extended my hand. He absently shook it. "I'm very sorry about your son."

"Yes. Well, thank you. Janine has been under . . . so much strain these last few hours. I'm afraid she's quite forgotten herself."

Kerstein said, "Perhaps a sedative, Allen?"

The husband shook his head in slow motion. "No. No, Sumner, I've tried, but she simply refuses. No one can make Janine do something she doesn't want to, you know." Van Horne turned to me. "Are you going to help us?"

"Your grandfather and I talked earlier. I'll be doing what I can."

"Yes. Yes, well, that's . . . good, good. I . . . I think I'll try to speak with him myself. If you think he's up to it, Sumner?"

"Perhaps not just yet, Allen. In the meantime, why don't you call the Foundation, be sure they won't be needing you over the next few days?"

"Yes. Yes, I should do that, of course. Thank you. And thank you, Mr. Langway, for whatever you can do for us."

He walked the route his wife had run, but continued on the ground floor and around a corner.

Kerstein said quietly, "The nominal head of the Foundation."

I looked at him, but didn't say anything.

We moved into the entrance foyer. Zoubek was still waiting by the front door.

Zoubek said, "Mr. Langway? Chief Turgeon say I call him when you coming. You wait here one minute?"

I said to both Zoubek and Kerstein, "I want to walk around the place before I bring my equipment in. I remember the bedrooms weren't locked but the wine cellar was. Any other doors need keys?"

Kerstein said, "I don't know."

Zoubek said, "You wait. I call Chief. He know."

The security man raised Turgeon on the communicator, ending the conversation with "Right, Chief."

Zoubek said to us, "The Chief come quick. He say you wait, please."

Kerstein said, "I've got my own calls to make. See me if you need me, Langway."

We nodded curtly to each other, and he walked away.

I said to Zoubek, "Czechoslovakia?"

"Yes."

"How long have you been in the States?"

"Fifteen year, three month."

"And working for the General?"

Zoubek saw something over my shoulder. "The Chief."

I turned. Turgeon was carrying an envelope with him. He walked like he was reluctant not to stand at attention and broke the pose only when absolutely necessary.

Turgeon handed me the envelope. "The list you wanted."

"Thanks." I put the envelope into my inside pocket next to the original contract. "Before I start checking the details, I'd like a guided tour of the place, with keys for any doors I find locked. You have a master set?"

"Yeah, but I can't leave central station that long."

"Can we step over here a minute?"

Turgeon glanced at Zoubek, who stared at the fleur-de-lis wallpaper like he might be tested on its pattern. Satisfied that he saved face before the troops, Turgeon said, "Okay, but let's make it quick, huh?"

We went past the staircase into the downstairs parlor. It was the size of two volleyball courts laid side by side, with clusters of sofas, loveseats, and chairs for polite chats over martinis and sherry. A fireplace large enough for burning heretics dominated one wall. General Alexander Van Horne as a mere brigadier stared authoritatively down from a portrait above the mantle, all other paintings and prints in the room magnitudes smaller in size.

I said, "Turgeon, we have two ways we can go here."

"What do you mean?"

"You can do what I tell you to do unless there's a good reason you shouldn't, or you can whine about it so I have to cut you down in front of your men."

Turgeon bristled.

I said, "Your choice. Either way, the General's going to back me on it, and we both know it."

He breathed hard. "What do you need?"

"I agree that with O'Meara at the gate and Zoubek at the door, somebody should be in central station. In fact, once I start checking the components, somebody's going to have to be there."

"There's nothing wrong with the components. Everything's working right and has been."

"Turgeon?"

He colored but didn't say anything more.

"That's the idea. Now, can somebody else take me around the place while you guys are on post?"

Turgeon thought about it. "Kerstein, the lawyer, I don't think he knows the house well enough. Maybe Willie?"

"Willie?"

"Willie Nusby. The houseman. Old black guy, him and his wife clean up, cook, that kind of thing."

I could just picture a faceless man with some kind of limp. "He have a set of keys?"

"Yeah. Needs them for things. His wife, too."

Turgeon tried to read my mind. "I figure they're clean, though. Been with the General since, I don't know, the forties, I think."

"Can you find Willie Nusby for me?"

"I can call him." Turgeon fiddled with his communicator box. "I put him on the net this morning. If he has it turned on." More formally, Turgeon said, "This is Chief calling Willie . . . Chief calling Willie . . . Come on, Willie, come on . . . Willie? Good. Where are you? . . . Well, get to the living room . . . I don't care, right now . . . Now, Willie . . . All right."

To me, Turgeon said, "He'll be here. Probably take a few minutes. He doesn't walk so good, from the war."

"I'll go with you down to central station. We can talk on the way, and I'll be back up here for him."

As we went by Zoubek, Turgeon told him to make sure Nusby waited for me in the living room. When we reached the door under the staircase, Turgeon opened it and went down, hoisting his M-16 so it wouldn't bonk on the steps.

The cellar was expansive, whitewashed walls and high ceilings. There were four doors off the bottom of the stairs, one marked with a capital "E."

"Elevator?" I said from memory.

"Yeah. Not used much, though."

"It'd be a help for me to use it with my equipment.

36

Doesn't need a key, right?"

"Right."

Turgeon approached the doorway immediately in front of him and fished around in his fatigue pocket.

Pointing to the other doors, I said, "Which is which?"

Turgeon gestured. "One on the right's the wine cellar. One on the left is storage."

I remembered a cellar full of stuff the Van Hornes probably could throw out. "Anything else?"

"The HVAC system's behind the monitoring room here so's nobody can get to it without going through us first."

Six months ago I insisted that heating, ventilating, and air-conditioning be controlled from security, but I let it pass. "Any prior threats. Letters, calls, anything?"

"Not that I know of."

He unlocked the thick, insulated metal door and we walked into the central station.

It really should have been called the security labyrinth. First was the monitoring room. Computer-chip panels with wink-out lights for the security devices throughout the house. Video displays of the front gate and all first-floor doors, panoramas of the grounds from cameras mounted under the eaves and elsewhere. I had recommended against long-range infrared sensors: with all the wildlife moving around the grounds day and night, the alarm would be sounding constantly.

Through one door off the monitoring room was the security suite, where the family could be gathered and maintained on a week's worth of air, food, and water. Through a second door would be the security staff's bedrooms.

Turgeon sank into a swivel chair and began niggling the dials on the monitors.

I said, "What's the story on Jaime Rivas?"

He played with the dials some more, then sat back. "He quit."

"Why?"

"Didn't say."

"He's the cousin of the au pair, right?"

"Something like that."

"Come on, lay it out for me."

"Like I said, he didn't say. You'll have to ask him."

I drew the impression that Turgeon was shielding Rivas rather than defying me. Loyalty to his men, even after they left on their own accord? I decided to leave it for now.

"Take me through the suite and bedrooms."

He used another key to open the door to the security suite. One large room, thirty-by-thirty, with floor cushions that could be used as mattresses and plenty of indirect fluorescent light to compensate for the absence of outside windows. Television, stereo, books, short wave. Arsenal box with M-16's, pump shotguns, and Colt and Browning handguns. Even a vault, the door to it four feet tall by three feet wide. And one foot thick, if I recalled correctly.

Only one bedroom, though. For the General, with attached bath. One other full bath and one half-bath for the rest of the family to use. Kitchenette with fridge and large separate freezer, microwave and convection ovens.

I said, "Now your rooms."

The security staff bedrooms radiated from one common bath off the hallway behind the second door in the monitoring room. At eight-by-ten with no windows either, each was a little smaller than the minimum the Supreme Court once said lifers were entitled to have in prison. Twin bed, desk, chair, bookshelves. A closet with built-in dressers. Monastic, except for the thirteen-inch color Sony with a single earplug in each room.

"The TV's standard issue?"

"General thought we all should have one, given the hours we put in. Bought them together for us and the up-stairs people, but we've got to use ours with the earplugs so we can hear the alarm or anything."

We went back out to the video room, where I stood with my hands on my hips.

Turgeon said, "Anything else?"

"All these cameras, and nobody saw anything."

"I was watching them, and I didn't see anything."

I filed that for later, too. "Kerstein told you about the statements I need?"

"He told me."

"Am I going to have them by tomorrow morning?"

"Do my best."

"I'm guessing it'll take me an hour to do the walk-through with Nusby, then however long to cross-check the system from the rooms."

"I'll be down here myself for the cross-check."

"Better warn the residents about the alarm going off."

Turgeon's eyes jumped.

I said, "What's the matter?"

"The alarm's not . . . Not all the detectors are connected anymore."

"What?"

"The upstairs bedrooms. I had to pull the circuit on the magnetic entry detectors on the windows."

"Why?"

"Because the god . . . because Kenny kept opening his window all the time to hear the alarm. He liked the noise."

"And the others?"

"The General told me to pull all them off, too. They still light up on the board here, so we can keep track of them.

They're just off the alarm circuit."

"Anything else I should know about?"

Instead of replying, Turgeon fixed me up with a communicator package. "Keep the power on, Channel Three. Just call when you're ready for the cross-check."

I left him and rode the elevator up alone, making sure I could still work it. No problems.

In the entrance foyer, Zoubek had been replaced at the front door. O'Meara beckoned to me, clicking off his transmitter again.

I said, "Doesn't that make Turgeon suspicious?"

"No. They go in and out, these boxes here." A cagey grin. "You need to know anything yet?"

"Let's start with Jaime Rivas. How did he come to be on the staff and why isn't he here anymore?"

"Jaime, he wanted to work in the States, get enough money to bring his family up. He was a good shit and a solid security guy, always awake, always alert. Did this kind of stuff—security work, I mean—down there in Bananaland, where it's the real thing. I'm not too sure about the immigration people, some angles I bet weren't exactly kosher, but between the General and Kerstein, the only guy they don't know is God, get me? So Jaime comes up."

"Because Gloria Rivas was here already?"

"Yeah. Gloria, she and Mrs. Van Horne are real—"

"Which Mrs. Van Horne?"

"Which?"

"Yeah. Janine or Lila?"

"Oh. Oh, no, you got it wrong. See, the General's daughter Lila, she took the name of one of the guys she was married to, so we call her 'Mrs. Underwin.' "

"Okay. So Gloria and Janine . . ."

40

"Right. Janine Van Horne and Gloria, they knew each other from the hospital."

"Hospital?"

"Yeah. They were nurses together or something like that. I think that's where Mrs. Van Horne met Doctor Allen. Anyway, when Kenny came on the scene, I guess Mrs. Van Horne got the General to hire Gloria to look after the kid. Then when Jaime wanted to come to the States, Mrs. Van Horne got the General to hire him. And he wasn't a bad guy, like I said."

"How's the pay here?"

O'Meara got defensive. "Could be better, but I can't complain."

"Come on, man. I consulted on all this, remember? You get twenty, room and board on top. Right?"

"So?"

"So where else is Rivas going to make that kind of money, he can afford to quit this job?"

O'Meara looked a little furtive. "This between us?"

"As long as it can be."

"Okay. The General, he gets upset about his daughter, Mrs. Underwin."

"What do you mean, 'upset'?"

"She kind of . . . cats around, you know? Her bed ain't always her own, and she makes a big stink about the Chief or one of us not letting her bring in some pretty boy through the front gate at three in the a.m., get me?"

"Rivas make trouble for her?"

"No. Other way around. Jaime was kind of her type, but with his family and all down South, she wasn't his."

"So Lila Underwin got him fired?"

O'Meara shook his head. "No. No, it wasn't like that. It was more Lila—Mrs. Underwin wouldn't leave him alone,

41

and he was afraid the General would pick up on it and blow him off with the Immigration Man."

"So what happened?"

"So Jaime left, everybody friendly and no waves with him staying in the States."

"When was this?"

"Two, three weeks ago."

"You seen or heard from him since?"

"No, but he's been by here."

I said, "How come?"

"He still drives up sometimes, takes Gloria down to the city. Go to church, have some fun with her own in Boston, you know?"

"Church. You mean on Sundays?"

"Yeah. That's Gloria's day off."

"You know where Jaime lives now?"

"No. Boston, I think. Gloria oughta know."

While I thought about it, O'Meara said, "Anything else?"

"No, thanks. You've been real helpful."

"Like I said, I help you, maybe you put in a good word for me." Again with the cagey grin.

"Oh, count on it," I said, grinning back.

Chapter Four

When I got back to the parlor, an older black man was standing next to one of the loveseats. It was hard to see how he could sit. His body looked as though it had been broken in half, then straightened again. He was bent over from the waist and pelvis so that his shoulders preceded his hollow chest. His legs looked skinny inside the union pants he wore, his upper arms the same where they came out from under his Red Sox T-shirt. The forearms were thick and muscular, though, giving him an oddly Popeye appearance. Clean-shaven, his hair under the headset was white in patches, his eyes alert. I realized I really didn't remember him from the prior April; maybe I'd just gotten a glimpse of him from behind or around a corner.

"Are you Willie Nusby?"

"Yessir. Chief Turgeon called me."

His voice was surprising, almost an anchorman's timbre and quality. I extended my hand. "Matthew Langway."

He took it. "Mr. Langway."

"Willie and Matt would be easier."

"Not for both of us, sir."

I wasn't going to argue with him. "Do you know why I'm here?"

"Zoubek just asked me to wait for you. Before he was relieved by O'Meara."

The way Nusby phrased it, I had the feeling he was remarking on overhearing O'Meara talking to me in the foyer, though nothing in Nusby's inflection or expression gave that impression.

I decided to change subjects. "Will you have keys to everything that's locked?"

"Yessir."

"You know the place better than I do. Any suggestions on where to start?"

Nusby watched me, perhaps trying to tell if I was putting him on. "Bottom to top might make sense."

"Let's go."

He led me back down the staircase into the basement. Pointing, he said, "Have you been in the security room?"

"Yes."

He jingled some keys on a ring looped through his belt. It had an elastic of some kind that let the wearer stretch the key from belt to lock without undoing the chain. He opened a door and flipped a switch that produced a dull glow. "Wine cellar. Watch your step, sir."

I walked down a short staircase into another room perhaps thirty-by-thirty. No natural light or outside exit here, probably so the surrounding earth could keep the wines cool for the General in particular and posterity in general. I moved through the stacks of bottles, on their sides but angled slightly off the horizontal. I pulled a few bottles out and whistled. Chateau Latour, Chateau Mouton Rothschild, Chateau Margaux. The first growths of Bordeaux, vintage after vintage.

Nusby had stayed in the doorway. I said, "These are awfully good, aren't they?"

"I don't know, sir. I don't drink. The General got to know wine when we were in France. He seems to like them."

I put a bottle back and kept walking, stooping once in a while to look at labels. "You were with the General in the war?"

"Yessir."

"Armor?"

"There was formal segregation in combat units then, sir. I was the General's valet."

I completed my circuit of the room and looked up at him from the bottom step. "How were you hurt?"

Nusby said, "Would you like to see the storage room, sir?"

I waited a moment. "Yes, I would."

"This way, please." He flipped off the lights before I reached the door.

Across the hall, the unlocked storage room had an outside storm cellar double door and three casement windows. The outside locks were secure, no tampering I could see. The room contained the sort of elegant crap you might expect an estate to generate and then replace over the years. Old wood tennis and badminton racquets, a croquet set, awkward golf clubs. Across the rafters overhead, a birch canoe with what looked like a cannon-ball hole in it. Cracked lawn furniture, moldy cushions, ancient motorcycle with sidecar, three bicycles of various sizes and apparent ages around it. All sorts of tires and a Jeep's fold-down windshield. Rolled rugs with fringes at each end. Rusting iron twin beds, a large table with canvas spread over it and lamps without shades resting on top of the canvas. I used one of the badminton racquets to poke around. Nothing.

"Anybody been down here recently?"

"As far as I know, just me, sir."

I put the racquet back on a nail and stuck my hands into my pockets to wipe them of dust.

"Next?"

Nusby said, "The first floor, sir?"

"Fine."

He declined to use the elevator. I was shown through the

kitchen and pantry. There was a panic button above the sink. Press it, and a subtle alarm went off down at central station, to bring the security staff at a run. I installed buttons in most of the rooms last spring.

Just off the kitchen was a small living area and door to what might have been a bedroom and bath.

I said, "Who lives here?"

"My wife and me, sir. Please feel free to inspect it."

I watched Nusby as he watched me. If I didn't look in his apartment, he'd disrespect me for being sloppy. If I did look, he'd disrespect me for suspecting him. I walked in.

Simple furniture, tidy and clean. I walked to the interior door, knocked first.

"My wife is shopping for food, sir. You won't be disturbing her."

Inside the door was a small bedroom with a nice window view of the back lawn. Curtains and bedspread in a matching blue print. Two bureaus, one closet, shoe racks.

I pulled open one of the bureau drawers. Nusby drew in his breath somewhere behind me, but didn't say anything. Everything in its place the way a former valet might insist.

I checked the bedroom closet and an even smaller one in the living room. Nusby and his wife lived lean in the clothing department.

Back in the kitchen, the man waited with consummate patience. I said, "Thank you."

Nusby showed me a sunroom, the dining room and three powder rooms. Next was a smoking room that reeked of cigars. Then the twelve-hundred square foot library, leather furniture and mahogany bookcases like I imagine they must have in the Algonquin Club in Boston's Back Bay.

Last was the mudroom. Hanging from a wooden peg were jodhpurs and riding boots that I didn't think were there when Turgeon brought me through earlier. The boots smelled more than faintly of manure.

"The General still ride?"

"Not for some time now, sir."

"Who does?"

"Mrs. Underwin started up when they moved back here."

"When was that?"

"Just after Labor Day, I believe."

"She the only rider?"

"Mr. Yale rides some, too."

"Mr. Yale?"

"Her stepson, air."

"Yale Underwin?"

"Yessir."

"Nusby, what do you think happened here?"

His expression was relaxed, even indifferent. "I don't know, sir."

"You didn't see anything, hear anything?"

"My wife and I get up early, so we turn in early. That's what I'll be saying in that paper I'll be writing for you, soon as you're finished with me."

"Upstairs?"

"I would advise the back way. It is steeper, but shorter."

I followed him up the stairs outside the kitchen to the second floor. He had no trouble negotiating the steps, and in fact opened a small lead on me by the time we got to the top.

I said, "There are three wings up here, right?"

"Yessir."

"Before we start looking in the bedrooms, can you describe the wings for me?"

"I'll try, sir. Over the front foyer, the library and parlor is what we call the front wing. It faces toward the drive and the fountain. That's where the General houses any overnight guests."

"Like Mr. Kerstein?"

"Yessir."

"Where does the General sleep?"

"The south wing, sir. His bedroom and sitting room both look across the rear lawn and toward the sea."

"Who else is in the south wing?"

"No one, air."

"What about the north wing?"

"Dr. Allen and Ms. Janine have the same rooms there the General has on the south."

"So that's where Kenny would be sleeping?"

"Maybe you should see for yourself, sir."

He led me down the north corridor to double doors at the end. The doors opened into a sun-filled living room that would have been just fine if you didn't compare it to the parlor downstairs. There were open doors off it to each side.

"Orient me."

Nusby pointed right and said, "Kenny," then left and said, "Dr. Allen and Ms. Janine."

I walked to Kenny's room, looked around it before going in. Fifteen-by-twenty with one large window and two smaller ones. Sesame Street wallpaper, double bed with matching comforter and countless stuffed animals jumbled around the pillows. Night tables, short-legged play-table with magic markers and other toys on it. Open-air closet with poles and clothes in no identifiable order. Pretty typical, until you noticed the twenty-nine-inch Magnavox with VCR. There were posters of real tanks on the wall and a pile of toy tanks on the floor, most of the latter with some kind of remote control wired to them.

I moved to the play-table. Every shade of magic marker, including purple. "The bed is where the note was found?"

"That's what I heard, sir."

There were three doorways off Kenny's room.

I walked to the one closest to me. It was to the bathroom. Sink, hopper, big Jacuzzi. To my eye, all marble, tub to ceiling. Grotesquely massive fixtures—Jesus.

I turned to the closer of the two other doors.

Nusby said, "That's the door to the corridor, sir."

"And this third door?"

"That's Gloria's room."

"The au pair."

"Yessir. She's out shopping with my wife. You can go in."

Gloria's door opened into a small studio. Twin bed, bureau with the usual thirteen-inch Sony, earplug attached. No night table, just the door to the outside hallway. You could see why Gloria Rivas might enjoy visiting the city from time to time.

I walked to her bureau. Grainy photos in Woolworth frames on top showing flat-headed, black-haired men and women of all ages with Latin/Indio features. Hairbrush, hand mirror, some cheap perfume.

I tugged on the knobs of the top drawer of the bureau. Nusby didn't make even breathing noises this time. I weeded gently through the undergarments, finding a black leather case twice the size of a change purse, coarse stitching around the edges. Inside the case were an eyedropper and several stoppered vials of opaque porcelain. I opened one. Liquid inside, a musky, mediciny smell.

"Does Gloria share Kenny's bathroom?"

"Nossir. She has one, other side of the hallway."

I put everything back the way I found it, then went through the rest of the drawers. Nothing of interest.

Closing the door, I crossed back through Kenny's room and by Nusby. From the living room, I could see the doorway to the other bedroom was ajar. I pushed it open.

Janine Van Horne glared at me over a Kleenex she held to her nose.

I said, "I'm sorry. I thought nobody was in here."

Behind me I heard Nusby rearrange himself, but not laugh.

Through the tissue, she said, "Look at what you have to and get out."

"I will, but I'll be back later with some equipment, and that will take longer."

Janine got up and moved toward me, the rustling noise of her clothes more pronounced than before when she'd hit me. I backed up a pace. She strided past me, crumpling the Kleenex and throwing it on the floor where Nusby could see it.

"Nusby, tell me when he's done. I'll be somewhere on the grounds."

"Yes, ma'am."

Nusby waited until she was out of the room before he moved deliberately toward the Kleenex. He lowered his body gingerly by bending only his knees, snapping the tissue up with one swipe, like a crab. Straightening without the support of a chair or table, he deposited it in a woven basket beneath the desk.

I said, "We going to run into anybody else?"

"Not that I know of, sir."

I went into their bedroom, nudging things around a little. Two doorways again. The first led to a larger version of Kenny's bathroom.

In the medicine cabinet were the usual items plus several syringes and some bottles with puncture tops. I read the labels. The ones I recognized were generic sedatives.

I left the bathroom and opened the second door. Huge walk-in closet, as though a bedroom like Gloria's had been pressed into service. I moved through it. On one side, seasonal women's garments up front on hangers, more shoes than Imelda Marcos. Sweaters on shelves, handbags in cubbyholes. At least a hundred blouses. On the other side of the closet, Allen's clothes took up less than half the space. Behind them was a store-full of things hanging in zippered, boxy bags of heavy, clear plastic. From the family's cruise wear in the first bag to the family's ski outfits in the last.

When I turned around, Nusby had inched silently to the closet door. I shook my head. "Why do they buy what they can't possibly use?"

"Mrs. Van Horne makes a good deal of her own clothes, sir." He waved his hand toward a cabinet table that I assumed contained her sewing machine, a wave that said he found it an odd trait for a woman who'd married into money and threw used tissues on the floor.

We moved back into the living room and then into the corridor toward the front staircase. "Who's in these rooms?"

"Next to Dr. Allen and Ms. Janine is empty. Extra guest room. Next to that is Mrs. Underwin's."

"And across the hall?"

"Next to Gloria's room is empty, also. Then there is Casper Binns and next to him, Yale Underwin."

We went through them all. Each had a bedroom and a modest bath.

Lila Underwin's chamber was done up in pink, with a canopy bed and plush armchairs. Her closet was normal in size and jammed with clothing. Even then, I had the feeling a lot was in mothballs someplace.

By comparison, Casper Binns favored austerity. Beyond the necessary furniture, just a bookshelf stereo system. Beneath the stereo, audiotapes in labeled cassette holders were arranged in neat rows. I picked up some of the tapes. Most were classical music, but two rows in the back had labels like "Kenny: Christmas, 1987" and "Kenny: General's B'day, 1988." The room smelled of stale cigarettes. On the night table, I found a mostly used book of matches with just the word "Fellas" printed in elaborate script. I pocketed it.

Yale Underwin had done up his room in early dormitory, with magazines and clothes, mostly of the sporting variety, everywhere. He had the standard Sony, but with a VCR hook-up instead of an earplug.

We moved to the front wing. Even in the empty suites, I went through bureaus and closets and bathrooms.

Past the central staircase was Kerstein's room, decorated like an old New England inn. Four-poster with pineapple tops, triptych dressing table, corner writing desk, midget bathtub. However, it felt more like a motel room used only for business. An attaché case next to the desk, a garment bag in the closet, and a toilet kit on the vanity.

I looked out the two windows. Kerstein had an expansive view of the fountain and the drive down toward the main gate.

Finally, Nusby said, "Anything else, sir?"

"Yes. The General's quarters."

"This way."

We walked around another bend in the corridor to the south wing. The double doors at the end opened into the architectural, if not stylistic, twin of Allen and Janine's suite. Masculine, simple, old-fashioned. Bedroom to the left, smoking room to the right, with a door in a different wall than Gloria's room next to Kenny's.

I moved to it.

"Knock first, sir."

I looked at Nusby, then knocked.

The General's voice said, "Who is it?"

"Matthew Langway, General."

"Come in."

I opened the door into what at first I thought was a darkroom, then changed my opinion to a screening room. A huge projection television, the kind you see in a sports bar, a stand of VCR equipment near it. Van Horne was seated in a cracked leather chair, oxblood with brass tack heads. In his lap were boxes of photos. He held a picture in each hand, as though he had been comparing them. Three snapshots were on the small cocktail table near his elbow. I didn't have to look to know they all were of Kenny.

Van Horne glanced up, impatient. "Need anything?"

"No, General, just doing a tour before I start checking the system itself."

He talked to the photos. "Don't let me stop you."

I turned.

Van Horne said, "Langway, do you need Nusby anymore?"

"Only his key ring."

Nusby appeared in the doorway before the General got to the point of calling him. The former valet unclipped the key ring and lowered it into my hand like a sleeping snake.

Van Horne said, "Can't get along without him myself, I'm afraid. Especially with the new-fangled devices." He looked up at the houseman and said, "The Fourth of July one, I believe, would be nice."

"Yessir," said Nusby, moving to a shelf of videocassettes.

I stuffed the keys into my pocket and moved to the door.

"Oh, Langway?"

"Yes, General?"

"Be sure to stop by and see me before you leave, now. For those photos you wanted."

"I will, General."

I closed the door behind me.

Chapter Five

After a quick walk-through of the other empty rooms in the General's south wing, I took the elevator down. Turgeon was waiting at the first floor.

He said, "I was wondering who was working this."

"Anything I should know about?"

"No. No contact, anyway. Everybody who's around is writing their stories of what they were doing last night. I'll have the rest for you by tomorrow morning. You going to run those tests now?"

"I'm going to check the outbuildings first. Then I have to get the stuff from my truck." I changed my tone. "With Rivas gone, how do you handle the shifts?"

"Man in central station, watching the monitors twenty-four hours a day. Man at the gate for daylight hours or when the General's entertaining. Third man's sleeping or off."

I shook my head. "Doesn't add up."

"It does if I pull double shifts and forget about my days off."

"Maybe so, but not forever. You been interviewing for a replacement?"

"I've got my feelers out. Don't want just anybody, you know."

Fingering the transmitter at my belt, I said, "I'll call you on this when I'm ready for the test."

I went down the hall to the front door. O'Meara had been relieved by Zoubek again, who just nodded to me. Outside, the weather had turned chilly, that first taste of

December in October. I moved around the house and slightly downhill. A grove of weeping willows sheltered the house from most of the sight and the smell of a stable.

I went in. A tackroom, four stalls, two horses. My presence made them nervous, high-stepping left and right like taxi dancers on a waiting line. I stayed as long as I could stand the stink, using the hand end of the pitchfork to probe around the piles of hay by the stalls and gear in the tackroom.

Back outside, I checked the video cameras. Everything looked as functional as the images on the monitors in the basement.

From the other side of the stable, I could hear the *thwock* of a tennis ball, but no sound of return. Given the spacing, someone was serving without a partner. I followed the noise uphill to a fenced, clay surface that would be a bitch to maintain properly. A black-haired woman was serving to an empty deuce court, her back to me. She wore a tennis skirt but only a halter-top.

I crunched a stone on the path and she turned around. Full make-up and earrings. A white Lhasa Apso sprang up next to one of the net posts and began yapping. It ran over to her, then careened in and out around her shoes like a miniature racing car on a figure-eight track.

"You're the detective, right?"

"Matt Langway. And you're . . ."

"Lila." She walked in tennis shoes the way a hooker does in high heels, slipping the latch that held the door closed, not caring if the dog ran free or not. "Lila Van Horne Underwin. I could probably dredge up the other married names, too, but they wouldn't help you much."

She gave me her hand, reached for mine, really. Her palm was sweating, moisture dotting the halter-top, letting me know what was underneath it.

Lila said, "Can you see through what I see through?"

She had a saucy smile, but up close she carried too many summers to quite pull it off. The hair had that high sheen of crow's wing and designer hair-coloring, the skin pulled a little more tautly across cheeks and neck than nature, left to its own, could manage. Her body was nearly perfect, however, both shapely and athletically toned.

I said, "Aren't you afraid you'll catch cold?"

"I don't. Even after four years in Malibu, I just don't much feel the cold. Can be quite a gift, making people feel warm when they're around you."

"I'll take your word for it."

The dog had transferred its attention to me, busily sniffing, skittering away, then returning to my pant cuffs.

"Yours?" I said.

"Yes. Mopsy, be a good girl now."

"Does Mopsy stay in the house?"

"Uh-huh. She sleeps with me. When there's room."

"Last night?"

"Unfortunately."

"She bark any time?"

"During the night, you mean?"

"Right."

"No."

"She usually this excitable around strangers?"

Again the saucy smile. "Just around the more exciting ones."

I wasn't sure why we were volleying, but I couldn't see getting much else useful from her. I told her to enjoy her game, and she told me to enjoy mine.

The cameras at the garages on the house side of the

tennis court were working fine. Inside were eight cars and two motorcycles. The winner was a breathtaking Rolls Royce followed by a convertible Mercedes 560SL and a BMW 733i, the last with California plates and a few dents and scratches. Next were a Chrysler convertible, a Chrysler station wagon, and a four-wheel drive Ford Bronco II. Completing the collection were two rust-patched heaps (a Pontiac Firebird and a Toyota Corolla). If it mattered, I could sort out which was whose later.

Though I doubted Lila or anyone else was trying to spy on me, I stopped by each car and looked in. Then I walked to its rear end, rocked it, and sniffed at the trunk seal. Nothing.

The two motorbikes were also at opposite ends of the spectrum. An 80-cc Honda scooter and a 1200-cc restored Harley, the latter a real muscle machine. I checked the storage rooms off the garage. Mainly landscaping equipment.

Walking back to the front of the house, I felt a chill. A lot stronger than the weather alone could be blamed for. I didn't like being on the General's estate.

At the rear of the Blazer, I used my own keys on the alarm and tailgate. I pushed the small suitcase with the Boomerang bug detector to the side. Then I eased the bigger carry-box toward me. Double reinforced aluminum, it was basically an airtight, watertight, and dust-tight foot locker. Filled, it could hold forty or so pounds of delicate equipment while I bounced to wherever a security system happened to be.

Turgeon called to me from the front entrance, Zoubek looking on. "Need any help?"

"No," I said, gently lowering it to the ground. "I'm used to it."

I locked up the truck and carried the box toward them.

Turgeon said, "You know, you don't have to lock your car around here. It's pretty safe."

I cocked my head at him, and he reddened as he realized how stupid he just sounded, especially in front of Zoubek. I hefted the box a little higher, lugging it over the steps and into the house.

Turgeon and I took the elevator to the basement. He went to central station, and I started with the storage room. Beginning with the storm doors and casement windows, I independently checked each security point, then crosschecked over the headset with Turgeon. Back to the elevator and first floor. Same drill. Then upstairs to the General's wing. I skipped the screening room, since it had no outside apertures, but otherwise went over everything, still coordinating with Turgeon. Then the front wing, focusing on Kerstein's room. Finally, the south wing. I saved Allen, Janine and Kenny's suite till last, spending twice as much time there as anywhere else.

The elevator brought me down to the first floor. I was sweating bullets moving through the center hallway toward the front door. Turgeon had beaten me there, replacing Zoubek.

I said, "They keep this place hot enough, don't they?"

Turgeon shrugged. "The General's got some kind of arthritis, on top of everything else. Heat helps it, I guess." In a different voice, tight from trying to be casual, he said, "Everything check out all right?"

I thought about what to say. "No problems I can see."

Turgeon seemed relieved, like what I'd told him was supposed to be good news. "General just buzzed me. I'm supposed to remind you he wants to see you before you take off."

I got the box to the truck and opened the tailgate. Sliding it back in, I pulled out the Boomerang this time. Locking up and wiping the sweat off my forehead, I began to wish I'd brought a change of clothes with me.

I pocketed the keys and walked back into the house.

Turgeon eyed my suitcase but just said, "Screening room."

"Thanks, I know."

"Please wait a moment, Langway. This one's nearly over."

Scenes of a party, apparently a birthday, played across the screen. I saw some faces I already knew, and some I didn't know yet. The camera centered on Kenny, wearing a glossy cardboard hat at slightly the wrong angle. The adults were dressed up, but there were no other kids in sight.

Kenny's right arm was bent at the elbow as he shook his hand reflexively, like he had just burned his fingers. His blondish hair was a little thin where it showed at the edge of the hat. He rocked side to side, his eyes flicking left-right-left in a predictable rhythm with no apparent purpose. He used his left hand to probe the plates of those around him, who tolerated the pestering partly for the lens but mostly for the General.

The retardation, if I could call it that, was apparent also in Kenny's voice, every other sound not quite a word. But, occasionally, the camera would catch him in repose, staring at his cake or a toy or the General, and for just a moment, you couldn't tell that anything at all was wrong with the happy, beaming child on the videotape.

The screen clicked to static snow.

Van Horne said, "Thank you, Nusby. Please rewind that

and leave us for a moment."

"Yessir."

Nusby closed the door behind him, the machine now making a soft, whirring sound. Van Horne turned to me. The lighting was dim, and I had to focus on the General to see him clearly from where I was standing.

Van Horne said, "Is it safe for us to talk?"

"It will be."

I lowered the case to the floor, opened it and assembled the Boomerang. More properly called a linear junction detector, it extends like a metal detector, emitting microwave beams to locate a bug.

I took off the communicator headset Turgeon gave me and replaced it with the Boomerang's earphones. After adjusting for volume and sensitivity, I moved around the room. Van Horne patiently watched me, as though I were searching for land mines. After fifteen minutes, I switched off the machine and took off the earphones.

"Well?"

"If there were a bug here, I would have heard a high-tone, constant squeal."

"And?"

"No squeal, no bug."

"Good." Van Horne hesitated while I got the Boomerang back into its case. "Are we going to have to go through this every time I want to talk with you?"

"For a while."

The General frowned, then said, "Could you come take these?"

I crossed the room, taking three photos from his hand.

"Those are the best, most recent ones of which I have duplicates. Will they be sufficient?"

For the sake of his feelings, I looked at each longer than

necessary. "These should be fine, General."

"Take this, too." Reaching down, he lifted a brown accordion file from beside his chair. "Your retainer, enhanced to fifty thousand, as agreed."

I laid the file at my feet. "Thank you, sir."

"I'd like a report now, Langway."

"Without Kerstein being here?"

The General just tilted his head to indicate I should stop farting around.

"Nusby showed me around inside the house. I went through the outbuildings on my own. Then I checked the entire security system. Every component in the house checked out perfectly. Front-line system completely operational, back-up system completely operational."

"That's what I was afraid of."

"One thing."

"What's that?"

"The upstairs windows aren't on the Klaxon alarm circuit anymore."

"I know."

"Turgeon said you told him to pull them off it."

"I did. Had to. Kenny couldn't leave his alone. Like a kitten with a ball of yarn."

"Why did you let Turgeon pull the other upstairs windows off as well?"

"Made sense. People, me included, liked a fresh breeze instead of the air-conditioning some nights. Your system was just too goddam tight for us, Langway."

I waited a moment. "General, it's possible that no insiders are involved. Maybe we're just going up against real professionals here."

"Meaning what?"

"You have a thin security staff, and all the bells and

whistles even you can afford can't stop the kind of people you used to deal with."

"Spell it out, Langway."

"When you were in the arms trade, you must have had competitors, dissatisfied customers or employees."

Van Horne shook his head. "I got out of all that ten years ago, Langway. The kind of people I dealt with before then settled scores quickly. They had to, the kind of business they were in. Pride and reputation was everything to them."

"How about people you didn't deal with?"

"I don't get you."

"Terrorists, relatives of victims your tanks rolled over."

"Again, too long a wait. Also, if real terrorists were involved, they would have left a manifesto, not a cryptic note on a child's pad. No, we're dealing with something criminal and personal here. Now, give me your real report, please."

I took a breath. "The way things check out, I think someone who was already inside the perimeter either did the kidnapping or at least participated by getting outsiders onto the grounds."

"How?"

"You never had the fence electrified."

"Hell, no. I'd have killed half the critters in creation every night."

"Then I'd rather wait on working out details for you until after I've had the chance to read the insiders' accounts and interview them."

Van Horne rubbed his palm impatiently on the arm of his easy chair, but said, "Understandable. Any sense from the . . . insiders? Nuance, emotions?"

"Nusby treated me like I was inspecting the place for cockroaches. Your—what is Janine, your grand-daughter-

63

in-law?—nearly took my head off when she ran into me. Your grandson Allen doesn't seem to have the strongest of grips. Your daughter Lila is polishing her tennis game. Turgeon is up to his eyes in covering his ass. Kerstein has his nose open, sniffing the wind. Other than a couple of sentences, I haven't spoken with anybody else yet."

Van Horne regarded me for a moment. "I'm not surprised that Paul Iannelli was sorry to lose you."

"You've got a good memory, General."

"I have an excellent memory, Langway. He recommended you, and I was impressed by your work here last spring. Thorough, professional, effective. You showed the same traits I looked for in an armor officer. Comprehensive but decisive. You acquired the information you needed, then made a decision, didn't sit around all the goddam day with fuel burning to hell under your tail. Iannelli told you I checked you out with him, didn't he?"

"Yes. You told me, also."

"That's right, I did. Tell me, did Iannelli go on to tell you that I checked you out afterwards, too?"

I felt a little ping, down in the stomach.

"No," said the General, sinking back into his chair a little. "No, I didn't think he would."

"Just what are we talking about, General?"

"After you consulted here last spring, I was so impressed with you that I got back in touch with Iannelli. I told him I was thinking about replacing my security chief with somebody like you. Iannelli said you wouldn't be interested."

"Iannelli was right."

"Oh, yes, he knows you well."

The General let that sit there for a while. I didn't want to pick it up.

"He even shared some of your background with me.

64

Both with the Bureau and before."

I still didn't say anything.

"Only after I urged him to share, of course. Iannelli is a very smart man. I like dealing with very smart men, Langway."

"General—"

"Iannelli told me you were a good soldier. He said your two-oh-one file was crammed with glowing reports of your efforts in the villages over there. How you handled difficult . . . what would you call them?"

I shook my head.

"Well, let's call them 'politicians' then. He told me how you handled the politicians who couldn't quite see the merits of doing things the way the regime we supported wanted them done. That you were an excellent persuader, and if persuasion wasn't enough . . ."

"General, I don't know what you're talking about."

His reply hit me harder than Janine's swing in the hall. "Don't try that shit on me, boy! Back in 'forty-four and 'five, I had more goddam people killed than probably live in your hometown!"

I didn't try to bait him.

He softened his tone to one of comradeship. "There wasn't much armor in your war, was there, son?"

I thought of the ARVN tanks that used to parade up and down the streets of Saigon, ostensibly to build morale, usually just intimidating. "Not that I saw."

"That's a pity. A real pity. There weren't many sights more . . . complete than fifty Shermans, lurching from a dead stop to twenty miles an hour across a meadow at dawn, spewing fire and death from their turret guns." He blinked.

Trying to keep him away from me, I said, "Is that how Nusby got injured?"

"What? Oh, no. No, Nusby got . . . We were going hellbent, leapfrogging town to town, our lead elements racing ahead. Trying to reach the bridges before the Germans had the good sense to blow them up. We were in a little town, village itself, really. Nusby was serving me a meal in what I believe was the mayor's house when the Germans hit us. Out in the street, I got a German halftrack on me before I knew it. Well, Nusby found a carbine—the colored, they weren't combat troops then, you see. Well, Nusby opened up on the 'track, drew it off me. Even got the driver with a lucky shot, but that made the driver wrench the controls. Wrenched right onto Nusby, death throe or vengeance, don't know which. That 'track pinned Nusby to a wall. Horrible sound, his being crushed. Miracle he lived at all, but was a tough bird. A tough one, all right."

Van Horne's eyes caught me again, the whites very visible in the darkened room. "Ever heard the term 'turnabout,' Langway?"

"No."

Van Horne spread his hands, then used them as though they were miniatures on a relief map. "Let's say you're outgunned, about to engage a superior force. But you've advanced so far you've outdistanced your own artillery. You can make a stand, and be annihilated, or you can turn tail and run. Well, a few of us figured a way to use that. The German tanks had more firepower, but our M-4's were more maneuverable. We'd dig in, like we planned to make a fight of it, so the German scouts would think we weren't going anywhere. But we'd just make it look like we were fortifying. Actually, it was kind of like a Hollywood set, you know? All fake fronts, not worth a Brit's shit. Well, we'd dig in like that, leave ourselves an easy, quick out. Then the Panthers would come. Oh, I tell you, any tanker claims he didn't wet his pants when he saw them rearing up and rolling, he's a liar. They were faster than a Tiger and had those long-barreled 75mm cannons on them. Adolph's best, they were.

"Anyway, we'd back out and turn tail and run, just letting the lead elements of the Germans get a look at us, a whiff of the blood, see? Then we'd go like hell for two, three kilometers, till the Germans' supporting artillery had to lift their tubes so the ordnance wouldn't rain down on their own boys chasing us. Then we'd wheel, maybe two-three-five degrees left. We'd drive on another half-kilometer, then wheel another two-three-five degrees left, slowing it down some. You following me, Langway?"

"You'd turnabout onto their advancing left flank."

"That's it! That's it exactly. We'd end up with our guns bearing down on them as they lumbered past us at damn near a right angle. Like a shooting gallery it was. Their Panther had great armor on its front but not much on the sides of the hull or turret. We'd kill the point and drag tanks first, then take our time with the ones trying to scramble like cows out from between them. Knock the tracks off the bogie wheels, mow down their crews as they bailed out. It was a killing ground, plain and simple. The Wrath of God Descendant."

"I don't see what you're driving at."

Van Horne lost his enthusiasm, leaning back in the chair and splaying his arms. "I wanted you here so you could tell me if what I figured had to be true was true. That this was an inside job. And you have done just that."

"Maybe. You also said you wanted me to look into the kidnapping itself. I still say you need the Bureau or at least a professional team—"

"God fuck the Bureau and professional teams, boy! I got

a goddam 'professional team' already, Turgeon and his playmates, and all he can think to do is run around like some Hollywood freak with an M-16 in his hand. Look, for the kind of problems I thought I still had, Turgeon and his men were fine. Scarecrows to shoo people away from the gates, keep vandals off the property, intimidate a burglar from even thinking about it. Fine. But now somebody's got my Kenny, and while I can still think straight about it, I want somebody who can get him back. And even if . . . even if I can't get him back, I want somebody who can take care of the people who took him. Get me?"

It was a minute before I said, "Turnabout."

"Exactly. Somebody who's killed before, who knows goddam well that he can do it and how to do it and expects to be compensated accordingly. In a word, boy, you."

"Why the hell do you think I would even consider that?"

"Cut the shit, Langway. Back when I was thinking about you for Turgeon's job, before I knew . . . back before I let things ride that didn't seem so important anymore, I had Sumner investigate you."

"You—"

"Oh, don't get all fussed up about it. It's not like we had you followed or something. Just financial, credit, the kinds of things bankers'll do for people who put the kind of money I do into their banks. We both know what I found out, right?"

"It's your fairy tale."

"Don't disappoint me now, Langway. Your partner, Fred Dooley, has been dipping and clipping for some time now. The details may be fuzzy, but you've got to know it's been going on. You've been carrying him while he's been bleeding you and maybe some of your other clients, too. And pretty soon the real investigators, the kind with badges, are going to be looking into things. Unless, of course, a transfusion of cash squares everything away."

I tried to think of how to play it, use it better. Instead I said, "How much of a transfusion?"

"One hundred thousand. That's a hundred over the fifty you already have by your feet."

"I get the fifty for looking into this . . ."

"And another hundred for the right result. No cops, no courts, no lawyers. Just you, leveling down on the ones who did this."

"And if you don't pay me?"

"I won't bother to look offended, Langway. I'm an honorable man. I'll pay you for the right result, and you know it."

I did. Something had to be said, and face to face, here and now, seemed like the best time to say it. "You realize, General, that the percentages say Kenny's already dead."

Van Horne's lips moved, but no words came out. He eased back into the chair and covered his eyes with his hand, as though shielding them from the sun. "Change the percentages, Langway."

I stood up, the Boomerang's case in my right hand, the accordion file under my right arm. I moved to the door and opened it. Nusby came forward from perhaps eight feet away. Farther than made sense unless he was trying to give me the impression he hadn't been listening.

He said, "May I have my keys back, sir?"

I returned them.

"Thank you, sir."

As Nusby entered the room, I heard Van Horne say, "I think the Christmas Eve, 'eighty-seven tape next."

I closed the door on Nusby's "yessir."

Chapter Six

I used the drive south to think about what the General had said. By the time I reached my house in Somerville, I decided a few more stops would be advisable.

Somerville is a blue-collar city stuffed between the poor section of Cambridge and the northern borders of Boston. An uneasy mix of student apartments and extended family three-deckers, leavened here and there with pockets of gentrification. I lived in one of the pockets near Union Square and next to a Portuguese neighborhood.

I had purchased my place just before the speculators found my street. Built in the 1880's by a mill owner for his workers, the house is only twenty feet wide but three stories tall. It has a party wall on the north side and a driveway on the south side narrow enough that I wished the Blazer didn't sport rearview mirrors on both front doors. I squeezed the truck through and around to the wider pavement at the back of the house.

Pulling into the garage, I decided to leave the fifty thousand in the truck's hidey-hole beneath the Boomerang case until I could get to the bank. I retrieved the larger carry-box, bringing it to the storm cellar doors. The previous owner had installed a lift down into the basement. Riding down would be a lot easier than negotiating the narrow staircase from the kitchen. I asked myself if it bothered me that the lift to the basement was about the only thing my house had in common with the General's. The sound and motion reminded me of the time I had made love on the lift. How long ago was that?

Thanks partly to the lumpy, concrete-and-gravel floor, the basement was ten degrees colder than the outside air. I put the carry-box on some shelves in the driest corner. Rooting through a few cartons, I gathered what I needed for the cross-frame trap into another, smaller case, then took the stairs back up.

Mrs. Pambeiro, all one-hundred-eighty-pounds of her, stood squarely in the large kitchen, a bread knife in her right hand, low just like they teach you at the academy. Quantico, however, was one place she'd never been in her sixty-some years on the planet. Using a knife was something she would have learned from her father. Or her mother.

"You know, Mr. Langway, someday I'm just gonna stab you, you sneak up on me like that."

"Sorry. I thought you'd hear the car."

She pointed to the silent Electrolux, still plugged in. "How'm I gonna hear your car, the vacuum on and all?"

"How'd you hear me coming up the stairs?"

"Didn't. Felt your invalid thing making noise from the basement. Man blessed with working legs shouldn't be using that thing anyways. Gets God to thinking about you."

"I sure don't need that. You finished with the third floor bathroom?"

"Yeah. You gonna scandalize me in front of my neighbors by taking a shower, I'm still here?"

"Don't you think I could use one?"

She made a face. "Not so much as your place here. It's been what, four, five weeks since I come in last time?"

"I've been busy, Mrs. Pambeiro."

"So busy, you can't pick up the phone? This place is a barn, the way you live here."

Some tumblers were drying in the rack next to the sink. "I'm going to be entertaining tonight. You do a clean sweep?"

She made another face. "You think I don't understand English or what? You say, 'clean sweep,' I give you clean sweep. Windows, handles, dishes, glasses, what do you think? You should live your life so clean."

"I'll be up in the bathroom."

As I climbed the stairs, her voice trailed after me. "I'm telling you, you don't want God to start looking for you."

The vacuum came back on.

I passed the second landing and the entrance to the second floor half-bath and my living room. The picture window at the back of the living room offered a view of my postage stamp backyard and, beyond a short fence, the rear porches of Mrs. Pambeiro's neighbors, daily wash flapping on a clothesline. The third floor was my bedroom and the full bath.

I stripped, showered, and braced myself for seeing Fred.

Fred Dooley lived in Saugus, about seven miles from our office in the commercial section of Somerville. Rather than fight the traffic, I stopped at the office. I didn't expect Fred to be there, and he didn't surprise me. I called the answering service, anyway. Nothing from Fred, but Dee Faber had left a message, confirming she'd see me at my place at eight.

I opened our mail, scanning it more than reading it. One of the letters was from a client, suggesting that the replacement parts we'd undertaken to obtain for a security system hadn't yet arrived, even though ("as the enclosed Xerox demonstrates") the client's check to us had cleared the bank nearly a month ago. I put it on the pile with the others.

I took out the list of phone lines and people Turgeon had made for me. I recognized all of the names except for a landscaper and appliance-repair shop. In effect, the list was an expanded security log, with times for each person entering and leaving the estate through the front gate. I ran off four copies on our Canon, then put the original in a separate letter-sized file folder in the General's overall legal-sized file in a cabinet. I marked up one copy, putting a hyphen next to the people I'd already seen and an F next to the ones I wanted Fred to pursue, mainly the service people and Jaime Rivas.

I closed up the office and headed to the bank with the General's accordion file. I didn't even consider bolstering the firm's checking or capital accounts. The courteous elderly man in the safety deposit department gave me a private cell in which to stuff the fifty thousand into my own box.

Leaving the bank, I was panhandled by a woman with a sweet face and crooked teeth. Maybe twenty-five, she said she was from Burlington, Vermont, and had lost her wallet when somebody slashed her purse open on the subway. She showed me where the razor blade had gone through the cheap vinyl on the side. She asked me if I could spare five dollars toward a bus ticket back to Vermont. Her tear ducts were just about to leak at the edges. Feeling flush, I pulled out a ten and gave it to her. She passed a shirt cuff across her eyes and asked me for one of my business cards, "So I can mail you a money order when I get home. I'll do it, too, mister." I told her to forget about it and wished her a good trip back.

Fred's place was on the wrong side of the tracks, literally and figuratively. The house kiltered toward the railroad's right-of-way, a vacant lot on the other side and a boarded-up trailer off its cinder blocks across the street. Fred's brown, faded shingles almost covered walls and roof, like so many tobacco leaves just pasted in place. His Plymouth was parked half in the gravel driveway, half on the dirt patch where the lawn had given up the ghost.

I knocked. No answer. I knocked louder, then just twisted the knob. The door wasn't locked, but I had to put my shoulder to it in order to overcome the warping effect against the jamb. The place smelled of Chinese take-out and pizza. Newspapers haphazardly overlapped each other near a gut-sprung chair. Across from the chair was a nine-inch black and white that was probably relegated to the kitchen counter in Fred's former house—before Mona learned to recognize an alcoholic when she woke up next to one every morning. Half the nights he'd find his own way home, the other half I'd drive him. And carry him. And alibi him.

Fred blamed the booze, and every other failing, on his leg. The left leg, the one that took two derringer bullets running straight and true for my chest, two steps below him on a porch near Porter Square. Fred and I were out with two Cambridge cops, routine pick-up of a fugitive from Virginia. Truck driver, the kind of guy who settled arguments with his fists. No past history of being armed. No future, either, after the two cops and I emptied our weapons into him. Fred couldn't quite qualify for disability, the one slug severing a ligament that just gave him a funny, rolling limp like Red Skelton clowning around.

The television set was on, some cartoon show from a UHF-station. Fred was passed out in the gut-sprung chair, an empty liquor bottle on its side at his feet, a .38 Detective Special partially hidden in the crack between cushion and chair frame. He hadn't shaved for a couple of days, his brown hair matted here and spiked there from turning his

head in what passed for sleep. A ball of wax was inching its
way out of the fuzz in his right ear.

I slid the revolver away from him. No response. Opening
the cylinder, I counted five live rounds, none under the
hammer. The old cops still did that, even with the half-cock
safety that keeps the firing pin from ever striking the
hammer round accidentally. I closed the cylinder and
walked over to the electric fireplace. I put the gun on the
mantel, between the photo of Mona and him and their sons
on the left and Fred's old Navy frogman team on the right.
You could recognize Fred from one shot to the other, but
you'd never match either with the lump in the chair.

I turned off the television. No response again.

"Fred."

I shook him gently, then harder until I had to stop because it was making me feel like hitting him instead. His
eyes fluttered open, then closed, then opened and perked a
little.

"What . . ."

"Fred, wake up."

"Matt . . . ?"

"We've got to talk."

"Sure . . . sure, Matt. Just give me a . . . minute, will
you?"

He tried getting up with one hand, then found he needed
the other. I'd seen him get up from a drunk more times
than I'd started a car, but he always did it the same way.
One hand, then both.

"Matt . . . you want something? Drink, maybe?"

"No. Neither do you."

"Aw, Matt, c'mon. You know how I get in the morning
if—"

"It's late afternoon, Fred. Another couple of weeks, it'll

be dark out this time. You ever worry about that, Fred? You ever worry about losing a whole day now and then?"

He reached down for the bottle at his feet, balancing himself after a fashion by holding onto the arm of the chair.

I said, "I worry about it, Fred."

"I can take care of myself." The last syllable came out a grunt as he heaved his torso back up. Fred examined the bottle, and saw it was empty. Because I was company, he restrained himself from just tossing it back on the floor. "C'mon in the kitchen."

I followed him, trying to remember how much more professional he could sound when he stayed off the booze. The kitchenette table and the sink were full of soiled cardboard cartons and flat, square boxes with somebody's house of pizza printed around the grease spots. Roaches played tag over most of the surfaces I could see in the sink. They were probably saving the tabletop for dessert.

Fred went to the refrigerator. I stacked the crap on the table, tossed it into the sink, and used a dishcloth from under the counter to wipe off the Formica surface.

Fred came back with two Classic Cokes. "C'mon, Matt. The caffeine'll cheer you up."

I let him pop the top on his and drink, the liquid overflowing his mouth and running down his chin like the wrong-colored blood in a cinema shoot-out. When he was finished, he belched.

"Fred, we have to talk."

"Matt, look, I know I haven't been holding up my end too good the last coupla weeks."

" 'Holding up.' That's a little too close to accurate, Fred."

"Jesus Christ, Matt. What do you want me to say? 'I'm sorry for all the shit I pulled'?"

76

"Fred. Being sorry isn't going to help. You've been dipping."

"What?"

"Dipping, Fred. Forging my fucking name to our capital account. Remember our capital account, Fred?"

"Matt, think about what you're saying here."

"I know what I'm saying, Fred. I'm saying you're a thief."

Fred winced and started rubbing his left leg.

"Forget the Danny Kaye routine, Fred. This isn't *White Christmas*, and I'm not Bing Crosby. I know you've been stealing. Stealing from me's bad enough. Stealing from our clients, Fred, that's not just between friends, get me?"

Fred buried his face in his hands.

"The clients suspect, Fred. You'd been coming into the office more than one day a week lately, you could read their mail, pick up their messages on the answering service. In fact, I could read their mail to you, Fred. Things they paid us money for that we haven't bought, much less sent them."

He talked through his fingers. "Matt, I swear to you, I'll make it up. I won't take a dime for the next—"

"Fred, you pathetic shit. You don't have any idea how much it is, do you?"

He took his hands away. "How much."

"Right, Fred. But you should ask it like a question. A very polite question, because I'm the only thing standing between you and a very substantial sentence right now."

"Sentence? Jesus Christ, Matt, you—"

"Stop whining and listen to me! You're an ex-FBI agent, you've fucking stolen people's money, and you used the U.S. mails to do it. You still got some brain cells left from the old days? You still remember how mail fraud is a federal crime, Fred? How long you figure it'd be before word got around the exercise yard? 'Hey, the new virgin, he used to be a fucking cop.' How long do you figure that would take, huh Fred?"

"Jesus, Matt, take it easy, will you? I'm . . . I gotta try to process all this, okay?"

"You gotta process it, alright. We get a big deal, we've got a chance of keeping you out of prison. We maybe even can save the business, pay back everybody in cash, smiles and handshakes all around. We don't, I'm out of work, and you're someplace where the lack of booze'll be the least of your worries."

His lips were quivering, his hands twitching. My stomach turned over.

"You got a way, Matt? You gotta line on something here?"

I told Fred what happened at the General's house, and his eyes got wide. Taking out Turgeon's list, I told him what we were going to do about it. His eyes got wider.

Chapter Seven

I tried Paul Iannelli's home number from a payphone on Route 1 and reached his wife, Stella. She assured me it would be fine to come to the house that evening, then apologized abjectly for not being able to fix a good meal for me. Her mother was recovering from surgery, and she had to go visit her at the hospital, which meant Paul would be with the kids and would welcome my company. I told her I'd be there about 6:30.

I called Dee Faber and got her telephone-tape machine. I left a message that I might be home a little after eight, but that I'd be there.

Crawling through the traffic, I got off Route 1 at Route 60, looping around Boston on secondary roads. The Iannellis lived in Wellesley, a chic suburb west of the city. Paul had bought his house before the boom, rolling an inheritance of Stella's into enough of a down payment to fool the bank into granting him a mortgage on a special agent's take-home. Or so he always told us. There was a whisper around the Boston office about Paul feathering his nest outside the payroll, but nothing tangible.

His small colonial was just past Wellesley College, enough bushes and lawn to require most of a weekend day to maintain. There was a nondescript blue sedan in the driveway, so I left the Blazer at the curb.

One of Paul's kids answered the door. Maybe fourteen, black curly hair done Boz style on the sides, ringlets down the neck. I struggled for his name, couldn't bring it back.

"Yes?" he said neutrally, his eyes sizing me up.

"I'm Matt Langway. I met you when I worked with your dad. Is he home?"

"Just a second." Then, louder, "Dad, you expecting somebody named Langway?"

A muffled voice from somewhere said, "Send him down."

The boy opened the door. "He's in the basement, building another model ship. You know the way?"

I nodded. From his expression, I gathered that son wasn't too much interested in Dad's hobby.

From the top of the steps, I could see Paul at the bottom. Pot-bellied from too much of Stella's cooking, wavy black hair, tenth-reunion grin.

"Matthew, Matthew! It's been a while."

"Too long, Paul. How've you been?"

I went down, took his hand. A little sawdust clung to my fingers and palm.

"Let me break from the model for a while. We can sit in the family room. Kids don't have much use for it anymore, so it's not the disaster area it once was."

Paul guided me around the corner to a linoleum floor with some bookcases over cabinets, a small Zenith, and what looked like the living room furniture of the 1970's. He took a chair, waving me to the couch.

"Beer?"

"Please."

He went to one of the floor-level cabinets, opened it to reveal a small refrigerator. "Miller Genuine Draft or Harpoon Amber Ale?"

"Miller's fine."

"Good thing. Don't know what Stella did with the damned church key, anyway."

He twisted off the caps, handed one bottle to me. "Cheers."

I took a swallow. "Stella said her mother was sick?"

"Yeah. Came through the surgery like a twenty-year-old paratrooper, though. I tell you, Matthew, when they can't kill her with knives, that's discouraging."

"Everything else okay?"

"Yeah. Stella and me are doing fine. How're you doing?"

"Fine, too."

"That's good, Matthew, that's good. You always were solid, you know that? Most people work only on what's urgent. You're one of the few agents I ever had who knew how to delegate the urgent and work on the important. So, what's on your mind?"

That's what most people noticed about Paul. That ability to put you completely at ease with the snappy patter and the smooth voice, then down to business before you could come up with more small talk to delay things.

"General Alexander Van Horne."

"Ah, the good General. And how is he?"

"Paul, just what did you tell him about me?"

Iannelli downed a little more beer, drew an index finger across his lips and settled back in the chair. "Matthew, we both going to play cop, or is one of us going to tell the other what's in the air?"

"You recommended me to him for that consulting job last spring. I appreciated that, telephoned back then to thank you."

"So I recall."

"You also recall you got another request from him or his legal gofer, guy named Kerstein, wanting a little more information on me?"

"After the consulting job?"

"Right."

Iannelli set the beer down on the floor in front of him. "I think maybe I did."

I drank some more. "There a reason you didn't let me know about the second call?"

Paul shrugged. "The General was in the market for a chief of security. Sounded to me way below what you'd be interested in, and I told him as much."

"You told him more than that."

"I told him enough so he wouldn't waste his time and yours on something that you wouldn't have considered, much less accepted. What's the problem here, Matthew?"

"The General knows about what I did in the Nam, Paul."

Iannelli thought about that. Brought his hand to his chin, scratched a little, then put an elbow on the arm of his chair, resting his chin on a balled fist. "I told the General some of your background in strictest confidence, Matthew. So he'd realize I knew you well enough to give him 'butt out' advice. He tells you what I told him, he has to be plenty interested in bringing you on for something, something a lot bigger than head gatekeeper for a nice house on the ocean. The question now is, do I want to hear about it?"

I cupped both hands around my bottle, bringing it to my belt as I leaned back in the couch. "The General has a problem. He doesn't want the authorities involved."

"So he turns to you."

"Right."

"But you might want a little back-door insurance. In case the shit hits the fan."

"That's about the situation."

"No, Matthew, that's your position. I still haven't heard about the situation, and I'm not sure I want to."

"Paul, the General has offered me a lot of money to do something for him. So far, he's the victim of anything he's told me about."

"Which you can't tell me about because the private investigator statute says you can't? Come on, Matthew."

"The statute talks about me revealing information only to the client or an 'authorized tribunal,' Paul."

"And I'm neither, right?"

"Right."

"What kind of bullshit we talking about here, Matthew? Grand jury, organized-crime unit, what?"

"Let me put it this way. A member of the General's household has disappeared under circumstances which suggest a kidnapping."

With a thumbnail, Iannelli worried the label on the bottle. "How strong is the 'suggestion'?"

"Like a note."

"Like that."

"Uh-huh."

"And X dies if the cops are called."

"Basically."

"How many kidnappings you handle when you were with me?"

"None."

"That's what I thought."

"Did work on the edges of one in Newark, another in San Antone."

"How much?"

"Ransom? I don't—"

"No, how much is the General going to give you here?"

"None of your business."

"Matthew. Just like it was none of the General's business about what you did in-country?"

"No, just like it was none of the General's business about Fred and me falling on hard times."

"Ah, and how is Fred? Still best friends with Jack Daniels and Jim Beam?"

"You can be a real shit sometimes, Paul."

"Hey, Matthew, drop the loyalty routine, okay? I vouched for both of you with the General because I wanted to see you get that consulting job. But a lush is a lush, Matthew. They cut Fred open, a sponge'd fall out."

"I'm not talking about the booze."

"Then what are you talking about?"

"What I think happened is, one of the customers you referred to Fred and me was unhappy about our work in some way, so you did a little discreet checking, burying something about us in a request for bank records, whatever. Lo and behold, you find we're a little cash short, so you check a little deeper."

"Maybe I ought to read you a Miranda card, Matthew."

"The point is, the General found out about all this a while ago, not this morning before he called me about his current problem."

"So?"

"So I think he got an update call, from an over-zealous guy who wanted to cover himself on any recommendation he gave the General."

"Maybe the General just has good connections in the banking industry."

"That's how he phrased it, too, Paul. You and the General should have worked out a little variation in the story there."

Iannelli took some more beer, then put the bottle down and resumed his relaxed look. "Your move."

"I'm going to try and straighten out what Fred's gotten us into."

"You gonna look after him all his life? He's a lush."

"He stepped in front of me once."

"Staggered in front of you, more like it. I had to kick him loose because of the booze. But you, Matthew, you could have stayed as long as you wanted."

"I'm still going to cover for it."

"With the General's fee for whatever it is I'm not supposed to know too much about."

"Right. And if I step in the shit, I want you to remember that everybody's got bank records, Paul."

His face tightened just the amount I was hoping for. "Better spell that out, Matthew."

"You give a lot of recommendations, don't you?"

"Always happy to help a friend."

"I'm not ungrateful, Paul. I'm just wondering if all the recommendations were for free."

His voice turned cold. "They were for you, Matthew."

"Maybe. But if I step in the shit on this one, I expect one stand-up guy to back my play, to put on the record that I tried to alert the authorities yet discharge my duty to the client. That I did my best with an impossible situation."

The cold voice remained. "So noted."

"I hope so, Paul. I hope to God it's so noted, because you can't afford to lose all this, and I can't afford to turn down the General."

"Anything else?"

"No." I stood to leave. "Thanks for the beer."

Iannelli smiled, used the smooth voice again. "Matthew, you ever have flashbacks?"

"Flashbacks?"

"To Vietnam, what you did over there."

"No."

"I hear a lot of guys do. I hear it really screws them up sometimes."

"Not me, but thanks for asking."

"Yeah. You see, if you did have these flashback things, I was just going to tell you, they're not real. You just have to say to yourself, 'I'm back in The World, so I'm safe, and part of the reason I'm safe is because nobody can do the kind of things back here that even I used to do over there.' You know what I mean, Matthew?"

I knew what he meant. I also knew what he really meant, and so did he.

When I turned the corner at the back of my house, Dee's Tercel was already there. She'd angled it so I could get the Blazer past her into the garage without either of us blocking the other in. Dee was nearly perfect that way: considerate to a fault, but always leaving herself an out.

From the kitchen, I could hear singing in the shower. I think it was a Chinese song Dee's mother taught her, but it also could have been a naughty French ditty from the Faber side. Given Dee's singing voice, it was tough to tell.

At the living room level, I took off my jacket and walked over to the stereo console. From a decanter on top, I poured a triple Scotch, telling myself I wouldn't like the look on Dee's face when she saw it, then convincing myself that after the sessions with Fred and Paul, I needed it more than I needed . . . what? More than I needed what?

Upstairs, the water sound switched from deflected spray to torrent, the singing stopping at the same instant. When she turned the water off, I yelled that I was home. She said she'd be right down.

Two minutes later I heard the clacking of high heels on the stairs. Dee languorously stretched a leg around the threshold, then slid into view, hugging the jamb like a burlesque queen at her stage-left curtain. She wore shiny, ebony high heels the color of her hair, which she'd wound into one long braid. The braid lay over one breast, soaking through the teddy she was wearing. She'd gone to some trouble for me.

Dee said, "You've got clean sheets, and I've got a dirty mind. Interested?"

Then she noticed the drink. And straightened up, crossing her arms. "I thought we agreed to try it this time without any booze first."

She hadn't spoken it like a question, so I didn't see a need to answer. Which made her stand there out of stubbornness. Except for the clothes, she looked a lot like she had the first night I met her, at a fashion show a year ago for which Fred and I had been hired as extra security. A buyer for a jewelry store downtown, Dee had been watching her wares like a hawk as the asexual models paraded detachedly along the foot-lit runway.

"Well, didn't we, Matt?"

"I've had a hard day, Dee, all right?"

"It's not your day we're trying to make hard, remember?"

"Clever."

Dee stomped awkwardly over to the decanter.

She poured herself a couple of ounces, straight up, and downed half of it, her back toward me, shivering a little. The teddy was the right size for her, the tail running just below her rump. Even at thirty-two, her skin had that burnished, Eurasian tint that taunts all white-skinned women to find the tanning method that can duplicate it.

Dee turned toward me, slow-stepping till she was standing in front, looking down at me. With her free hand she took mine, squeezing insistently. "We've got to figure this out, Matt. Work it out somehow."

I squeezed back, then shifted my position on the chair to break her hold. She sighed, sat down on the floor, Indian style.

I said, "You'll freeze it off that way."

She didn't reply.

"Look, Dee, it's just one drink. Take the edge off my worries, okay?"

"I'm not accusing you of being an alcoholic." She caught herself. "I'm sorry, I'm not accusing you of anything."

"I know."

"These worries. Can you tell me about them?"

"No."

"Matt—"

"I can't, all right? It's confidential. Professional, confidential stuff."

She lowered her voice. "It's just, well, it was so good at the beginning. I don't pretend to be any kind of expert, God knows the nuns at school saw to that till I was twenty. But I never felt it was better with anyone. And I still think we can deal with this, but we've got to start eliminating possibilities, Matt. Like the booze, even in small amounts."

"I told you, I don't think it's the booze."

Dee stayed patient, that reasonable executive manner that can drive you nuts sometimes. "You didn't think it was anything, remember? We went through this for two or three months before you'd even see a doctor."

I thought about that charade. Having to see the urologist's assistant first, a woman of maybe twenty-three with an East Boston accent you couldn't dent with a sledgehammer. Talking with her, oh so clinically. Then the urologist himself, reading his assistant's notes, nodding politely, scheduling tests I knew would show nothing physical was wrong.

"Matt?"

"Sorry. Slipped away there a little."

"That's the real problem, you know?"

"Huh?"

"You're slipping away from me. All because of your . . . not performing right with me. The sex is a big part of why I think we're so good together, I can't deny that. But it's only a part. I really think I . . . care for you, Matt. But we have to work this thing through together."

"Or else we're through together?"

"Matt, don't say that. Please don't."

Dee took my glass gently from my hand, placing both her drink and mine well out off flailing range. Then she began undressing me. Tugging off my tie in that herky-jerky way women who've never worn one assume it has to be done. Then undoing my shirt buttons, clicking her nails like knitting needles. She dragged the nail of her middle finger vertically down my chest as she worked her way south.

Dee undid my belt, trying not to notice the roll of fat above it. After unzipping me, she took off my loafers, rolled down and off my socks. She slid her hands, nails down, under my pant legs and up my calves, very lightly touching rather than massaging or even scratching. Then she leaned forward, pressing her breasts against my knees as she lowered her head to kiss through the opened fly.

Dee whispered to me. "Why don't we continue this in the bedroom?"

"I want to."

She stood, took my hand and led me upstairs. Dee used every part of her that could lick, nip, and coax on every part of me. At one point, I thought I was stirring, and I pushed her onto her back so gravity could give me a helping hand. But I knew as soon as I tried to enter her that it was no good. I could feel her straining beneath me, willing herself to be as wet and welcoming as possible. But it was no good.

As I rolled off her, Dee made a sound deep in her throat, like a cat that can't jump through a windowpane to catch a bird.

For a moment all I could hear was breathing, hers shallow and quick, mine deeper, more resigned.

"I could stay the night," she said. "If you want to . . . try it again?"

"I don't think so."

Dee laid her hand on my shoulder once. Then she left the bed. There were little snap and swish noises as she got dressed.

The mattress rocked as she sat down to put on her shoes, her back to me. "I have to be in New York tomorrow and Wednesday, but I'll be back Wednesday night. Here, say around eight again?"

I thought about it. "Sure. Have a good trip."

"Yeah. Good luck with . . . your worries."

There was something going wrong with Dee's voice for the last few words. She hurried from the room without kissing me good-bye.

Her steps on the stairs grew progressively muted. I heard the kitchen door slam, then the sound of the Tercel, starting up and tracking around the driveway until I lost it in the street noise.

I turned on the light and checked the clock. Then I went downstairs and found my copy of Turgeon's list. I dialed one of the General's numbers.

"Hello?"

"Turgeon?"

"Who is this?"

"It's Langway."

90

"The General wants to know if you're coming back tonight."

"Any word from our friends?"

"Our . . . no, no further communication of any kind."

"Then I'll be there tomorrow. Eight a.m. You have everybody's written statement?"

"Everybody who's here."

"Meaning?"

"Meaning all the people here. Family, staff. The only ones on my list that I don't have statements from are Ethan—that's the other grandson up in Maine—and Jaime Rivas. They just aren't here."

"All right."

"Oh yeah, and Kerstein. He left before I saw him, but I'm figuring he'll bring his up tomorrow."

"I'm going to want to talk to all the people on the estate. Be sure they're available from eight on. Anybody gives you any trouble about that, go directly to the General and tell on them. Got it?"

A pause to unlock his jaws. "Got it."

"I may want to talk with some of them more than once, depending, so tell them not to make any other plans for the day."

"Right."

"I may also need a room there for tomorrow night."

"I'll tell Nusby and his wife."

"See you in the morning."

At least Turgeon had the satisfaction of hanging up first.

I inhaled another scotch, then a third. Bringing the list upstairs, I put it in the nightstand drawer next to my Smith & Wesson Chief's Special.

I took a hot shower and went back to bed. Trying to remember what life was meant to be like, I fell asleep.

Chapter Eight

I am on the plane, the commercial flight carrying me toward Ton Son Nhut airbase. I am surprised that the Army is not using military aircraft to bring us into the country, a convex crescent sort of like a mirror-imaged New Jersey. A stewardess is asking if I want anything. Then she turns to a first sergeant sitting across the aisle from me. I begin to relax. If we're flying in commercial, stewardesses and everything, it must be safe, right? We must be winning after all.

My mood doesn't seem to be shared by the others on the plane. Most are enlisted men, half of them black or Hispanic. Seventeen, eighteen, nineteen years old. Somber, with shaved heads just sprouting some growth.

"Gonna waste them gooks!" An immature white voice, two rows in front of me, cracks a little at the end.

A jaded black voice replies. "What kinda shit you slinging, man?"

"Lost my best buddy from home to the gooks."

"So you thinking, 'vengeance is mine,' huh?"

"You got that right."

The black voice says, "How many you think you gonna get?"

"I dunno. Hope it happens soon, though. Don't wanna be a virgin too long."

"Bad weapon, the 'sixteen.' "

"The baddest. It'll open a hole like a baseball on the other end of you."

"Other end of the gooks, you mean."

"That's what I mean."

92

"Them gooks, they don't stand a chance, you around."

"We be home by fuckin' Christmas."

"Easter, very latest."

I notice the first sergeant across the aisle a little more now. Black, blocky head, fist-flattened nose. Short-sleeved khakis, a chest full of ribbons. He's fidgety, sweating profusely even in the air-conditioning.

A debate breaks out up front over the proper pronunciation of the last three letters of the country we were going to fight for.

Righteous White Vengeance says, "I'm telling you, my buddy was there, and he said it's 'Viet-NOM,' " the kid making it rhyme with "Mom."

Jaded Black Philosopher says, "Look, man, my brother, he done two tours, and all the time he say it be 'Viet-NAM,' " now like "Ma'am."

"Hey, man, I'm telling you, it's 'Nom'."

"And my brother say it be 'Na'am.' You calling my brother a liar?"

"No way, man. It's just . . . Hey, we can settle this. I'll ask the top kick there."

A seat buckle unsnaps, and the first sergeant next to me stiffens a bit as White Vengeance comes down the aisle.

"Excuse me, Top, but can you settle this for us? Is it—"

The kid stops talking when he sees how the sergeant's hands are shaking, fumbling with his own seat belt. Finally, the top stands up, facing White Vengeance from three inches away.

"Get back to your seat."

The kid scampers back.

The sergeant, grinding his teeth a little from the shaking, raises his voice. "Now I'm only gonna say this once. Something like six thousand GI's was dead by the time I left this place the last time. If I hears one more word about combat, or killing, or anything else from you green little turds for the rest of this here trip, I'll do you myself. This airplane be the last time I'm gonna have peace or quiet for three-hundred-sixty-five fuckin' days, and I'm gonna have it and I'm gonna enjoy it. Is that clear?"

A smattering of weak, uncoordinated voices. "Yes, sergeant."

"I said, 'Is that clear?' "

One strong response, in unison, "Yes, Ser-geant!"

The top sits back down, manages to buckle back up. He hyperventilates three, four, five times. I'm about to ask him if he's all right when he turns to me.

"Sorry, sir, it's just that—"

"Don't worry about it. They were starting to get to me, too."

He nods, rocking his head back against the cushion, trying to come back down.

I wake up to the clock radio. Some punk station Dee set a week ago that I haven't bothered to change because the music is so bad, I can't loll around listening to it. I try to rub the memories from my eyes and think about what I've got to do at the estate that morning.

The General handed me a stack of handwritten pages and said, "Langway, I hope you're ready to start now."

"I'd like a place off to myself for seeing the people. Where I can keep it formal or sidle up to them, based on how I want to handle it."

"How about my library?"

"Good. I need to install the cross-frame trap in there anyway."

Van Horne looked at Kerstein across the dining room table, still set for the numerous people who didn't share the General's penchant for dawn breakfasts.

Kerstein said, "You'll want to review the statements first, I take it?"

I thumbed the edges of the stack Van Horne had given me. "That would make the most sense, I think."

"Sumner, show Langway to the library. Have Nusby bring him whatever he needs. Langway, who do you want first?"

"You, General."

"Call when you're ready for me."

In the corridor I told Kerstein I could find my own way to the library. I asked him to keep everybody off the phones until I told him otherwise. He said he'd need five minutes worth to contact his office. I said fine.

Once in the library, I spent the five minutes moving around, getting a sense of the room beyond the walk-through with Nusby the day before. It smelled a lot like the interior of a new car. Fresh leather, citrus polish for the wood furniture, faintly coppery smell of something meant to take any offensive odors out of the air. Shelves lined with bound classics of English literature, Greek philosophy, ancient military history.

Behind the glass panels, some relics of more recent armed efforts. From what came to be called the First World War: a helmet that looked like it gave better vision than protection; a forty-five automatic, chips knocked from the handle; a diary with an uneven brown cover; a letter on curling yellow paper, the irregularities and blotches of an old fountain pen giving it a strange fascination. I guessed the General would have been too young for that one.

From what began for us in 1941: A Walther, with black SS holster; an Iron Cross; a Wehrmacht parade cap; photos of starved, wild-eyed creatures in dingy, striped uniforms you had to look at twice to be sure were human, staring from behind a wire fence that some GI's in the foreground were cutting while trying not to look at the camp survivors watching them; a lean, mean Brigadier General Van Horne standing in the hatch of a tank, binoculars in his hands, regarding with determination whatever he had been seeing through them.

From the first war I remembered being called a "police action": a sandy brown, ear-flapped cap with a red star where the forehead would be and a ragged, blackened hole just above the star; a map of South Korea, with some grease pencil overlays showing artillery emplacements and infantry assembly areas; a photo of a Korean woman of indeterminate age carrying a baby shy both arms below the elbow . . .

The last was too close, even without any photos of the second war that supposedly never was a war. I cleared my mind by installing the cross-frame trap.

Finished, I sat down, skimmed all the handwritten reports, cursing over one until I realized another wasn't there. I checked again. Same omission.

I thought about how to use that, then focused on the General's version.

ACCOUNT OF THE NIGHT OF
SUNDAY, 16 OCTOBER

I write this detailing my movements on the assumption that you can rely for the movements of others on your own checking of Turgeon's list and the other accounts you have requested. Based on Sumner's suggestion, an invitation was extended to Ethan to come down for Sunday dinner. We made awkward small talk over cocktails until 1800 hours, when dinner was served. In attendance for at least part of cocktails and the meal were Ethan, Janine, Allen, Kenny, Lila, Sumner, and myself. I believe Lila's boy, or stepson, now I see why you wanted this in our own hand-

writing, spontaneity might perhaps cause one to slip. Good idea, Langway. Lila's boy, Yale, was off somewhere, I believe. The dinner turned rather sour, me trying to draw Ethan into conversation, him giving his usual one word answers and displaying his I'm-above-all-this attitude. I didn't like it, thought it neither in the spirit of the invitation to him nor his acceptance of it, and said as much. That produced a shouting match, and he left the table, stalking off somewhere. Dinner broke up without dessert.

Allen had some Foundation event to attend. Sumner stayed here, meaning in the library, reading the draft of an instrument he needed for a meeting the next day. Janine had to bathe Kenny because Gloria, his au pair, had come home here from visiting in Boston with some kind of flu, and I didn't want her near Kenny. Janine groused about it, naturally, but eventually took Kenny upstairs with something approaching good humor. Lila and I took brandy in the library, she talking in a way that seemed to me intentionally to bother Sumner. At some point, Ethan burst back in on us, saying he couldn't see the sense of staying the night after all, me saying that was fine. I finished my brandy, leaving Lila and Sumner in the library.

I went to bed at approximately 2200 hours, though I was not looking at any clocks. I was at the breakfast table the next morning at approximately 0630 when Nusby, who was serving me, and I heard screaming from upstairs. By the time he and I reached the staircase, Sumner, Allen, Lila, and perhaps others were all at the head of the stairs, passing a piece of paper back and forth, everybody talking at once and Janine just screaming.

After conferring with Sumner and Turgeon, you were

contacted at approximately 0900 hours on Monday, 17 October.

Van Horne, Alexander M.

"Well, Langway, was my account satisfactory?"

"Better."

"You needn't flatter me. I need you, and you need my money. That's sufficient for both of us now."

I set his report aside. "Any further ideas on the kidnapping?"

"Is this room . . . clean?"

"Swept it already."

"Then, no. No further ideas." He took a breath, expelling it slowly. "Why have they let a full day go by without contacting us?"

"Hard to say. Maybe the drop they're planning takes some setting up. Probably they know that getting the ransom together might take some time, even for you. Kerstein on that?"

"Yes. We discreetly tapped four different bank presidents who owe me more than just confidentiality, but even with armed messengers, it took most of yesterday to assemble a million dollars."

"Denominations?"

"Tens, twenties and fifties. That's . . . customary, isn't it?"

"Yes. Are you going to leave it with the banks until we get the call?"

"No. We're having it brought up by armored truck. Sumner's idea. In case the estate is being watched from outside, the truck will show we're serious."

"Fine. But that means you'll have to leave a man on the place you're keeping it here."

"I've a vault in the security area downstairs."

"I saw it."

"Only Sumner and I can get into it. The man on the security room can watch it as well as it can be watched."

I laced my hands on the desk. "General, I'm going to tell you some things I'll keep from the others. First, my partner, Fred Dooley, is going to be doing outside inquiries, following up anything I develop here."

The brow furrowed. "You believe that's wise?"

"I believe that's necessary. I explained to him the situation you have us in, and he's willing to do most anything to save his own skin."

"So long as that doesn't make him . . . desperate."

"No more desperate than you are."

He just watched me. "How much did Sumner tell you about my . . . condition."

"Just that you were sick." I paused. "My guess from your appearance is cancer."

"Lymphoma, Langway."

He said it like he was ordering pie in a restaurant.

"Where?"

"Everywhere."

"General, I'm sorry. Truly."

"Thank you. If it makes a difference to you, to your investigation, I mean, the high estimate is three months, the low a matter of weeks."

I just nodded.

"I think the low doctor believes I'll commit suicide from the pain, thereby letting him win a bet with the high doctor."

"General—"

"I plan to keep him from winning that bet, Langway."

"Yessir."

"And I want Kenny with me for as many of the good hours as possible."

"Yessir."

"Anything else from me?"

"Not just now."

"Who do you want to see next?"

"Turgeon."

"Done."

Chapter Nine

REPORT OF MY ACTIONS OF
SUNDAY, 15 OCTOBER

I got up at 0600, ate breakfast, and toured the perimeter fence like always. Nothing unusual was observed. O'Meara had the day off. O'Meara was on duty Saturday from 1600 to 2400. I reviewed his log. Nobody came in or out on Saturday, 14 October, after 1800. Zoubek was on duty from 2400 Saturday to 1600 Sunday. I reviewed his log. Ms. Lila Underwin entered the grounds at 0330 Sunday. Gloria Rivas left the grounds at 0820 Sunday.

At your request, I gave you the log list for all subjects that came to the estate on Sunday, 15 October. The only persons not resident were Ethan Van Horne, resident of Maine, and Sumner Kerstein, resident of Brookline, Massachusetts. Sumner Kerstein was checked into the estate by Zoubek at 1408 hours. Ethan Van Horne was buzzed in by me at 1648 hours.

At 1724, Gloria Rivas was checked in by me. She looked sick, so I drove down to the gate and brought her back to the house. Gloria told me she got a ride to the estate by Jaime Rivas. Jaime was not at the gate when I got there to let her in. At 1736, Yale Underwin was buzzed in by me.

At 1850, Dr. Allen Van Horne was buzzed out the front gate by me. At 2141 Ethan Van Horne was buzzed back out the front gate by me. At 2339, Dr. Allen Van

Horne was checked back in the front gate by me.
            Submitted by Turgeon, Gilbert

Turgeon just sat there, watching me read his account. I kept my eyes on it for a while after I finished reading it. He never moved.

Without looking up, I said, "Not much emotion here, Turgeon."

"You asked for a report of actions. You got one."

"Why did you think I meant my remark as a criticism?"

He smiled, smug. "We playing some psychological game?"

I put the report to the side. "You ever in the service, Turgeon?"

"If you mean the armed forces, no. If you mean security services, I was with—"

"No, I meant the Army, Navy—"

"Then no, I wasn't."

"Why?"

"Why?"

"Yes. You seem to love all things military. The way you dress, who you work for, how you write a report. Why no service connection?"

"That's my business."

"Maybe the General—"

"Then call him on it, goddammit!"

Hitting a nerve is sometimes a lucky thing. Stepping back from it a ways, using it later, is sometimes a smarter thing.

"Your report ends a little early, doesn't it?"

"You said you wanted through Sunday. That's what you got."

"What did you do Monday morning?"

"After we . . . after Kenny was gone?"

"After he was discovered missing."

"I briefed the General kind of quickly, then went to central station. I told Zoubek and O'Meara to get their weapons and check the fence. Took them a while to do that. Everybody else searched the house. Nothing."

"Any chance Zoubek or O'Meara might have missed something along the fence?"

"No. They both went to the main gate and then headed out separately along the fence, different directions, till they met each other again out by the cliff. Then they doubled back to the main gate along each other's trails, so they could check each other out about things along the fence. Nothing."

I said, "How about more generally?"

"I don't get you."

"How was the security staff deployed here?"

"Like I told you."

"Tell me again."

Turgeon sighed. "With Rivas gone, the three of us had to pull double shifts. I did most of it. On weekends, one of the men, Zoubek or O'Meara, was off each day. This past weekend, Zoubek had Saturday off, O'Meara Sunday."

"When were you off?"

"I wasn't. Haven't been since Rivas left."

"Come up with any reason why he left?"

"Like I said, he quit, I didn't fire him."

"And he didn't tell you why?"

"No."

"Why do you think he left?"

"I don't know."

"Doesn't sound like great executive supervision there, Turgeon."

"Then it doesn't."

I asked myself again whether I liked the way Turgeon was covering for both his former employee and the amorous Lila. I decided to let that ride for a while, too.

"So, you were on midnight Friday to eight a.m. Saturday, and eight a.m. Saturday to four p.m. Saturday?"

"Right."

"Except for daylight hours, the man on duty would be in central station, right?"

"Right. Watching the monitors and panels."

"Watching, right. When somebody comes to the gate?"

"We have a way to buzz them in."

I thought back to April. "I recommended that be disconnected."

"Yeah, you did. But with only the three of us on board here, we reconnected it. Had to, otherwise the guy in the security room has to come to the front gate and then nobody's watching the monitors and panels."

"Just like when you went to the gate to let Gloria in."

"Like I said, she was sick. It wouldn't have been right to ask her to walk all the way up to the main house."

"She told you Jaime drove her back from Boston."

"Right."

"Why wouldn't he have just driven her up to the main house?"

"I don't know."

"Let me guess. I should ask him."

"Right."

"Was letting Gloria in the only time you left the security room that night?"

"No."

I referred to his report. "Sometimes you say you 'buzzed' someone in, other times you say you 'checked' someone in."

"That's right."

"Buzzed in means you used the buzzer and didn't leave central station?"

"Right."

"And checked in . . ."

"Means either the man at the gate checked the person in, or that the gate was unmanned, meaning the monitor room man had to leave the basement and come down to the gate to let the person in."

"So on Sunday night at about 9:40, Ethan Van Horne was buzzed out, but on Sunday night at about 11:40, two hours later, you went down to the gate to check in Dr. Allen Van Horne."

"Right."

"Why?"

"Why?"

"Yes. Why didn't you just buzz Allen back in?"

"Car trouble."

"What do you mean?"

"Dr. Allen had car trouble. Engine flooded. He's a real . . . he's not too good around things. Mechanical things. I am so I went down, got the wagon started for him."

"Wagon?"

"Yeah. The Chrysler wagon's the one he drives."

"Which vehicle is yours?"

"We use the Bronco."

"Yes, but aside from security work, which car is yours?"

"None of them."

"None?"

"Right. The Harley's mine."

"And the little Honda scooter?"

A trace of a sneer. "Yale Underwin's."

"Match up the other vehicles for me."

Turgeon held up his hand to use his fingers. "Ernie, he—"

"Zoubek?"

"Right. Zoubek, he doesn't own a car. The Rolls is the General's, the BMW's Lila Underwin's. The Chrysler convertible goes with Janine Van Horne, the Toyota is Casper Binns. The Chevy Cavalier, that's the Nusbys'."

I hadn't seen the Cavalier yesterday, but then Nusby said his wife and Gloria were out shopping. "How about the Pontiac Firebird?"

"Oh, right. That's Tim's."

"O'Meara."

"Uh-huh."

"When did O'Meara come on duty?"

"On Saturday, now?"

"Yes."

"At 1600, the end of my double shift."

"Where was Zoubek?"

"Off."

"Yes, but off where?"

"Ask him."

"All right. On Sunday, why did you reverse the shifts?"

"I don't get you."

I picked up his report. "It looks from this that Zoubek checked people in from midnight Saturday till you kicked in at four p.m. Sunday. How come?"

"Day after a day off, the guy who was off usually takes a double shift, like Zoubek did on Sunday. That's so I can get some down time, even if I'm not leaving the estate."

"And that's why O'Meara was on the front gate Monday morning?"

"No. Things weren't exactly 'usual' Monday morning."

"Who came on at midnight, Sunday into Monday morning?"

"I . . . I had to stay on."

"Why?"

"O'Meara didn't get in till almost two, oh-two-hundred, I mean."

"Meaning his day off ended at midnight Sunday, and he wasn't back till two a.m. Monday?"

"He wasn't . . . he wasn't in any shape to go on duty."

"He was drunk."

Turgeon looked uncomfortable, then nodded.

"So you pulled double-duty again, from four p.m. Sunday to eight a.m. Monday?"

"Right."

"Staring at the panels."

"In central station, right."

"With the upstairs entry detectors connected only to the panel lights, not the Klaxon alarm."

"Right, right. Like the General told me."

"Double-shifting like that, staring at the panels, you didn't maybe nod off?"

"No."

"Not once, Turgeon?"

"I said no. I stayed awake."

"Awake enough to notice O'Meara down at the main gate at two a.m. into Monday morning."

"Right."

"And you buzzed O'Meara in?"

"No. No, I went down and checked him in."

"Why?"

"He looked so stiff on the monitor, I was afraid he'd run off the road between the gate and the house here."

"Even so, on the log you don't show O'Meara coming in, buzzed or checked."

Turgeon shook his head.

"Why?"

"I was already short one man, Rivas. I couldn't . . . I was barely getting enough sleep as it was . . . I left his name off the log so the General wouldn't fire him."

Turgeon passed his hand across his eyes. I got the queasy feeling that he just barely kept himself from crying.

I said, "O'Meara's not the only one you forgot to log."

"What?"

"There's no entry for Kenny leaving, either."

Turgeon jumped up and left the library.

TIM O'MEARA, ACTIVTIES FOR SUNDAY

Im not so good at report writing, so its probably a good thing this is short. I was off on Sunday. So I got in my car and drove out of the estate around three. I went down to Boston. Spent some time in the bars. Watching football, then dinner. Went to a cuple other places. Drove home to the estate. I got here and went to bed. Didn't hear a thing till Chief Turgeon got me up Monday morning. I guess thats about it.

Tim O'Meara

"Sorry there isn't much there."

I said, "Not your fault."

The flashy grin. Probably how he'd gotten through life so far. "Anything else I can help you with?"

"How about you telling me your sense of everybody around here."

"My sense?"

"Yeah. Confidentially, how do you peg the people who could have been involved?"

"Where do you want me to start?"

"Whoever comes to mind first."

O'Meara leaned forward. You could get tired watching him think.

He said, "The General, he's a good guy. Tough man to work for, but he lets you do your job, you know?"

"That's exactly the kind of thing I want to hear. What about the others?"

"The others. Well, Mrs. Underwin, I already told you about her and Jaime, right?"

"Right."

"Okay. Her son, Yale, he's okay, I think."

"How do you mean?"

"Well, he's just seventeen, maybe. But he's got the world by the balls. Rich kid, good-looking chippies hanging off him."

"So you don't see him being involved in all this?"

"No. Just don't see him stopping with the tennis and the boats and all long enough."

"Who do you think of next?"

"Dr. Allen, I guess. He's not . . ."

"Not what?"

"Not . . . look, this here is confidential, right?"

"Right."

"All the way? I mean, nobody but you and me, right?"

"Right."

O'Meara blew out a breath. "Okay. I get the feeling that Dr. Allen and his wife don't get along so good."

No surprises so far. "How do you mean?"

"In the sack. I heard she had a thing with this tennis pro guy from one of the country clubs, you know?"

I cleared my throat. "Anything ever come of it?"

"Well, I figured Mrs. Van Horne had to be punching this tennis guy, but real . . . there's a word for it, like when somebody's having an affair with somebody else but they're being real careful about it."

" 'Discreet'."

"Yeah, 'discreet.' Yeah, well I guess she was being real discreet about it, but the General found out anyway and—"

"How?"

"How?"

"Yes. How did the General find out?"

"Don't know. I just know he hit the fucking roof about it. Around Christmas time, I remember, you could hear him yelling his lungs out all over the house."

"That stop the affair?"

"Far as I know."

"Any other affairs?"

"Not that I heard about."

"Anything else about Janine Van Horne?"

"Well, I don't think her and the kid get along too well, either."

"She's his mother, though, right?"

"Yeah, but the girl, Gloria, she's with the kid most of the time. For Janine, it always seemed to me kind of like Kenny was this dog her husband always wanted but never walked, you know?"

"I get the picture. How about Gloria?"

"Gloria? Ah, she's okay. I mean, for an immigrant like her, don't speaka the English too good, she's doing fine."

"How does she like Kenny?"

"Pretty good, I think. I mean, I see them all the time together, playing little games he likes."

I glanced down at Turgeon's list. "How about the tutor, Casper Binns?"

"Casper? Well . . . Casper."

"What is it?"

"Casper's a little on the strange side."

"What kind of strange?"

"Like . . . well, he never approached me or anything, but I always got the impression he, well . . ."

"Come on, O'Meara, what the hell are you talking about?"

"I guess I always thought there was this hint of mint about the guy."

I thought about the matchbook in my pocket. "You mean he's gay?"

"Yeah. Nothing he ever said or anything, but you know how some of those guys like the big muscles?"

O'Meara seemed to do an involuntary flex. I kept from smiling. "Yeah."

"Well, I get the sense, like you said before, that the guy's queer, but I can't give you any proof of it."

"How about Sumner Kerstein?"

"Smart J . . . He's real smart, been around a long time. General seems to trust him."

"But you don't?"

"I . . . I never liked his looks."

"Meaning?"

"He always seemed to me like a guy who was trying to be something he wasn't."

"And what was that?"

"Somebody who wasn't a Jew when he was around people who weren't Jews."

"You know Ethan Van Horne?"

"The other grandson?"

"Yes."

"Never met him. Black sheep, I guess."

I realized I hadn't been thinking about Nusby and his wife. Bad lapse. "What about Willie Nusby?"

"Willie? He wishes people would call him 'Mr. Nusby,' but nobody ever will. I don't see him being able to get the kid out, but you never know. A lot of the jigs, they're wiry strong, they surprise you."

Consistent son of a bitch, this O'Meara. "And Zoubek?"

O'Meara seemed taken back. "You don't figure Ernie's in on it, do you? I mean, he's one of us."

"What do you figure?"

"Ernie." O'Meara shook his head. "I can't see him doing something like this. He's like, too loyal in the old-country sense, you know? I could see him standing with a spear at the castle door, dying so the head shit and his family could get out the back way."

"And Turgeon?"

"The Chief? Come on, he really takes this stuff seriously. He couldn't be in on it."

Which left, if I believed him, just Jaime Rivas and O'Meara as people with detailed security information. Either O'Meara was awfully stupid or awfully honest. With some people it's hard to tell, with others it's both.

My name Ernst Zoubek. On duty from midnite Saterday to four o'clock in the Sunday afternoon. Mrs. Lila and Mr. Kerstein the lawyer and Mr. Ethan I never met before come then to the estate. I go to my bed at maybe ten o'clock in the Sunday nite. After my supper. I don't know nothing wrong before I am awake from Chief Turgeon. He telling me Ernie, get up, get up, Kenny is gone. That is Monday in the morning early. I don't hear nothing when I asleeping.

I tell you one thing, I don't know what happen. I swear to God.

"I am sorry for my English."

"Nothing to be sorry about."

"It is not so good in the writing, but I can talk better. You have questions?"

"Yes. I'm told you were off on Saturday?"

"Off, yes. You bet."

"What did you do?"

"When I am off Saturday?"

"Right."

"I go to hike. In the woods. Good for you. This good job, but you too much sit and stand. No good for the body."

"Where did you hike?"

Zoubek shrugged. "Over here, over there." He shrugged again.

"You came back on duty at midnight on Saturday?"

"Saturday, yes."

"I understand that Lila Underwin didn't come back onto the grounds until about three-thirty a.m. on Sunday morning?"

"You right. I write down when anybody come in or go out when I am on duty."

"She usually such a night owl?"

"What is the 'night owl'?"

"Is she usually out so late?"

"Oh. Yes, she . . ."

"Please, go on."

"She . . . Mrs. Lila . . . she go out a lot of times."

"And stay out?"

"I don't know that."

"But you do log her in pretty late sometimes."

"Pretty late sometimes, yes."

"Did you buzz her in or go down to the gate and let her in?"

"I buzz."

"How about Kerstein?"

"Mr. Kerstein the lawyer come to visit the General a lot of times."

"On Sunday, I mean. He arrived at . . . a little after two in the afternoon?"

"Yes, you bet. He come in, thank me for letting him in gate. He always polite to me, Mr. Kerstein."

I leaned back in the chair. "You say you don't know Ethan Van Horne, the General's other grandson?"

"No."

"Do you know of any reason anybody would have for taking Kenny?"

"No."

"What do you think happened?"

"Happen? I don't know."

"No idea at all?"

"I asleeping in my bed, like I tell you there in the writing. I don't hear nothing when I asleeping."

"Did you hear O'Meara?"

"Timmie? Timmie, I hear."

"When?"

"Sunday night."

"What time?"

"After I go to my bed."

"What did you hear?"

"I hear Timmie sick with throw-ups."

I pushed his report to the side. "What did you do in Czechoslovakia?"

114

"Do? What I am told to do. Like here, but not like here. I tell you one thing, here you told what to do on your job. That is okay. Over there, you told what to do for all things. That is not okay."

"What was your job over there?"

"I was soldier."

"Army?"

"Yes. Soldier in army."

"What kind of soldier?"

"Good soldier."

"What was your job in the army?"

"To be . . . oh, you mean, what I do on duty in the army?"

"Yes."

"I was mountain soldier. You don't understand the word for it, but we was soldiers, go in the mountains, fight anybody coming into country through the mountains to fight us."

I thought about the cliff off the General's ocean view, the cliff down to the sea and the rocks.

"You ever rappel, Zoubek?"

"Rappel with the ropes, you mean?"

"Yes."

"Ho, boy, I tell you, we rappel all the time. Like goats, we rappel."

I saw a happy, open face. Simple features, trying to please. "Anything else you can help me with here, Zoubek?"

"I don't know." He seemed to struggle with something. Then, "I can ask question?"

"Sure. Go ahead."

"You know about these things. You think Kenny . . . you think Kenny all right?"

Zoubek was in some pain. He seemed as straight and

real to me as a clump of soil in a farmer's fist.

I said, "Nobody can know that but the people who have him."

Zoubek nodded vigorously. "That is right. I am sorry. You got any more questions for me?"

"Not just now. You think you could find Sumner Kerstein for me?"

"Mr. Kerstein. Sure, you bet."

Chapter Ten

"You want to talk with me next?"

I looked up at him. "No. I want your advice."

Kerstein smiled, the *that's-what-I'm-here-for* smile you see from polished professionals as they turn on the meter. Sitting, he said, "About what?"

"Yesterday, Janine Van Horne didn't exactly welcome me to the hearth. I'm wondering if we know her current state of mind?"

Kerstein looked pensive. "With Janine, that can be hard to tell."

"I may have to ask her some tough questions about Kenny. You think it would help to have her husband with her?"

"Allen? I don't find Allen to be much of a help with anything besides shaking hands at fund-raisers."

"It is their child we're talking about. If you don't see any objection, I'd rather talk to them together."

Kerstein stared over my shoulder. "I don't see what harm it could do. She was pretty hysterical yesterday morning. Maybe having Allen in the room would bolster her a little, prevent a recurrence of . . . what happened between you two yesterday."

"See if you can find them for me, then."

"Right."

He stood to leave.

"Oh, and Kerstein?"

He didn't turn right away, like he wanted it to sink in that I wasn't supposed to address him that way. "Yes?"

"I don't see your summary of what happened Sunday night."

"Now why do you suppose that is?"

"Do one."

"You can't be serious?"

"I am. The General took the trouble; I didn't tell him that you hadn't. That's one you owe me, counselor."

The lawyer bit the inside of his cheek. "Half an hour."

"That should be fine."

MY REPORT OF SUNDAY EVENING LAST

We all gathered for a Sunday dinner, as in the old days, I suppose one could say. Sumner's idea, actually, toward effecting a reconciliation between Ethan and the General. Ethan behaved rudely during cocktails and saw fit to continue his behavior during dinner. There was a tiff, and he left the table, rather in a snit and quite the worse for it, I thought. There was a charitable event that required my presence on behalf of the Foundation, but Janine wasn't feeling up to it, so I left on my own. I didn't really notice the time, but I'm sure the security staff can fill that in for you.

I returned to the estate sometime near midnight, I believe. I was let in by Turgeon from the security room. I crept around so as not to disturb anyone else, but I did look in on Kenny, who seemed sound asleep. I then went to bed.

I heard nothing further that night. Early on Monday morning, I was awakened by Janine's screaming. She ran up to me and then out into the corridor of our wing, clutching this piece of paper which I soon discovered was the ransom note.

I would be happy to speak with you about anything else you think important.

Allen Van Horne, M.D.

JANINE V. H.:

Sumner and the General were trying to get Ethan to come back into the family, instead of playing hippie in the woods. He came for drinks and dinner on Sunday, and acted like a jerk. After dinner, I took Kenny upstairs for a bath and bed because Gloria had some kind of plague she caught down in the city. I think she was asleep in her room. I put Kenny to bed, then stayed up in my room. I read for a while. I fell asleep sometime, I don't know when. But I woke up for a minute when Allen came in. I don't remember saying anything to him. Something else, I don't know what, woke me up early on Monday. I got up to see if Kenny was okay, since I didn't think Gloria would be up yet. I opened the door to his room. And he was gone. I didn't think too much of it, because he sometimes gets up early and roams around, looking for the General. His window was open, though. And since it was blowing cold air, I went over to close it. That's when I saw the note. I don't remember much except screaming and running around after that.

Janine V. H.

Allen Van Horne, M.D., sat in his chair like he was trying to make a good impression at a prep school admissions interview. Janine slouched in the other chair. They were both dressed in a variation of the clothes they'd worn the day before. She probably could dress like that for three months and never wear the same outfit twice in a row.

119

Janine said, "Can we get on with this?"

Allen shot his wife a pained look, but he immediately seemed relieved that she hadn't seen it.

I said, "I've reviewed both of your statements."

Allen said, "Yes?"

"Mrs. Van Horne—"

"Oh, for Christ's sake, don't you think you could call me Janine by this point?"

I took a breath, Allen seemed afraid to.

I said, "When you put Kenny to bed, did he say anything?"

"About what?"

"Anything he was planning to do, maybe anything he was afraid of?"

"Kenny never says too much that makes sense."

"Dear, perhaps Mr. Langway could—"

Her look cut him off. "Allen, *Mis*ter Langway can speak for himself." She looked back at me. "Kenny's speech patterns were . . . are pretty . . ." Her eyes clouded up. She pulled some Kleenex from a pocket before Allen could clear a handkerchief from his. "My God, I'm already talking about him like he's dead."

I found myself fixing on Allen's statement. "Dr. Van Horne, you say Turgeon let you back into the estate?"

"Uh, yes."

"Personally?"

"Personally . . . ?"

"He came down personally to let you in?"

"Oh. Personally, yes. Yes, he did."

"Why didn't he just buzz you in?"

"I was having car trouble. It . . . it seems the car floods or something when I try to start it, you see. It's been giving me fits for a week or so, but I never seem to get around to having it seen to."

"Why did you have to start the car?"

"Why . . . ?"

"Yes. Why did you turn the ignition off outside the gate?"

"Oh. Oh, I didn't. It stalled."

"It stalled."

"Yes. Yes, and when I tried to start it again, it just . . ."

"Flooded."

"Yes."

"So Turgeon came down."

"Yes, and he was able to get it started for me. Wonderful chap around things mechanical. Not me, I'm afraid."

"You also say here that you looked in on Kenny when you got back Sunday night."

"Yes. Yes, it was late, so I didn't want to wake him. But I knew that Gloria had come back rather under the weather, and I just wanted to see that he was all right."

I snapped up to him. "You saw Kenny, then?"

Allen looked pained again. "That's what I keep asking myself, you see. I keep trying to recall the picture of what I saw. I really only glanced at his bed, you know. From the connecting door between our parlor and his bedroom. I really didn't go in his room, because I didn't want to wake him. Kenny gets . . . cranky when he's awakened during the night. But I thought I saw his head, his hair, really, on the pillow through the moonlight from the window."

"The window in his room?"

"Yes."

"Was the window open at all?"

"Open?"

"Yes. Open."

"Why . . . why I don't know. Why would it be open?"

"Could you feel a draft?"

"Draft?"

"Yes, Doctor. Draft. Cold wind blowing in."

"Oh. Yes, draft. No, no I . . . well, I suppose I'm not sure now. With trying to remember if it was Kenny or just one of his animals I saw . . . I'm sorry, I just don't know."

I looked over at Janine, who seemed to have recovered somewhat.

She said, "I wrote down the window was open because it was. The big window, maybe three inches. His room was cold from it. I didn't imagine it."

"I'm sure you didn't."

"Yeah, well be sure of something else, too. I haven't been a very good mother to Kenny. I wouldn't be a very good mother to anybody, retarded or not. But I love him and I want him back. Do you understand me?"

Her eyes were so intense I had trouble meeting them. The good doctor didn't bother to try. He'd given up that joust a long time ago.

For the sake of consistency, I asked both of them if they heard anything during the night. Allen shook his head, Janine said "No."

CASPER BINNS: SUNDAY NIGHT

I understand you wish a report of what each of us was doing on Sunday night. I'm afraid that I haven't been asked to participate in something quite like this before, so please make allowances accordingly.

Sunday was quite nice weatherwise, and since my tutorials of Kenny are limited to weekdays, I thought about driving to the beach. It is so much nicer this time of year, what with all the crowds returned to their autumn pursuits. However, I compromised by merely sitting out on the promontory, as I call it, overlooking the ocean and content with my own thoughts of the moment.

As I'm sure someone else has told you we (meaning "the staff"—nice euphemism for us servants, don't you think?) can take our meals through the good offices of Marcella and Willie Nusby when we don't dine with the family. I ate at approximately four, so that the Nusbys would not be too put out by me as they were preparing le grande meal du jour for the prodigal grandson. I went up to my apartment shortly afterward, hearing some spatting through the doors to the library where I assume cocktails were being sipped.

I stayed in my room, listening to music on my stereo and reading. Since I was wearing earphones, I really didn't hear anything thereafter. I showered and retired by ten-thirty, and frankly didn't even hear the great uproar the next morning at dawn. Sound sleeper, I imagine.

I'm afraid that exhausts my memory on the subject.

Casper Binns
Tutor-in-residence

"You don't write like a servant, Mr. Binns."

He was shorter and slighter than I am, with big eyes and a carefully groomed look to his hair, sweater, and slacks. He settled back into the chair, crossing his legs. "Really?"

"Really. You sound more like a social commentator, dropped undercover into the household."

He smiled. "Some societies bear more commentating than others."

"Especially small, closed societies?"

"Especially."

"Like a near-feudal manor."

"Now you've got it."

"Feel free to smoke, if you'd like."

"No, thanks. For me, it's a pleasure, not an addiction."

I slid his account into the file. "What are the chances of getting you to level with me?"

"Miniscule."

"Mind telling me why?"

"Yes."

I took the matchbook from my pocket and tossed it on the desk in front of him so that the "Fellas" script was visible.

Binns looked at it. "Are you a patron of that establishment?"

"No, I'm not."

"But you are familiar with it."

"Yes."

Binns leaned his cheek onto his right hand, the index finger pushing up on his right eyebrow. "Then tell me, are you one of those law enforcement types who believes every gay is really a pedophile?"

"No, Mr. Binns. Are you one of those gays who believes every cop is a basher?"

A sour smile this time. "No. But then, you're not a cop, are you?"

"Not anymore. I'm just here at the General's request, asking questions of those who want to cooperate."

"Oh, nicely *put,* Mr. Langway. *Nicely* put. As though we free citizens of a great democracy have more of a choice than the turkey does at Thanksgiving."

"You don't give a shit whether Kenny comes back or not?"

"Uh-oh. Interrogation technique number two, eh? Change of tack noted, sir."

I dropped my tone a couple of notches. "Tell me about Kenny."

" 'About' him?"

"Yeah. Just tell me what he's like, what I'm looking for."

"Seriously?"

"Seriously."

Binns straightened, folded his hands in his lap. "Kenny has a form of . . . do you care about developmental jargon here, Mr. Langway?"

"No. Just be descriptive. Capture him for me."

"He suffers from a condition that we know more about treating than we do about curing or preventing. Somehow, children like Kenny come out with normal features, but are severely . . . limited in their learning capacity. He recognizes those around him easily, can distinguish animals, even plants. He's quite a happy child most of the time, spared by nature and circumstance of a concern about food and shelter for the morrow. His speaking voice would give away . . ."

"I've seen some videos."

"Yes, well I've worked on filing the edges off that, using audiotapes and making games of improving him that keep his attention long enough for slow, and I mean *achingly* slow, progress. I've been here for nearly two years now, and I'm good, yet I've made only small advances to date."

"Anything recently that was odd about Kenny's behavior?"

"Recently. No."

"How about not so recently, then?"

"Some days Kenny was . . . sharper than others, with no good explanation for the difference."

"Any bad explanation?"

"Kenny can be hyper-kinetic, which has been known to upset adults around him."

"Leading to what?"

"Perhaps some kind of . . . pacifier."

"You mean drug?"

"Perhaps."

"You ever pursue that question?"

"No."

"Why not?"

"His father's the doctor."

"How outgoing is Kenny?"

"Outgoing? Do you mean demonstrative?"

"I mean would he go off willingly in the middle of the night with a stranger?"

Binns said, "You know, I've thought about that. You must understand, Kenny appreciates far more of what goes on than most adults credit him. It's an easy thing to do, to underestimate someone you know to be your intellectual inferior beyond a shadow of a doubt. But Kenny really does follow language far better than he can articulate it. And he is simply marvelous, nearly extrasensory, about perceiving emotions, even playing on them. But no, no, I don't think a stranger could have fooled him into going out the window."

"Why do you say 'window'?"

"Why do I . . . ?"

"Why did you say 'out the window'?"

"Oh. I don't know, just a figure of speech." Again the smile. "How did they take Kenny out, anyway?"

I smiled back. "Do you spend most of your weekends off here at the estate?"

"Some. Not that much to do around here once you've taken in the local color."

I had the feeling he wasn't referring to the foliage. I tilted my head toward the matchbook. "Go to Boston much?"

"Now and then. Expensive city."

"Can I ask you another serious question, Mr. Binns?"

"Yes."

"What do you think happened up here?"

He seemed to have thought about that, too. "I think the best, most loyal subject in the manor got kidnapped, Mr. Langway. And I don't have a clue as to who, how, or why."

Chapter Eleven

I was thinking about seeing Lila next, but I needed a break. My watch said only 11:05 a.m. I thought back to what Kerstein had said about the estate's dinghy down at the harbor. Good excuse for getting out for a while.

In the kitchen, Nusby said a bacon, lettuce and tomato sandwich on my return would be no difficulty. I chose the perfect tour guide on my own.

Like, I don't know what you want me to say. I was out all day on the boat. Nice day like this, we won't see too many more till next spring and I was with this fresh chick. And her and me were really messing. I was like planning to go out with her on Sunday night too but I got this head from drinking the hard stuff on the boat you know so I didn't. Found out Monday when I got up that I slept through all the stuff about Kenny. Guess I can't help much.

Yale Underwin said, "Hey, man, that's pretty cool, you know?"

"What is?"

"Driving and reading like that, all at the same time."

"Not as cool as your Sunday was."

"Yeah, well, you know, the sun, the booze, the sex, after a while it takes it out of you."

I glanced across the Blazer's console at this seventeen-year-old, the face of a kid, the soul of a satyr. Surfer blond hair, still streaked from the Southern California sun. Husky in that baby-fat way that goes to pot in the mid-twenties. Sly smile, attract the girls like honey if the appearance of money didn't take care of that already.

"So, like what else can I tell you?"

"When did you and your mother arrive here?"

"She's not my mother."

Yale's voice was kind, not defensive.

I said, "Sorry. Your stepmother, Lila."

"Which time?"

"Which time?"

"Yeah, like we come back here every time one of her marriages hits the rocks. Which time you talking about?"

Interesting. I had just assumed that he was the son of Lila's most recent husband. "This time. This last time."

"Oh, let's see. Maybe September, I guess. Yeah, if this is October, right, then yeah, last month sometime." He changed his tone. "Uh, you want to take this right here. No, not . . . right, that's it."

We went by a red brick building just off the town green. "School?"

"Guess so."

"No. I meant, is that your school?"

"No. Don't go to school."

"At all?"

"Man, I been around to so many, one more couldn't help much, you know?"

He had me there. We angled down toward the harbor, passing a bunch of trendy restaurants, art galleries, one bank, one drugstore, and a handful of bars.

I said, "What do you do during the day?"

"What everybody wants to and can't. Tennis, sail, ride. I was never much into the riding, but the General has these bitchin' horses, man, it's like they're riding you, they're so well trained."

"What happened to swimming?"

"Got to go with the flow, man. Water around here'd freeze your nuts off. I tried diving, even a little wind-surfing, but I gotta wear a full wetsuit for both of them, and that's kind of a drag."

"You miss Southern Cal?"

"No more'n any other place we been to and left. Lila's good that way. She hooks up with a different guy, different kind of guy, each time. Like she's working her way through some psychological profiles or something. We change our name, get to see a different part of the world each time. It's okay, better'n most get."

It shouldn't have troubled me that he took all the up-heaval in his life so easily. It should have reassured me that any creature is adaptable to any circumstance. But it didn't.

"Where does the money come from?"

"Don't know, man. Never had to think about it."

"And never want to?"

He shrugged. "What do you need money for, anyway? The General gives us this place to live here, picks up for the boat and all. Nusby feeds us real good, lots of different kinds of food. His wife's great with the cakes and pies."

"What happens when the General dies?"

"Lila gets her chunk of it."

I decided to find out what he knew. "How much is that?"

"Not sure, but I get the *Cheoy Lee*."

"The sailboat?"

"Yeah. The General, last time we were back here, before he like got sick and all, him and me took it out. Hit kind of a blow, but with me helping, we got it back in, no damage. He said—what the fuck was it? Oh, yeah—he said he was 'impressed with the way I handled myself.' Told me he was gonna leave it to me, like in his will, you know?"

"That bother anybody else?"

"Doubt it. With the General sick and all, I'm about the only one uses it." Again the sudden change of tone. "Uh, pull up over there."

I eased onto a wooden access wharf that rumbled and clopped under the car's weight like an old covered bridge. We got out of the Blazer.

"There she is."

I followed Yale's hand to a dark, single-masted hull moored to a white spherical buoy twice the size of a basketball. The boat was at least a hundred yards out, but even at that distance it looked over thirty feet long. A blue bonnet stretched on its boom to protect the lowered mainsail from the elements. She was rigged with a furled jibsail at the bow and an encircling lifeline banister, pickets three feet apart, at the stern.

"General named her the *Remagen*. After some place in Germany."

"A bridge there."

"Yeah, well, I always thought it was like a funny name for a Chinese boat, but then, it's his boat. Know much about them?"

"Boats? A little."

"No, I mean like the *Cheoy Lees* themselves."

"No."

"Great boat. Old-time good, all teak and brass and shit. It's a bitch to keep up, but you keep it up, it looks like a million dollars. Not so fancy maybe, only thirty-five feet and a small engine, but it'll do six knots under jib and mainsail. It's something you can . . . I dunno . . ."

"Be proud of?"

He shrugged again.

The *Remagen* was one of only thirty or so boats left in the harbor. Literally hundreds of buoys bobbed empty in the light chop. Surf broke on either end of a rocky barrier island maybe half a mile due east, I assumed giving the harbor its sheltering effect.

"Everybody else out sailing?"

"What . . . Oh, no. It's the end of the season up here. Most of the boats got lifted out already. Like . . ." he scanned the harbor and pointed again. "Like that one. See?"

At one of the wharves a crew of two men were coaxing a boat into a sling and derricking it up onto a huge cradle. Like an iceberg, the boat seemed much bigger below the waterline than above it.

I said, "How come the General's boat is still in?"

"The way he is now, he doesn't worry much about it anymore. Besides, I figure, he's so sick now, like maybe he'll die before it gets too cold for me to sail her to Florida."

I tried to imagine sailing that boat in late October or November down the east coast.

"What if you wait too long?"

"Not that much of a problem. Takes a while for this harbor to ice up. I just bring it in here to the yacht club dock, and they take it from there."

Nodding my head, I said, "The dinghy?"

"Oh, right. Over here."

He led me to a flotilla of black and gray rubber rafts, each differentiated from its cousins by varying outboard motors and markings I couldn't decipher. The rafts were strung together between land and a long, sinuous dock that branched out here and there to enclose more and more of them.

Yale said, "This one's ours."

Black, with a twenty-five-horse Johnson mounted on its wooden stern transom. A bright orange gas can was connected to the motor by a twisted, bulbed black hose. Some kind of suction pump floated in the three inches of water sloshing around its floor.

"How long since this has been used?"

"Sunday. I went out and back to the *Remagen* in it."

"You got back when?"

"I dunno."

I thought back to Turgeon's report. "How does five-thirty sound?"

"Probably right, I guess. I was pretty juiced. Lucky I didn't total the scooter between here and the estate."

I pointed to the Johnson. "Can you tell from the amount of gas left whether anybody's used it since?"

Yale hopped down, dancing to balance on the gunwales in a way that kept his shoes dry. He checked the bubble in the top of the gas can, then hefted the can itself using the handle on top. "Can't tell for sure. I filled it that morning, and it's still pretty full."

"Could it have gone from here to the cliff at the edge of the estate and back?"

"Could it . . . Oh, wow! You figure that's how they got Kenny out? Like down the cliff?"

"Could it?"

He did some kind of calculating in his head. "No. No, it'd take at least a quarter of a tank to go out and around over there. And even then . . . ."

"Yes?"

"Well, even then, there'd be a hell of a surf to bounce through. These things are okay up to maybe two-foot seas, if you hold on and know what you're doing. Rougher than that, I don't see anybody risking the cliff and back."

I looked around the harbor. Couple of lobstermen, working their wooden boats with the phone booth cabins disproportionately forward of midships. One was close by, pulling traps. The other was chugging near the barrier island, taking the channel north of the island out to the open sea. Quiet, even in the middle of the day.

"You want me to like, show you anything else?"

"No, thanks. That ought to do it."

Back in the Blazer, I started up and maneuvered us back onto the street, climbing away from the harbor.

After a while, I said, "How do you feel about Kenny?"

An arch of the neck. "About his being gone and all?"

"No. About him, personally."

"Kenny." A quick laugh, as though I'd asked about some anecdote from summer camp that amused him. "Kenny's like this little dog, you know? Always wants to be where you are, tagging along kind of."

It struck me that both O'Meara and Yale thought of Kenny as a dog.

"He's a pain sometimes, but most times Gloria's keeping him out of the way, and the General's just about in love with him, the way he plays games with him and all."

"You don't resent Kenny being the center of the General's attention?"

"Resent? Why would I resent what an old guy like him wants to do with a retard?"

"You know any reason why Kenny would be taken?"

134

"Shit, no. For money, I guess. People who need it more than I do."

He looked at me, all innocence, but he couldn't quite keep the sly smile from toying with the corners of his mouth.

Chapter Twelve

When Yale and I reached the gate, Turgeon and Kerstein were standing there. Kerstein fuming, Turgeon grinning just a little, his eyes covered by the aviator shades.

Kerstein said, "What the hell do you think you're doing?"

I said, "Calm down, counselor."

"Calm down? What if the call had come while you were off gallivanting at the yacht club?"

"Did it?"

Kerstein sputtered, then said, "No, it didn't. And I didn't tell the General you were gone." He turned away, walking to the Mercedes I remembered from the garage, now parked next to the guardhouse. Over his shoulder, he said, "My statement is on the library desk."

I guess that meant he thought we were even. Turgeon's slight grin grew a little as I drove past him up the drive.

I suppose I should feel honored: this is the first time in years anyone has cared about what my *opinion is on anything. Well, here goes.*

I was in the library having drinks with the rest of the functional antiques when Ethan stormed in. No, that's not fair. When Ethan came *in; it was going out that he was storming.*

He made what I thought was a reasonable effort to start a conversation with Father—or should I call him "the General," too? In any case, the available, noncontroversial subjects were rather quickly exhausted, and we gratefully turned our attention to dinner. There was some uproar about something, but fortunately I already had ingested sufficient stimulants (or I guess I should say depressants, since it was just scotch and wine) that I wasn't paying quite the attention I could have. In any case, then Ethan did his hurricane imitation, and Father, Sumner, and I repaired to the library. Father wanted the company of the one person who never contradicts him, and I wanted someone to tease. Sumner was the perfect choice for both of us.

At some point, Ethan made a brief appearance for dramatic effect, then took to his dogsled for the mush northward. I stayed on in the library with the brandy until I grew bored even of bothering Sumner. Then I went up to bed. Alone, more's the pity.

I would be happy to elaborate at your place or mine.

Lila

"You play much tennis, Matt?" she said, toying with the racquet.

"No."

"Do you *mind* that I call you Matt?"

"No."

"Please call me Lila, then."

"Fine."

"Don't you have any questions for me?"

"When you're finished."

She gave me an appraising look. In a different tennis outfit, this one with a pleated, cheerleader miniskirt, she shifted in her seat so I could now see the right leg crossed over the left. "Am I losing my touch?"

"Maybe we just have different views on what's important right now."

"Right." Lila saluted me. She didn't seem drunk, just playful. "This kidnapping business has us all *so* upset."

"Does your sarcasm suggest that you don't think this is serious?"

"Ah, finally the detective asks a question. I don't think most things are serious, Matt. I live for myself, I always have. It's probably the one useful thing I ever learned from dear odd Dad."

"You weren't living on the estate when I was here in April."

"How nice of you to notice. No, I was still with Number Four, living the hedonistic life in the land of the sun."

"Malibu."

"Malibu. Not what it's cracked up to be, by the way. Phony houses, all built to look like they were some place else. Phony people, all of them trying to give you the idea they're in show business when most of them peddle plumbing pipes or office supplies. Even phony money, it just doesn't go as far out there."

"So you came back home."

"Only temporarily. It remains one of the aspects of my lack of character that I understand the least, but whenever a marriage breaks up, I head for the bolt hole, the good old hearth and home. Then after a couple of months, I bravely gather my rags and strike out anew."

"About—"

"Probably be New York, this time."

"I'm sorry?"

"New York. Where I'll go this time. Beacon Harbor is so boring, you have the same *dreams* every night. That ever happen to you?"

"Sometimes."

"Well, New York is the place to go when your money outlasts your looks."

She paused for me to reassure her. When I didn't, she huffed and went on.

"Yes, New York. My second was in the art business. I met some of the most wonderful people there, cosmopolitan, international, charming. Some phonies, too, but where are you ever safe from them?"

"Not even in Beacon Harbor."

"No, no that's quite right. Not even here. Ah, but Manhattan. New York and our fair village may share the same time zone, but the Big Apple is in a different *dimension*. You've been to the Museum of Modern Art?"

"Once."

"Oh, I would go weekly. I never tired of it. Never. Degas, Monet, Gauguin. Mondrian, Pollock, Picasso. And my favorite, Max Ernst. People walking around looking so bizarre you half expected to see them hanging from a hook on the wall in the next viewing room. A Bell helicopter suspended over the escalator to the fourth floor. A peppermint-red Pininfarina sports coupe from the forties, looking twice as sleek and sexy as anything I've seen on the streets in twenty years."

"Don't they also have glass cases with vacuum cleaners and stereo receivers inside them?"

"Yes," impatiently.

"That would bother me. Seeing things I grew up with in a museum."

Lila began to straighten the strings on her racquet. "Very well, why don't we get down to business, then."

"What do you think happened?"

"What everyone else does, I imagine. Some stealthy men

of ability and daring snuck in here and kidnapped Kenny for ransom."

"You told me out by the tennis court that your dog didn't bark."

"That's right."

"And you yourself didn't see or hear anything?"

"No. I'm just relieved."

"Relieved?"

"That they took Kenny rather than me. I'm not sure the General would pay a million to get me back."

I looked down at her statement. "Why did you want to bother Kerstein on Sunday night?"

"I didn't want to 'bother' Sumner in particular. I just felt like tweaking *some*one after the scene with Ethan was so badly mishandled, and Sumner is a perfect choice."

"Because he's the one who arranged for the attempt at reconciliation?"

"Not really. Just because I make him nervous."

"Why?"

"Do I make him nervous?"

"Yes."

A coquettish lift of the chin. "A deep, dark secret."

I waited.

Lila said, "Aren't you going to ask me what it is?"

"You'll tell me anyway."

She laughed, a braying barroom laugh that was sincere, if unattractive. "You're right, you know? I will. Then I'll tell Sumner, and then you'll make him nervous, too. Be good for him, keep him thinking."

I still waited.

"You see, Sumner and I are . . . some years apart in age. One rainy Sunday, when everyone else was off and he was twenty years old and I much younger, too young as he would later study in law school, he was my first lover."

I guess I shouldn't have been surprised, but I was. A little. "Anything still there?"

"Emotionally, you mean?"

"Yes."

"Let's see . . . Guilt on his part, amusement on mine. They're emotions, I suppose." She leaned forward. "That was my 'college-boy period,' you see. Sumner was the first, but not the only for long."

"What period are you in now?"

Again the laugh. "Yale calls it my 'blue-collar period.' "

"Like Jaime Rivas?"

"Ah," spinning her racquet, as though she were contemplating return of serve, "you *are* quite the detective, aren't you?"

"Have you seen Jaime since he . . . left?"

"No, but replacements abound."

"Like Turgeon and O'Meara?"

She sighed. "Turgeon is a nerd, and O'Meara is a fool. Jaime had a certain . . . edge to him." The boredom left her face. "So do you, Matt, if you'd care to move to the front of the audition line?"

"Your stepson took me down to the harbor."

"Glad you're getting to mix some pleasure with business."

"I got the impression Yale was hoping for Florida over New York."

"Nothing about my life is written in stone, Matt."

"Was he here that night?"

"Yale? How would I know?"

"You're his stepmother. I assume he's your responsibility."

"My . . . ? What a quaint notion. You're not joking, are you?"

"Do you know where he was?"

"No, I'm afraid I don't."

"There a reason why he came back home with you rather than stay in California?"

"Just tradition. He's always come with me. Yale is the son of number . . . just a minute now. Number *Two*. Yes, number two, the New Yorker. His father died shortly after the divorce, and I felt obliged to . . . well, be responsible for him, I suppose."

She broke eye contact for a moment, as though she really had never thought about it that way before.

"Lila?"

"Yes?"

"What kind of independent income do you have?"

"Independent? Independent of what?"

"Of whatever the General gives you."

"I don't see that's any of your business."

"It is if Kenny's disappearance turns out to be more than temporary."

"Ah, the *estate plan*. Motive, right? Well, if motive can hang me, start knotting the rope. I couldn't stand the poor creature, made me shiver just to hear him try to talk. And I assume many of us would be better off without him in the line of descent from the General's mountain of gold. But I believe I consumed enough spirits in the presence of enough people to rule me out as a co-conspirator. Anything else?"

"Not just now."

"Perhaps some other time, then. When you're not so focused on 'what's *important*.' "

She swished out of the room, smacking the taut strings of the racquet off the palm of her left hand. Like someone applauding her own shot.

★ ★ ★ ★ ★

*Please, excuse the English. I am in this county now 9 year.
I work the week. But Sunday I don't. I go to Boston. See
my friends. Jaime give me his ride back here in the
afternon. I am sick. So I go to bed with pills Dr. Allen he
give me. I don't wake up before I hear Janine. Sound
terible to me. Kick on my door. I come out. She run
away, Dr. Allen and everbody come out. Kenny is disappeared. I don't know nothing for me to say.*

"Are you feeling better, Ms. Rivas?"

"Si, yes. Thank you, *señor."*

"What was wrong?"

"You mean, why I am sick Sunday?"

"Yes."

"I don't know. The bug."

"Like a flu?"

"Yes, the flu. I am sick with fever and, *como se dice,* the
bad stomach?"

Gloria Rivas sat stiffly in the chair, as though she weren't
used to sitting while others were. If you could use only one
word to describe her, it would be "stubby": body, legs, fingers, even features. It pushed her face toward homely, even
primitive, but with that earth-mother quality that told you
she'd be good around kids. Maybe especially around kids
who wouldn't disappoint by growing up. Her eyebrows
were sparse but her hair was glossy, black the way Lila's
stylist would like to duplicate and done up in a prom queen
style that made it look like a coifed wig.

"Ms. Rivas, how did you first come to the estate?"

"Janine and me, we work for the hospital. She in the office, director's office. I see her sometime in the cafeteria."

"What did you do?"

143

"I work there with the sick kids. The ones can't talk English."

"Is that where Janine met Dr. Allen?"

"Where, *señor?*"

"At the hospital?"

"Oh, *si, si*. Dr. Allen and Janine, they fall in love there."

"And when Kenny was born?"

"They bring me here to help. Then they . . ."

"They found out Kenny was . . . slow?"

"*Si,* yes. Slow. But I am good for him. Play with him." She sniffled. "When I am not sick from flu."

I said, "How did you go to Boston?"

"I am not so sick then."

"Yes, but how did you get there?"

"Oh, I am sorry, *señor*. I catch the bus."

"Where?"

"In Beacon Harbor. By the mail office, the bus stop and go to Boston."

"Where in Boston were you?"

"With my friends."

I picked up a pencil and drew a pad toward me. "What are their names?"

Gloria Rivas stared at my hands. "You write down there the names?"

"Yes."

"Some . . . The General, he tell me to tell the truth to you."

"You should do that."

"He say . . . The truth is the people I know, they are not to be here."

"Immigration problems?"

She nodded.

"Ms. Rivas, I won't tell anyone else about them. I just

need all I can get to find Kenny."

When her face came up, there were tears in it. "For Kenny?"

"For Kenny only."

Rivas gave me a list of six names, none of them sounding related.

"Was Jaime there, too?"

"No. He come later."

"When?"

"When I am sick. He come to give me his ride back to here."

"When did he pick you up?"

"At my friends?"

"Yes."

"He come maybe . . . I don't know."

I pointed to her statement. "You say here that you got back to the estate in the afternoon."

"Yes."

"Chief Turgeon said he checked you in through the main gate at about five-thirty."

"Yes."

"So Jaime picked you up about four-thirty, then?"

"I think. He say in the car it, *como se dice,* it is shame that I must come back so early, he look at his watch."

"He looked at his watch?"

"Yes."

"Was there anywhere he had to go after that?"

"After . . ."

"After he dropped you off here at the estate."

"Oh. No . . . I don't know about those things."

"Those things?"

"Those things Jaime do now, when he not here no more."

"Where does Jaime live?"

"In Boston."

"Address?"

"He live at Cooney Street."

"House number?"

"He don't got no phone."

"No. His address on Cooney Street."

"Oh. The house has number one-twenny-seven."

"In Dorchester?"

"I don't know."

"Why did Jaime leave here?"

She answered quickly, expecting that one. "I don't know."

"He didn't tell you?"

"I don't know. You maybe ask him?"

I pointed to her statement. "You say here that Dr. Allen gave you some pills?"

"*Si,* yes. For the flu."

"What kind of pills?"

"I don't know."

"Pills to make you sleep?"

"I sleep."

"But you don't know if the pills did it?"

"Make me sleep? I don't know, I was sick."

"Why didn't you take your own medicine?"

"My medicine?"

"Yes. Your eye-dropper medicine."

Rivas got nervous. "I don't got no medicine."

"In your room. In your dresser. In the leather case."

She licked her lips. "That is not my medicine."

"Whose is it, then?"

"That is for Kenny."

"For Kenny?"

146

"*Si,* yes. For Kenny when he . . . *como*—when he jump around too much."

I upped my opinion of Casper Binns. "The medicine calms him down."

"*Si, si.* It make him happy to sit, not do nothing for a while."

"Where did you get this medicine?"

"From . . . my friends."

"And where did they get it?"

"Is from Colombia."

"What is this medicine called?"

" 'La Flor Blanca'."

The White Flower. I tried to remember if I'd ever heard the expression down in San Antonio. No bells, but then we dealt mostly with Mexicans, and folk remedies change names over distance more often than streets in Boston.

"When you give this medicine to Kenny, how much do you give him?"

"Just the drop. In the glass with water."

"When was the last time you gave him the medicine?"

"I don't know."

"No idea?"

"Maybe last week?"

"What day?"

"I don't know. I am sorry, the days, they are all the same here."

"Does Dr. Allen know you give Kenny the medicine?"

The gaze dropped again. "Janine, she know, *señor.*"

Which probably meant Janine was really the one who gave the "medicine."

I didn't speak until the au pair looked back up at me. "Ms. Rivas, do you know who took Kenny away?"

She started crying, hard enough to dislodge her hairdo. I asked her if she wanted to help get him back. She bobbed her head, the lacquered hair bouncing on her forehead. I told her how she could help, and when.

ACTIVITIES OF MARCELLA AND WILLIAM NUSBY ON THE NIGHT OF SUNDAY, OCTOBER 16, 1988

We prepared drinks and dinner for the family on Sunday afternoon into evening. After dinner, several of the family left, several stayed for brandy in the library. We cleaned up and went to bed. We slept until we rose early Monday morning to prepare breakfast. During breakfast, we heard screaming and ran with the General to see what happened.

Respectfully,
Marcella and William Nusby

"The General said that he believed it would be all right for you to see both of us together."

Nusby said it flatly, no inflection of either question or command. Just as though he were describing the color of the walls.

I looked at Mrs. Nusby. She seemed very nervous and very glad her husband was there to answer questions.

"Your report is concise."

"Thank you, sir," he said.

"You saw nothing unusual?"

"Nossir."

"No one unusual?"

"Nossir."

"Ethan Van Horne was unusual, wasn't he?"

"I don't understand, sir."

"Ethan wasn't usually around for Sunday supper, was he?"

"Nossir."

"How did he seem to you?"

Nusby blinked twice. His wife hadn't blinked since she'd sat down.

"There is unhappiness between Mr. Ethan and the General. I don't think I can say anything more than that."

I said, "Does anyone here have any reason to . . . to want Kenny out of the way?"

Mrs. Nusby drew in her breath. Nusby didn't even glance at her.

"Nossir."

"Everybody loves him."

"I can't say, sir."

"You love him?"

Mrs. Nusby brought a hand to her eyes, realized there was no tissue or hankie in it, and brought it awkwardly back to her lap.

Nusby said, "Kenny is one of God's children, Mr. Langway. He doesn't have all of the things some of us have, but he has some of the things few of us have. He loves everyone, and I certainly return that love."

Nusby's voice was quiet, respect for life in every word. I had the distinct feeling I'd been put in my place.

"You didn't hear anything that night?"

"Nossir."

"No one moving through the house?"

"Nossir."

"Mrs. Nusby, do you have anything to add?"

She said "no" like she'd been practicing it for years but never had to perform in public before.

"There's nothing either of you knows that would help me?"

Nusby watched me. She watched him.

Finally, he said, "Nossir."

Chapter Thirteen

STATEMENT OF SUMNER KERSTEIN
UNDER PROTEST THIS 18TH DAY OF OCTOBER
REGARDING MY ACTIONS OF
SUNDAY, OCTOBER 16TH

*As indicated above, I am providing this statement
under protest but at the request of my friend and client,
General Alexander Van Horne, in this terrible time of
stress for him. I hereby reserve the right to review and
revise this statement in any way and to object to its use,
in whole or in part, in any future matter, regardless of
forum.*

*I arrived at the estate on Sunday at approximately
two in the afternoon. I spent the day speaking with the
General, walking the grounds, and playing tennis with
Lila Underwin. I joined the family for cocktails at approximately five p.m. Ethan's potential reconciliation
did not progress as I had hoped. After he left us, I attempted to work in the library, but both the General and
Lila felt in need of company, so I spoke with them instead.*

*I retired to bed at approximately eleven p.m. I re-
viewed some papers, then fell asleep. Like the rest of the
household, I was awakened in the very early morning by
Janine's screams. I rushed into the corridor, catching up
to her and the others at the top of the staircase. I managed to get the note from her before it was mangled beyond use.*

After conferring with the General, you were summoned.

Under protest as above indicated,
Sumner Kerstein

"Satisfied?"

I said, "No."

Kerstein scowled. "What more can you possibly want?"

I held up his statement. " 'Under protest'. Three times in maybe two hundred words, counselor. Cute, but what the fuck does it mean?"

His nostrils flared like a horse sensing fire. "It means, Mr. Langway, that I am not providing that statement of my own free will."

"What, we beat it out of you?"

No response.

"I guess what I want to know, and wouldn't have to ask except for the dimestore legalese in all this, is why you're so touchy about giving a statement for your actions on the day and night in question."

"I've given you my statement. Under—"

"—Protest. Right." I tapped a button on my belt rig, heard a faint beep.

I said, "Turgeon, how do you find the General for me? . . . Because I need to speak to him . . . Fine, I'll hold . . . Okay." I looked at Kerstein. "He's going to call us."

Kerstein gave me his best lawyer's look.

The telephone made a noise I remembered from *Star Wars*. I picked it up. "Yes, General . . . No, nothing yet. I have Mr. Kerstein here, and he's being more than reticent about his activities on Sunday . . ."

I swiveled the receiver end away from my ear. "No, General, I'm sure he can hear you from where he's sitting . . .

152

Yessir, I believe he's reminded of that now."

I hung up.

Kerstein managed to say, "Ask your questions."

"Why didn't you do the paperwork during the afternoon instead of walking and playing tennis?"

"When you've practiced law as long as I have, you find you work better in rhythms, different times of the day for different tasks. I'm a better reviewer of documents after dinner."

"More reflective mood?"

The tongue moved around against the inside of his cheek. "Something like that."

"But Lila was bothering you in the library?"

"After dinner . . . As I stated, the evening was a difficult one. Since the suggestion of Ethan coming down was mine, I felt . . . well, responsible in a way for the family's discomfort, and I felt I should provide a sounding board in the library for whatever they had to say."

"Anything left between Lila and you?"

Kerstein's ears reddened. "No."

"Your guest suite upstairs—"

"I said there was nothing left between us."

"Not what I meant, counselor. Looking out the windows of your room, you have a pretty fair view of the fountain and drive?"

"I suppose so."

"You happen to notice Turgeon going down the drive toward the main gate?"

"No."

"No?"

"No, Mr. Langway."

"Aren't you even going to ask me when?"

"When what?"

153

"When I'm talking about Turgeon going down there?"

"It doesn't matter. I didn't see him. And when, or if, he did go down there, every front wing room has basically the same view mine affords."

"Why did you suggest Ethan come here from Maine?"

"Why? Because I thought dinner on Sunday, the family together again, might be conducive to warmer feelings."

"Why did you want the reconciliation in the first place?"

"What kind of question is that?"

"My kind. What do you gain from a reconciliation?"

"Gain? I never . . . Have you ever heard of human compassion, Mr. Langway?"

"Books, movies."

"But never in real life, is that it?"

"Right."

"Well, let me tell you something. It won't do any good, but it needs to be said. That man, the General, our mutual meal ticket as you no doubt are about to remind me, is a very sick and a very sad old man. He was a giant in his time. Thanks to men like him, you didn't have to take German as a second language in school. Most of my family made it out of the Fatherland and its soon-to-be satellites in time. I've spent my adult life watching his family decay from the centripetal force of money. Money's like a drug, Mr. Langway, a drug to which you can build some resistance if you are exposed to it only incrementally. If you have it all at once when you're born, more than you can count while you're still in the womb, you can't deal with it. Either you scorn it, like Ethan, or you worship it, like Lila, or you're baffled by it, like Allen. But you can't deal with it. So people like me are around, people to watch over and after the heirs and the spendthrifts, the people with more assets than brains, until they pass from us. And if I can do something on the side, something to make the General's last few months a little easier, then I'm going to try it. That's why I did what I did with Ethan, but I don't expect you to believe it."

The telephone made the *Star Wars* noise again. I pushed the blinking button and picked up the receiver. "Hello?"

"Get General Van Horne to the phone. Now."

The sound wasn't quite a voice. More a scrambling and reassembling of phonetics, a cross between a robot and Woody Woodpecker. Hard listening but easy to understand.

I said, "Hold on." After hitting my beeper again, I covered both ear and mouthpiece on the telephone.

"Security, Turgeon."

"It's Langway. The call's coming in."

Kerstein stood up.

Turgeon said, "Which line?"

"Fuck which line! Get Van Horne to the library. Now!"

"Right."

I held the receiver and scanned my equipment from where I sat. Kerstein for once had the good sense to remain silent.

The General took the receiver from me, Turgeon hovering at one corner of the desk, hand on the grip of his sidearm. I moved to my equipment, changed headsets, and nodded to Van Horne.

The General nodded back and said into the phone, "This is Alexander Van Horne. Where is Kenny?"

"Takes you a long time to get to the phone, old man."

"I'll speak to him before we go any further or we go no further."

There was a sound like a hang-up. The General took the phone away from his ear, looking first to Kerstein, then

155

back to me. I shook my head, pointing to my headset. Van Horne had just returned the receiver to his ear when I heard, "Hi, Gra-da, s'me, Kenny."

The General seemed to be lost between death and heaven. He squared his features somehow and sat straighter in the chair.

There was a hang-up noise again, followed by the original sound. "That's your taste, old man. Now we deal."

Van Horne said, "State your terms."

"First, no police."

"None have been summoned."

"No word games. Are police of any kind involved in this?"

"No. No police at all."

"Second, one . . . million . . . dollars."

The amount was said with feeling. Even through the scrambler, you could hear the hunger.

"We have been gathering it."

"What denominations?"

"Tens, twenties, and fifties."

"No good."

"See here, they're all used bills. It's taken—"

"No good."

Van Horne fought with himself for control. "What do you mean?"

"The money has to be in cash in one hundred dollar bills, all used, no consecutive serial numbers."

"I . . . I have to speak to someone about that. It may—"

"Two days."

"What?"

"You have two days. We'll call again then."

"Wait! You can't leave me hanging like that—"

"Two days."

There was another sound from the other end as Van Horne mouthed the word "Please." But he'd heard the sound too, and didn't continue.

No one spoke. The General lowered his face to his left hand, extending the receiver into mid-air. Turgeon snapped it up and placed it back on its cradle.

A long minute went by. I pretended to monitor my equipment.

Then, "Langway!"

His eyes were bright, piercing. Ready for battle.

"Yes, General?"

"Why did his voice sound that way?"

"Can't be sure it was a he."

"What do you mean?"

"Whoever it was used a scrambler box. It distorts the voice so that only the syllables and none of the signature comes through."

"So you can't tell who did it?"

"No. Neither could the Bureau or the cops, even if you'd called them."

"My mind doesn't require any easing, thank you." He turned. "Sumner."

"Yes, General?"

"How quickly can we get the million we've gathered changed into hundreds?"

"Into . . . ?"

"Hundreds. Goddammit, hundred dollar bills, man. Used, no serial numbers in sequence. How soon?"

"I . . . I don't know, but—"

"Well, goddam find out and be goddam quick about it!"

"Yes, General."

I heard Kerstein in the corridor, then just his voice saying, "I don't think now would be—" before Janine's voice cut through it with a "fuck you" they could hear back at the Foundation.

She burst into the room, her face on fire, her arms slashing the air. "That was them, wasn't it?"

She clearly spoke to the General. He waved her off. "Not now."

"Not now? Not now! When the fuck, then? Why didn't you call me?"

"Because you wouldn't have helped, and you're not helping now. Please leave us."

She simmered, her blouse wavering around her torso like the lid on a pot on the stove.

"Please leave us," he said at that same, order-within-a-request pitch.

Janine spun on her heel and stalked out.

Van Horne said to me, "I want to talk with you. Will Turgeon be helpful?"

Turgeon just stood there, like the piece of furniture the General took him for.

"You'd do better at central station," I said to the space between them.

Turgeon said, "I'll be there," and left.

"Fine vice, pipe tobacco. Should never have given it up."

Still in the library, Van Horne held a pipe that might have been older than he was. A scent like baked Alaska wafted by me, then got pleasingly denser. The General was in the chair I'd been using. I sat where the residents and guests had for a good part of the day.

He said, "Your opinion?"

"Of pipe-smoking?"

The General left the pipe stem in his mouth, speaking

through clenched teeth. "Don't be an asshole, Langway. I need you."

"If they checked it out, they might know that it takes that long to rake together one million in existing hundreds."

"Be a damned stupid thing for them to do, check it out."

"Agreed. Unless one of them is familiar enough with banking to know that."

"But even so, why bother to mention it? Why not just say they'd call tomorrow, and if we haven't got it, give us the extra day then?"

Van Horne seemed animated again, alive as I remembered him the previous spring. "I don't know, General."

He took out the pipe, played around inside the bowl with some kind of tamping tool. "What do you think of the percentages now, Langway?"

"They're better."

He arched an eyebrow, concerned over a bad bottle of wine served a guest. "Why only 'better'?"

"I don't like the two days."

"Explain that."

"The voice was Kenny's?"

"No question. Not just some old fart being irrationally hopeful, either. Kenny's."

"Then they run the risk of something unexpected happening the longer they hold him. He's like an atomic bomb they're hoping to unload sooner rather than later, before somebody notices they've got it."

"Notices?"

"Somebody sees them bringing in food when they always ate out, somebody remembers they never liked hamburgers with cheese before, somebody hears a noise. Kenny . . . Kenny doesn't sound like most kids, sir."

"Finish your point."

"Somebody hears him, they think something's awfully odd. They call someone else, maybe the landlord, maybe the cops. Why run the risk?"

The pipe went back in, another match crackled and hissed to ignite it. Through the puffs, Van Horne said, "They have him somewhere isolated. No risks like that."

"But close enough, they can put him on a payphone?"

"What makes you think it was a payphone?"

"They were too tolerant of us keeping them on. My equipment showed a lapse of four minutes, thirty-two seconds."

"And?"

"And that's a twitchy long time to be on an unbroken line you've already rigged with a scrambler box."

"Perhaps they just broke in somewhere, used a phone in someone's home."

"Like stealing a car to commit a robbery?"

"Right."

"Not likely. More risk, since they'd have to be bringing Kenny along. Outdoors, where people might see him. Remember, they can't be certain you haven't gone to the authorities."

"But I haven't."

"General—"

"You're right, you're right." A few more wisps of smoke. "So then, what do you think?"

"I think maybe they're setting up a drop that takes them some time."

"Money drop, you mean?"

"Yes. They're setting something up that takes time to set up. The two days is more for them than for us."

Van Horne thought about it. "But you still don't like it."

"No, I still don't like it."

He thought some more. "Can't be helped. You'll stay the night?"

"It might help."

"You ready to give me your report on how they got Kenny out of here?"

"Almost."

" 'Almost'? Is there anyone you haven't seen yet?"

"I'd like to finish with Kerstein."

"Finish with him?"

"We were interrupted by the phone call."

"One of his goddam lackeys can swing the cash. I'll find him, tell him to finish with you. Now."

Kerstein came into the library and took his old seat, since I was back in the General's.

He said, "The money will be ready by Thursday at ten."

"That was quick. What does 'ready' mean?"

"It means here. A million in hundreds is ten thousand individual bills." He dropped his voice a notch. "Several bank officers are . . . winking at severely explicit regulations to do this for us. Even then, some of the bills will be new and in sequence, though the banks can dirty and shuffle them a bit." The voice rose again. "Why in God's name would they want hundreds instead of denominations they could pass more easily?"

"Maybe it's the way they see it."

"See what?"

"Kidnappers, they have this vision of the whole thing, beginning to end. Oh, there might be surprises along the way, ad-libbing required, but on the whole they have this grand view of what's going to unfold."

"I thought you didn't know that much about kidnappings."

"I don't, directly. You just hear things, tendencies, like hunters talking about deer. Maybe this bunch just always wanted hundreds in their wallets."

Kerstein shook his head. "It must be more than that."

"When we got the call earlier, you were telling me about easing the path for the General."

"I said more than I intended about that. What else do you want to know?"

"Lila."

The ears began flushing again. "What about her?"

"You said she loves money."

"The word I used was 'worship'."

"How much of it does she have?"

"How would I know?"

"You'd know."

Kerstein resettled himself in the chair. "Not much. Perhaps three, four hundred thousand."

"Not much."

"A woman like Lila goes through that in nine months to a year, depending on vacation choices."

"Any independent sources of income?"

"Not that I'm aware of."

"Yale told me he gets the boat."

"The *Remagen*? Yes, he does."

"I thought you said that people got only 'tokens' under the General's estate plan?"

The superior smile seemed happy to return to his face. "Mr. Langway, when you're talking about a hundred million, even big toys are tokens."

"Anyone else stand to get these tokens?"

"Certainly. The Nusbys, even Binns and Turgeon. A lot of people receive what you might think are handsome dollar legacies. However, the question you asked me out by the cliff was whether anyone was better off given the General versus Kenny dying first. The only ones really affected by that are Janine and Allen on the one hand and Lila on the other."

"And Yale."

"I told you. Yale and everybody else does as well either way."

"I mean indirectly, Counselor. If Lila benefits, then so does Yale indirectly as her stepson."

Kerstein waved it away. "I suppose."

I clasped my hands behind my head and leaned back in Van Horne's chair. "I don't see this as one person."

"You don't."

"No."

"Because it's too difficult for one person to watch the boy and do everything else?"

"Partly."

"What's the rest of it?"

"I don't know. It just feels like more than one person, that's all."

Kerstein looked wary. "And you're confiding this intuition to me."

"Have to trust somebody, Sumner."

He pretended I hadn't used his first name. "What about your partner? You've stopped trusting him?"

"No. I called him earlier. He was out, but I gave the answering service Jaime Rivas' address. Fred'll check it out, along with the bakers and candlestick-makers who were by here last week."

"And meanwhile?"

"Meanwhile we wait."

"We wait."

"Yes."

163

"And you trust me."

"Right. The way you've set all this up, Sumner, a nice but not embarrassingly large chunk of the hundred million falls into your lap no matter who's done what."

"And that's why you trust me."

"That's why."

"Why did you want to see me again so soon?"

"You may be worth your hourly rate after all."

Kerstein just drummed his nails on the desktop.

I said, "If the General thought Kenny was dead, would he still go through with the ransom?"

"You have evidence—"

"Please. For now, just answer my question. If Van Horne thought Kenny was dead, would he go through with the kidnappers, anyway?"

Kerstein let his eyes roam over the shelves behind me. "Unless you presented irrefutable proof that Kenny was dead, I believe the General would go through with the ransom. It is one million against his many millions, his short remaining time, and a boy he loves. Now, why do you ask?"

"You said before that you wanted to make Van Horne's remaining time easier."

"Yes?"

"So do I."

"Therefore?"

"I can't be sure of this, but both my machine and I listened to that telephone call."

"And?"

"And I haven't told the General this, because it isn't proof that Kenny is dead, just not proof that he's alive."

"What the hell are you—"

"Kenny's voice on the phone. I think it was a tape recording, and my machine does too."

Chapter Fourteen

Van Horne put his drink on the desk and took the chair I'd come to think of as mine when he wasn't in the library.

"Let's have your report, Langway."

"Everybody claims they were asleep or otherwise engaged from ten p.m. Sunday until Janine discovered Kenny missing early Monday. Nobody has an alibi worth much since we don't know for sure when the child was taken."

"No way to pin that down?"

"There's some indication your grandson Allen saw Kenny still in his bed when Allen got back from his Foundation function around midnight. But he only got a glimpse in bad lighting and could have been seeing one of the stuffed animals."

"Go on."

"So I've been approaching it from the other aspects."

"What other 'aspects'?"

"First, if this was outsiders, how did they get on the property and when?"

"I thought we agreed it must be insiders?"

"Bear with me for a minute, please."

"All right."

"The way I see it, outsiders could have come over the fence anywhere along the perimeter, since the fence isn't electrified. They didn't cut through, or if they did, they did a hell of a job of covering it, since both O'Meara and Zoubek walked the perimeter Monday morning and neither saw anything wrong."

"That assumes neither one's a turncoat, though."

"If either of them is, then the team could have come in anytime the turncoat was on duty."

"All right, Langway. Could they have come up the cliff by the sea?"

"Possible, but I doubt it."

"Back during the war, in England, I watched Darby put his Rangers through cliff drills, both climbing up and rappeling down."

"Yes, but I examined the cliff face, and I didn't see any marks or chips from any equipment."

"And therefore you think they would have had to come over the fence."

"Not necessarily, but if they did, they could have been on the grounds for a while."

"A while."

"Turgeon walks the perimeter every morning, but if the team, or even just one kidnapper, was already on the grounds, he or she could hide pretty effectively for a day or two given all the wooded acreage."

"But if they didn't come over the fence?"

"Then we're dealing with an insider using outside help, and somebody could have come through the main gate at any time in the backseat or trunk of the insider involved."

"At any time?"

"And hidden out for a while."

Van Horne took a sip of his drink. "I don't see how all this about how they got in is helping us any."

"I'm just trying to be comprehensive here, General. If we can't pin down how or when they got in, then put those aspects aside for a minute and examine another. Can we determine how or when they must have taken Kenny out?"

"I thought you told me you couldn't do that?"

"We can back into it. No question Janine puts Kenny to

bed after dinner. How do they get him out of his room?"

"Just windows or door to the corridor."

"Right. And probably not through Janine and Allen's living room. So that leaves Kenny's own windows, Kenny's door to the north wing corridor, and Gloria Rivas' room and corridor door."

"Gloria?"

"It's a possibility, because her room connects to his. But there's a problem with the window. In fact, with any window."

"The video cameras outside."

"Partly. When an upstairs window is opened after the security system is armed for the night, no alarm goes off because the mag entry detectors on the windows aren't tied into the Klaxon circuit anymore. But a light goes off on the panel Turgeon would have been watching, and that would focus him on the videos."

Van Horne considered it. "Then that means they took him out through the corridor. How the hell did they get Kenny out of the house once they got him out of his room?"

"Turgeon left central station at least twice. Once at about 11:40 p.m. Sunday to let Allen back in, a second time about 2:00 Monday to let O'Meara back in."

"O'Meara?"

"Yes."

"Goddammit. They could have gone through a door while Turgeon wasn't there to watch the panels and monitors, then."

"Right, or even lowered Kenny from a window. But while they had their choice of windows on the upper floor, they would have been stuck with the front door to the house."

"Why?"

"Because the alarm would have sounded if any other first floor door, or window, had been opened once the entry detectors there were armed for the night."

"And the front door wouldn't have tripped the alarm . . ."

"Because Turgeon would have cut it from central station before he went up and out that door to go to the gate for Allen and O'Meara."

The General sank back in his chair. "If anyone approached the house while Turgeon was in central station, Turgeon should have seen them."

"On the video monitors."

"Then they came into the house when Turgeon went down for Allen, and they left the house with Kenny when Turgeon went down for O'Meara?"

"Unless Turgeon nodded off some other time and missed something on the panels or monitors."

"But nobody could rely on that. Predict it, I mean."

"No. Unless Turgeon is involved."

"But even . . . even Turgeon wouldn't know when Allen and O'Meara would be coming back to the estate."

"That's right. But if Turgeon is in on it, the possibilities are endless."

Van Horne came forward. "Very well. Assume for now that Turgeon isn't involved. Where does that leave us?"

"The random opportunities of Allen and O'Meara arriving whenever they might are a tough bet."

"Meaning?"

"Meaning I don't see this as outside professionals without inside help."

"Goddammit, Langway, that's what I thought before I brought you into this!"

"All I'm saying, General, is that the facts bear you out."

"So an insider is involved. How?"

"First, in helping with the selection of this weekend.

Ethan coming down and all. Lots of activity, lots of distractions. At least one security man off the estate at just about all times."

"Back up a minute. If Turgeon's not involved . . ."

"Then I see the insider as getting Kenny away from his bed. Asleep, drugged, maybe even wide awake and playing a game."

Van Horne winced. "And then?"

"Kenny is taken out of the room, by window or door, when Turgeon's out of central station. The insider passes Kenny to some outsider, who either came over the fence or is waiting on the other side of the fence."

"How does the insider get back inside the house?"

"Maybe he or she doesn't have to. They just wait in one of the outbuildings till morning and slip back inside the house in the general commotion."

"Or they would had to have timed Turgeon going down for Allen or O'Meara."

"Depending on whether Allen is right about seeing Kenny, and Janine is right about the window, and Turgeon is right about not falling asleep, and—"

"Enough, Langway."

This time, Van Horne sagged back into the chair and picked up his drink from the desk. "I'd hoped for more . . . elimination of possibilities."

"I have all the handwritten versions of what happened. I'll reread them, check them against the note, but I can't promise anything there. I'll also call my partner, see how he's doing."

"One thing, during the call, that . . . voice. He — it, goddamit, asked me if we'd brought in the police."

"Yes?"

"Why ask that if an insider would already know you're here?"

"They know independent kidnappers would have asked that question."

"So they'd have asked the question even if they knew we hadn't alerted the police."

"Especially if they were trying to cover an insider who'd already leaked my being here to them."

"Lord almighty." He set down his drink, shakily. "What do you plan to do next?"

"Have dinner here, go into town tonight."

"Town? You mean Beacon Harbor?"

"Right. See if I can pry something loose without giving away too much."

"What good would it do you to run the risk of something getting out? Something that could get back to the authorities, I mean, and spook the kidnappers."

"I won't know what good it'll do until I poke around a little. I'll be careful."

"Be more than careful. What about tomorrow?"

"They said they wouldn't call back till Thursday. That gives me all day tomorrow basically free of having to be here."

"And?"

"And I figured that it would be a good time to drive up to Maine and see your prodigal grandson."

Van Horne turned baleful. "I would prefer you didn't make jokes about my family in my presence."

"Sorry, General."

"You think Ethan can tell you anything?"

"He and Allen were the only two who clearly were both in and out of the estate that night."

"I just can't see . . . What about Rivas? Didn't he drop Gloria off?"

"Yes, but that was earlier in the day, the afternoon."

"He could have hung around, outside the fence."

"Gloria gave me an address on him, in Boston. Fred's trying to run it down."

The General picked up his drink, paused with it halfway to his mouth. "Straight on, Langway, what do you think the chances are that somebody in the family's involved in all this?"

"You've got at least two people involved. The insider to get Kenny out of the house, an outsider to spirit him away from the estate. You can figure the odds on whether the insider is family as well as I can."

"Shit." The General scoffed the rest of his drink. Glancing up at the clock on the mantel, he seemed to brace himself in the chair. "Time to put on a brave face for dinner. Come on."

The entree was roast lamb. Since this wasn't a formal reconciliation, everybody but security was in the room, and everyone in the room except for the Nusbys was seated at the long rectangular table. The General was at the head, I was at the foot. The pairings across the table were Allen and Janine, Kerstein and Lila, Yale and Gloria. Casper Binns was odd man at my end, seated to my right. I had the feeling that Kenny's place would have been closer to the General rather than the empty seat next to Gloria.

Willie and Marcella had served the soup, a thick cream concoction with generous chunks of at least three different kinds of mushrooms. A small scoop of sherbet in a delicate crystal goblet followed to cleanse the palate. Apparently the salad would come after the lamb dish, French style.

We'd already had two different wines, and the General advised Nusby that it was time to bring out the decanted third. I began to appreciate the board, if not room, benefits, that Binns had raved about to me. Otherwise, however, it was as though we were eating exceptionally well at an unusually quiet Irish wake.

The General said, "Allen, anything of interest happening at the Foundation?"

"The Foundation?"

I thought Lila was about to say something like, "You know, that boondoggle that justifies your existence," when Kerstein said, "Perhaps the salamander project, Allen?"

The General said, "Salamander project?"

"Oh, uh, yes. We've just approved a grant to a research physician at Rutgers Medical School. He's hypothecated the most marvelous potential relationship between the way salamanders metamorphose and the way human tissue regenerates after a thermal trauma."

Lila said, "Allen, you're paying this guy to burn little lizards?"

The General grunted and Kerstein clamped down on a laugh, but Yale roared out loud and Binns broke a smile. Janine's eyes scoured everyone except Gloria, who seemed not to get it, and me, my best poker face sutured on tight.

Binns raised his glass melodramatically. "This is a superb Bordeaux, General."

Van Horne appeared pleased, as much by the distraction as the compliment. "Haut Brion, 'seventy-six."

"Magnificent," said Binns, finding comfort in redundancy.

I said, "I'm planning on seeing Ethan tomorrow. Sorry to turn this into a working dinner, but does anybody know anything I should ask him?"

Only Lila was smiling this time around.

I said, "If you think of something, please let me know."

At which point Kerstein remembered a fascinating anecdote about a foiled corporate take-over, which filled the void till brandy time.

Chapter Fifteen

I parked the Blazer outside the first bar I came to. It was at the end of the restored street of tourist rip-off shops offering maple syrup, seascapes, and scrimshaw. Though they were closed, it looked like all of them carried the same merchandise.

A phone booth stood vacant on the corner. I scooped up enough change to call Fred in Saugus. I talked to him in the clear about what I'd learned so far, and how we could use it. After hanging up, I thought he sounded sober and scared. Just as he should.

Inside the bar, it was quiet, three couples in Boston fashions finished with dinner and lingering over wine or coffee but no cigarettes. There was one woman about my age sitting at the bar who didn't look like she wanted to talk, and one old guy three seats away who did. They weren't hitting it off.

I sat next to the old guy on the side away from the woman. He wore a stained captain's hat cocked back on his head. The old guy's hands were gnarled, but the fingers didn't look as though he'd spent his life fighting the sea.

I tapped him on the sleeve, and he turned to me. "Yeah?"

"I'm wondering what you recommend having here."

He nudged his brow toward the steaming mug in front of him. "Hot buttered rum. Chipper does a great job on it. Hey, Chipper?"

A bartender who looked as though he could have been the woman's husband came over. Gaunt, not too friendly, and definitely not in love with the old guy calling him by a nickname.

"Chipper, give the gentleman here a hot one, on my tab."

I already had the twenty in my hand. "No, please. On mine. I insist. And make that two rums, please."

Chipper nodded and got to work. The old man squinted at me and offered his hand. "Whit Damon, pilgrim."

I shook with him. "Lang Matthews."

"What brings you to our fair city, Lang?"

"Sight-seeing. Just got transferred in from San Antonio, thought I'd take in some of the coast."

"You've come to the right place, then. I know this part of the Maritimes like the back of my hand, and there's no prettier section than ours."

Chipper brought the rums and escaped as soon as possible. Whit and I clunked our mugs, he slurping down a quarter of his, then pouring half of what was left into his first mug. Or, more likely, his other mug.

I said, "I'd heard the same thing."

"The same thing?"

"That Beacon Harbor was scenic. Had some trouble seeing the ocean, though."

"Trouble? What kind of trouble?"

"Well, I got my bearings and tried to drive down to the water, but I kept getting stopped at the gates."

"Ah, yes. Our landed gentry."

"One place in particular. Kind of open-looking place, but the gate was still there, back up in a stand of trees aways."

"There are lots like that. Our upper crust, they do like their illusions of democracy."

I had the feeling that if I followed old Whit home, I'd see

him pass through one of those gates himself. Instead, I said, "There was a guard and everything, though. Looked like a goddamned army post."

"Ah, the General, then."

"General?"

"General Alexander Van Horne. Not quite from around here originally, but rich enough to blend right in."

"You know much about him?"

"Enough." Another noisy slurp. "Military industrial complex and all that."

"Huh. Must have a lot of enemies, he keeps his place protected like that."

"Enemies? Don't see how, really. He keeps pretty much to himself. Has a *Cheoy Lee* at the club that you could just cry over, but doesn't use it much himself. Mainly some younger generations aboard when I've noticed it going out. You ask a hundred people in the center on a Saturday if they've ever actually seen old Van Horne, I doubt two could answer yes. Some of us have really pissed the townies off by soaking up the best of everything they had around here, but Van Horne bought a place that was closed off so long ago, nobody thinks of it as having been theirs once."

I thanked Whit for his company and got elaborate directions to the roads, "Two of them still unpaved, Lang," that offered the best access to rocks and surf.

The next place I stopped was a step down. Nets, floats, and lobster pots on the walls. Patrons dressed like cops and schoolteachers, out for their one restaurant meal of the week. Or month. A blackboard had a few daily specials chalked on it, with "Chicken Lobster" already scratched through. I wondered why they didn't just erase it.

The bartender looked under-worked and talkative. The

Bruins game on the overhead TV was entering the last minute of the second period. I took a stool away from the set, and he pushed his rump off the shelf of bottles and came over, sliding a coaster in front of me.

"What'll you have?"

"Draft?"

"Michelob, Bass, Harpoon."

"Harpoon."

He brought back the reddish ale. "You a hockey fan?"

"I like to watch it at the Garden. Too early in the year to be playing, seems to me."

He warmed to that. "You're telling me? For crissakes, we ain't halfway through the NFL yet, and the World Series just ended. I can't handle that, myself. Baseball on one channel, hockey on another. Just don't make sense to me, having both of them on at the same time."

"Remember when we were young? Remember how there'd really be those seasons, baseball ends as football starts up, football ends as basketball and hockey kick in. Now, it's hard to know what's going on, where in the year you are."

"You got that right. I have this theory on it."

Oh boy. "What's that?"

"I got this theory, it's because there's so many people living down in that Sun Belt now."

"The Sun Belt."

"Yeah. It's like this. Back when they just had the snakes and the Apaches there, we didn't have none of this football in August, baseball in winter kind of shit. But now with all the population moving down there, they don't know what time of year it is anymore, see? They don't have no way of knowing what month it is, 'cause all the months are the same fuckin' frying pan outside. So, they got when they're supposed to be playing what all screwed up, see?"

"Interesting theory."

"Yeah. Yeah, I think so, anyway."

"I'm up from Boston, myself, just driving around, you know?"

"You're lucky this is October, pal. Summers, it's like New York City up here."

"That because of all the rich people?"

"Nah. The rich ones, they pretty much stay to themselves, you know? Gin and tonics and badminton on the lawn. They don't fuck things up so much. It's the fuckin' tourists. Not like you, pal. I mean from New York, New Jersey, everywhere down there. They've fucked themselves with this hospital tide shit in their water and on their beaches, so they come up here for vacation. They're ticked about how long it took them to drive here, ticked that Boston isn't within walking distance, and ticked that we got greenheads the size of your thumbnail that'll tear the flesh from your bones even after you've swatted them flat. Then they try to swim in the water, and it's freezing compared to where they're from, and there aren't any waves, and the sand is more like gravel than sugar. Then, after they get soused and bored from sitting around their screened porches all day, they come down to us. They start demanding all kinds of shit, like they owned the place and was holding a competition to see who got fired and who got raises. You make a fuckin' fortune summers here, but I gotta tell you, I'm not sure it's worth it anymore. Not sure at all."

"I went past one place today, all gates and guards and what not."

"We got a bunch of them. Playing badminton back there, like I said."

"I heard it belongs to some general."

"Oh, yeah. General Van Horne. He's been around a while. Got some family comes into town, I hear, but I don't know much about him. Another Harpoon?"

"No. Got to be going, thanks."

"Hey, watch the papers, huh? Fuckin' Red Sox probably be starting up before Christmas soon."

The third place was so many steps farther down it was off the staircase. A block in from the wrong side of the harbor, there were a dozen trucks and utility vehicles in the lot, most smelling strongly of dead fish and infrequent washings. One beat-up Ford pick-up had a bumper sticker that read "COMPLAINTS ABOUT MY DRIVING? CALL 1-800-EAT-SHIT."

I walked into the place, the door broaching its hinges as I closed it. Heavy clouds of cigarette smoke, jukebox going. The Bruins game had come back on, ghost images of no cable hook-up making the screen so snowy the existence of the puck was an article of faith. Loud talk, cursing, clinking. You couldn't exactly say an odor of beer piss hung in the air: it was the air. Blue-collar dive on the way to black-and-blue, everybody waiting for tonight's excuse to drop the gloves.

"Hey, Matthew!"

I turned, my eyes adjusting. Lila was sitting at a table, three beers in longneck bottles in front of her, five more next to her where a chair was pulled out.

"Come on over, Matthew."

She was just loud enough to turn heads. I decided it was better to sit down with her.

Two fresh beers appeared. The bartender said, "Buckie ordered these on his way out."

I said to Lila, "I don't want to break anything up."

"You're not. Buckie gets back, we can order some more. They got a freezer full of these, right?"

The bartender left us, shaking his head.

Lila clinked her Bud against mine. "What brings you down here?"

I took a sip. "You first."

She sassed her head, left to right and back. "Uh-uh. I asked you before you asked me."

She was drunk. The dangerous, I-can-handle-it-and-anything-else drunk you don't like to see in a place like that.

"I was just calling it a night, myself. Can I give you a ride back to the estate?"

"Shush," drawing her hand to her mouth and stretching out the syllable. "I'm slumming, and you're gonna blow my cover."

She was in jeans, tight fitting, and a turtleneck Mohair sweater that probably cost what the barkeep grossed on New Year's Eve. "I don't think you're fooling anybody."

"Maybe not," she hooded her eyes and made little patterns on the table with her drink. A family trait. "That's just one of the things that sucks nowadays, you know?"

"Lost me."

"Well, back when you and I were growing up, back in the late great sixties, there was all this shit about money and position and who was who, but then we blew all that away with the protests and the music and found ourselves, and everybody could get together and just get it off without all kinds of hang-ups, you know?"

Her vocabulary seemed to be following her mind back along the time trail. "Things change."

"Yeah, they sure do. Back then, it was different. The

drugs were grass or acid, and the love was free. The drugs made you feel good, the sex made you feel better. Now what do the kids have? Crack and AIDS. The drugs kill you, the sex kills you. What have they got to hope for?"

"Maybe things will change back."

"But that's the problem. Don't you see it? We have changed back, but the wrong way. With Reagan in the White House, we changed back to the fifties, shit, the Middle Ages, with our attitudes about not helping people and all, but now the drugs kill and the sex kills, and . . ."

"At least the tennis is still good."

Lila scrunched up her face. "You're making fun of me, aren't you? Little Miss Rich Bitch, crying in her beer over how the revolution didn't change shit. Well, let me tell you something, a good forehand isn't shit compared to good foreplay, and that's something you don't have to be anybody's heir to figure out." Her face changed and her mood seemed to swing. "Hey, Buckie told me this great joke."

"Just who is Buckie?"

"What's the . . . no, shit, that's not right. Oh, yeah, how do you practice Polish birth control?"

"I don't know."

"The girl keeps her legs spread and the guy keeps his fingers crossed."

I was letting her get over her laughing jag when I heard from above and behind me, "The fuck is this guy?"

I edged my seat back just enough to give my knees free space to move. He sidled into view, looking from me to Lila and back again. Maybe six-one, two hundred in shape, two-twenty with the gut straining against the chamois work shirt and his belt. Hands with more scars on them than the old pick-up outside.

Lila said, "This guy's been bothering me, Buckie." She

180

gave me a dazzling smile. "And he spit in your beer."

Buckie squared to me and said, "I'll let you get up first."

Which meant, of course, that he planned to swing on me as soon as I put my hands on the arms of the chair to stand. I put my hands on the arms, and as he cocked his fist, I punted up with my right foot, catching him just a little too high in the groin. He wobbled, then sank to his knees, clenching and groaning. By then I was up, but he was waving me off and sinking lower, onto his side.

To Lila I said, "Ride's still good."

Her eyes were glazed, a sheen of perspiration on her upper lip. "You bet."

I moved sideways to the door, my palm on the bend of her elbow, in case one of Buckie's buddies decided to escalate.

Outside, she turned and pushed into me for a kiss, smothering my face with the pong of stale beer over expensive perfume.

Lila broke off and said, "What's the matter?"

"I wasn't competing, and you're not the prize."

"I have my own car, thank you very fucking much." She wheeled and stomped away, but not back into the bar.

I got to the Blazer, started up, and drove around the harbor for a while before heading back to the estate.

Chapter Sixteen

I am in-country less than a month. A colonel thinks what I need is combat experience. "Toughen you up for what's to come, Langway." I draw an experienced platoon in an infantry company sweeping a heavily rice-paddied sector. Until I arrive, the platoon has been led by a sergeant named Lau, a maniac. He tells me we can't walk along the paddy dikes because they are too often mined.

"Yessir, L.T.," he says, using the grunt's stock abbreviation for lieutenant. "We may get our fuckin' feet wet, but at least they'll be fuckin' wet at the end of our fuckin' legs where they fuckin' well belong, yessir."

The platoon starts across another paddy. Stands of bamboo, coconut palm, and banana trees are broken and uprooted along one side of the water. My briefing had placed a Marine artillery battery on the ridge far to our left. The trees were likely recent victims.

We slog along with Mosher, the point man, maybe thirty meters in front of me, the rest of the men spread at five-meter intervals. In addition to C-rations and canteens, each carries eight pounds of rifle, another eight or ten of extra ammo, five pounds of helmet and liner, seven pounds of flak jacket. The RTO humps twenty-six pounds of the PRC-25 radio and battery, the machine-gunner nearly forty pounds of M-60 and ammo belts. The air is thick, a withering heat. The milky water is nearly to our knees, the mud below sucking at our boots with every exaggerated forward swing of a leg. I don't understand how the RTO and M-60 keep their sanity.

I make the mistake of looking down into the water. It moves,

even when you don't. Not from any current, mind. It moves be-
cause a billion larvae from a hundred species of bug swim there,
ready to beat the leeches to your flesh or catch you on the fly after
they grow wings. My legs, especially my calves, are itching like
crazy, even through my boots.

We've gone through half a dozen paddies when we approach
a ragged old man to our right. He is slowly, patiently tending the
edge of the dike. Maybe deaf, maybe just used to soldiers, the old
man never even turns around to look at us. His way of life is
bending over, straightening, shuffling a few steps sideways, and
bending over again. He wears a conical hat of woven straw, a
burlap bag on a makeshift sling around his shoulders. Mosher
keeps his M-16 leveled at the man as the rest of us advance on
an axis parallel to but twenty-five meters or so to the ridge side of
the farmer.

As Mosher draws even with the old man, the farmer suddenly
pitches forward, arms akimbo, face down into the dike. We all
drop to our knees, the barrels of our weapons swinging slowly left
and right in interlocking arcs. My heart is trying to break out of
my chest, getting in the way of my breathing.

Mosher looks back at me. I wave him over to check the
farmer. Motoring across the water like a beaver, Mosher cheats
on the swimming by using his hands and knees on the bottom.
He reaches the farmer, using his weapon to prod the man.
Mosher sloshes back to me as Lau edges up so the three of us can
talk.

The point man says, "He's dead, sir. Round in the back."

"Round?" I say. "But nobody fired."

Mosher jerks his head up toward the distant ridge. "There
are Marines up there, sir. Artillery. Probably just some sentry
with a sniper rifle."

"What?"

Lau says, "L.T., gets pretty fuckin' boring, sitting on one of

183

those fuckin' hills all day. Some jacked-up jarhead's jerking our chain."

The shock must be jumping off my face.

"You're right, sir," says Lau. "Dead on fuckin' right. We are too fuckin' close to that gook for those guys to be shooting at him. Way too fuckin' close."

I look into Lau's face to be sure I am hearing him correctly. I am. What bothers him is our proximity to the target, not the act itself of shooting at the old farmer.

"Langway, can I speak with you?"

A male voice on the other side of the door, then more knocking.

I was covered with sweat, my calves itching insistently. "Who is it?"

"Casper. Binns."

"It's open."

Binns came into my room. He was wearing a white terry-cloth robe and beach thongs, his hair wet.

"I'm sorry to bother you, but I just noticed something I think you should know."

Awake now, I levered up onto my elbows. "What is it?"

"It would be easier for me to show you. In my room."

"I'll meet you there."

After he left, I pulled on a shirt and pants. When I got to the turn in the corridor, his door was open.

Binns was standing in front of the stereo display. He beckoned me over and swept his hand at the shelf of audio-tapes. "Notice anything strange?"

I let my eyes follow his hand, checking a few of the labels randomly. "Looks the same as when I was in here on Monday."

"That's right. It looks fine. But notice." He picked up

one of the plastic cassettes and shook it. "Nobody's home."

I held out my hand, and he placed the plastic in it. Very light.

"Empty."

Binns smiled. "Two others the same way."

I read the label. " 'Kenny—General's Birthday.' These are the audiotapes you make to help Kenny's speech patterns?"

"Yes. And no. *Most* of the tapes are just that. Sort of a spoken version of somebody learning the piano by playing the scales. The one you've got there and the other two were ones where Kenny was taping kind of a speaking card for the General. Birthday, Christmas, back from a trip."

"A chance for Kenny to just sort of talk to him?"

"Yes, but also a chance for Kenny to feel proud of the progress he was making."

I looked back at the shelf. "How often do you check these?"

"I don't, really. Given all that's happened though, I thought I would try to find one that might make the General feel a little better. I heard that he was up in his screening room watching videos of Kenny, and, well, I thought this might help, too."

"So the actual tapes could have been taken when?"

"Just about any time, I suppose, but I can't see a reason for it. Unless . . ."

I handed him back the empty container. "I'm listening."

"Well, if *I'm* the kidnappers, I have to think I would want some of Kenny's voice on tape. Just in case I needed to show someone that Kenny sounded alive and fine over the telephone."

I watched him till he blinked. "And if you're in with them, tipping me to this earlier rather than later might make you a less likely suspect."

Affronted, Binns said, "I was merely speaking hypothetically, trying to help."

"Thanks."

I went back to my room to shower and shave.

"More coffee, sir?"

I said, "No thanks, Nusby."

"General?"

"No, Nusby. Leave us, please."

"Certainly, General."

Van Horne watched the door to the kitchen area swing closed. He pushed his cup and saucer to the side. "How are you going to approach Ethan?"

"According to Kerstein, there's no phone up there. I got driving directions, so I think I'll just pop in and surprise him."

Somehow, I didn't think that was the question on Van Horne's mind. I sipped my coffee, some kind of almond with chocolate, fresh-brewed, and waited him out.

"Ethan doesn't give a tinker's damn about money. Or how it's divided among the family when I'm gone."

"People say that a lot."

"What?"

"That they don't care about money. Give them a taste of it, though, and they can change their minds. Like ordering dessert in a fine restaurant."

Van Horne shook his head. "No, I just don't see it. Ethan and I have never gotten along. Oil and water, ever since he was a young boy. I couldn't see much of him back then, but I made sure he was provided the best, him and Allen both. Neither turned out . . ."

I didn't say anything.

Finally, "Neither turned out the way I expected. Bad thing, expectations."

Finishing my coffee, I said, "Any suggestions for what I should say to him?"

Van Horne seemed to come back from somewhere. "Ethan?"

"Yes."

The General got up, walked to the doors to the patio while taking out his pipe. "Just tell him that I'm sorry, would you?"

He stepped outside, closing the door in a way that kept me from seeing his face.

I took 1-95 North to where it becomes the Maine Turnpike. There was some foliage, but except for the Portland area, most of the next hundred miles cut through evergreen forests lining the highway.

About twenty minutes into the trees, I noticed something. I was relaxing, my breathing deeper, the diaphragm reaching maximum lift, then sliding back down from my chest to rest. A bone in my neck made a crickling noise, my shoulders aligning with the contours of the upholstery. My mind seemed to clear, worries and contingencies sloughing off like a bird molting feathers.

I left the interstate at the Augusta exit and meandered roughly north and west for another forty minutes. Even with Kerstein's directions, I had to stop at a gas station and a general store for corrections.

Half a mile down the right fork of a rutted, seemingly seasonal, road, I came to a hand-painted sign that said, "OLDE COUNTRY FURNITURE." I turned into the driveway of a weathered board house. The main wing and the addition were different colors, and both looked home-made. A sagging porch with railing jutted out toward the road. The railing was shy a few pickets.

I parked the Blazer next to a pitted Subaru pick-up with grossly oversized tires and more dirt than paint showing. A hound of sorts came out from under the porch, baying and examining me sidesaddle in that mournful, distrustful way they have. While I was watching the hound, a male voice said, "Help you?" and the hound immediately shut up and slinked back under the porch.

The man was about six-two, thick through the shoulders and hips, in worn jeans and sweat-stained lumberjack's shirt. He was working a dirty strip from an old towel over his hands as though he were lathering them with soap. His hair was brushed straight back from his head, gathered in a spiky ponytail, and the beard had that unkempt, prospector look. It was the features that marked him a Van Horne, though. The beak and burning eyes of the General, none of the paleness and uncertainty of Allen.

"Ethan Van Horne?"

"Uh-huh."

"Mr. Van Horne, my name's Matthew Langway. I wonder if I could talk with you a minute."

Ethan nodded, but more like he was thinking than assenting. He slapped the cloth against his thigh, then folded his arms. Waggling his butt against the railing on the porch, Van Horne inclined his head an inch toward my car. "Mass plates."

"Yes."

"That plus your calling me Mr. Van Horne, makes me think this is kind of official."

"It's about your nephew."

"My . . . ?"

"Kenny."

188

"Oh, Kenny." He shifted his feet, pawing the dirt a little. "What do you have to do with him?"

"I'm a private investigator from Boston." I moved forward a couple of steps and gave him my ID. The dog growled somewhere, out of sight.

Ethan's nails were cracked and bumpy as he turned the plastic laminate over and back. "Private investigator."

"Your grandfather's asked me to try to find him."

Ethan squinted. "Find him?"

"Kenny. He's missing, Mr. Van Horne."

"Christ." He remembered to give me back my ID. "Come on in."

He tromped up the steps to the front door. It opened into a large sitting room with a wood stove and one piece of what I'd have called living room furniture, an old, lumpy couch. Otherwise, the space was filled with hand-hewn chairs and tables. The chairs were twisted saplings of birch or cherry, tied down to make large, uncomfortable looking seats like backwoods peacock chairs. The tables seemed all one piece of trunk, carved, whittled and polished into monstrosities that wouldn't seem to fit anywhere.

"Those are mine," Ethan said, a layer of modesty over the pride in his voice.

"Impressive. Take a long time?"

"Most of a week each for the chairs. Longer for the tables, but then they're a labor of love."

As if on cue, a woman appeared from what looked like the kitchen area. Framed in the doorway, she had long brown hair, parted in the middle and falling down past her breasts. Peasant dress, no stockings, something like Timberland moccasins on her feet.

She stared at me. I got the impression she wasn't expecting to be introduced. Then she turned to Ethan and said, "Got to go to the store."

"Then go."

"Got to have some money."

"Gave you some yesterday."

"Day before. It's long gone, Ethan."

"Gone? How could—"

"Gone for beer."

"Christ." He dug into his jeans, cowboy style. Came up with some change and a few bills, folded in no order. He kept one bill and two quarters, dumping the rest in her hand like one child transferring a prize bug to another.

She put the money in a scruffy leather handbag that looked like it last served as herb pouch to a Neanderthal. "Keys?"

He made a grunting noise, but dug into the other pocket and came up with car keys.

She walked past me and out the front door, jingling the keys in her hand and singing what sounded like Joni Mitchell's "Court and Spark."

Ethan said, "Why don't you take that one? It's the best one I got out here from the shop."

I settled gingerly into one of the braided chairs. It was surprisingly comfortable, even without a cushion on it.

"Set in that long enough, it'll mold itself to you. Real one-man chair."

Before he could offer me a discount on it, I said, "I understand you were at the estate on Sunday."

"That's right."

"When did you arrive?"

He started to say something, then broke off. Reassessing me, he said, "What does where I was have to do with Kenny running off?"

"He ever run off before?"

"Wouldn't know."

"We think he was kidnapped, Mr. Van Horne."

"Kid—Keeeerist Almighty! How?"

"That's what I'm trying to find out."

"But—you've been there? To the estate, I mean?"

"Yes."

"It's like a fortress, man. Nobody could get in *or* out.
Unless . . ."

"Unless."

He regarded me a little more warily. "Want a beer?"

"No, thanks."

"Mind if I do?"

"Not at all."

He disappeared for a minute. My eyes wandered around
the room. Rifle and shotgun over the wall behind the
woodstove. Sisal rug, filthy from stains and probably very
little upkeep. No prints or paintings on the wall, no knick-
knacks. I had to look around again. No television, stereo,
even radio. No electric lights, just a couple of small propane
lamps with little keys sticking out from their sides. No elec-
tricity. I didn't even want to see the plumbing. If Ethan
cared about more than food and beer money, his lifestyle
sure didn't betray it.

He came back in from somewhere beyond the kitchen,
twisting the top off a bottle of generic. "Dug a cold cellar
underneath the back there. Keeps things just right."

"If I can get back to Sunday?"

"Why would somebody kidnap Kenny?"

I tried to decide if he was being disingenuous. "For
money, we believe."

"Yeah, but why Kenny?"

"Because the General dotes on him."

Ethan took a swig of his beer and coughed. "Don't seem
right."

"That they'd choose the boy?"

"No, that Kenny's got to go through all this just because my grandfather is loaded and can pay."

"Money's important to a lot of people. More important than a little boy's feelings."

"And whose fault is that?" Ethan said, straightening up.

I had a feeling I was about to be treated to a reprise of Sunday's flare-up. "Whose fault?"

"Yeah. My grandfather's, that's who. He got famous killing people with tanks, then he got rich selling them to people who want to kill other people, and now he's just rich. Him and all the ones like him, just sitting back after the country's been raped and pillaged so he can have a private army and electrified fences around his mansion."

Except the fences weren't electrified. "I take it dinner on Sunday fell apart over the money issue?"

"You know about that, do you?"

"I know what I've been told. I'd like to hear your side of it."

"My side?" He put down the beer. "My side is that everybody at the estate except maybe the Nusbys is crazy for money. My parents were killed because they could afford more car and booze than my father could handle. Then my grandfather, the revered General, has all these plans for Allen and me. Only they didn't work out like his battle plans used to, and that pissed him off royally."

"He mentioned something about 'expectations.' "

"Yeah, 'expectations.' You in business for yourself?"

"Partnered."

"Even better. Listen to me, you'll learn something. You enter a contract with a guy, you figure, the agreement is what's written down, right? I mean, he's got to do what he writes he's going to do, and I got to do what I write I'm going to do."

"Go on."

"Well, it wasn't that way with the General. He was so used to being the General, so used to everybody just doing what he told them to do . . . If something wasn't right or wasn't enough, the people would go back and do it again or do more so the General was satisfied. The problem is he got used to a world where he got to re-write the contract, you know? He had all these expectations from a contract I never signed, never even discussed with him, and then he'd get pissed if I broke it or wouldn't change it to suit him."

"Like for instance?"

"Like for instance, he had this thing, this view of the future, that Allen would be the doctor and me the lawyer. So each of us could serve the family, in sickness and in wealth. Now Allen, he was scared of his own shadow growing up, so there was no way he could be the lawyer. Fine. But I didn't *want* to be the lawyer. I didn't know what I wanted to be, but it sure as shit wasn't some guy in one of his twelve suits he couldn't tell the difference from one to the other without a fashion consultant. And I hated paperwork, hated it. But no, I was going to be the lawyer, and Allen the doctor."

"So what happened?"

"So Allen keeps the contract, and goes on to medical school and fuckin' freaks out the first time he's got to touch a body. A cadaver, or whatever you call it. I mean, they've got to pry him off the wall with like a crowbar. And I flunk out of enough pre-law programs, I took the same courses so many times, I probably know enough about law school to advise kids on why not to go to it. And Allen winds up in some medical school where *Ingles* is not the native tongue and heading some dip-shit foundation so he can look useful. And I end up . . ." he waved his hand around the room, "living lightly on the land, you know?"

I let the silence sit a minute. He retrieved his beer and chugged the rest of it.

Ethan wiped the back of his hand across his mouth. "I'm going to get another."

"I'll join you."

Ethan seemed to hesitate a half step as he realized I meant to join him literally. He continued through a primitive kitchen with a tacky plastic cloth over the table and a couple of chairs painted a smoky white. We descended eight solid wooden steps into a damp, clammy pit, shored up here and there with irregular pieces of knot-riddled scrap lumber. Food was stacked in uneven jumbles of cans, containers, and boxes.

It was at least twenty degrees cooler than the air outside the house. "Things stay pretty cold down here?"

Ethan yanked two beers out of the cardboard case. "Not below freezing, but good as any refrigerator. Don't have the power out here, don't really need it for my work. And you can stuff those propane jobs. They still cost hard money."

He handed me a bottle, his eyes a window into a mind trying to figure me out.

As we moved up to the kitchen, I said, "You happy here?"

He didn't answer until we were back in the living room. "I'm happy to be away from what the General had all planned for me. I'm happy making custom-made furniture for me, and selling it to people who aren't asking me to sign any contract for what they want but are just satisfied getting what they can see I already did. I'm happy . . . Look, I know the guy is dying and all."

I tried my beer. Flat. I didn't say anything.

"I mean, I know he hasn't got all that much time left, and I'd rather see him happy than not. That's why I listened to Kerstein about coming down on Sunday. Rocks in my head. From the second the General saw me—in the best of these kind of clothes I own because these are the only kind I've got anymore—he took one look, and I could see it in his eyes, the old unwritten contract, the old unfulfilled expectations, and I decided then and there I wasn't going to take any more of his shit, because he can't bargain with me and he can't persuade me and he can't even threaten me because the only leverage he's got is his money and who he's going to leave it to and I couldn't give a shit about that, and he knows it."

"When did you get there on Sunday?"

"Oh. I don't know, man. I was supposed to be there around five, but I got down to Beacon Harbor about four, no traffic even with the foliage freaks out. I didn't want to be early, so I farted around Beacon Harbor for a while, just getting more convinced I didn't want any part of it all even before I saw him."

I sipped enough beer to be polite. "When did you leave?"

"Don't know. We started arguing over drinks and kept it up over dinner. I walked out on everybody before we were finished, and I tried to walk it off around the grounds . . ." Ethan shook his head. "The grounds. Sheee-it, I've never even gotten over using the right words, have I? Anyway, I walked around for a while, trying to cool off, but it was no good, and I knew it. I went back in, just to tell everybody I was leaving so they didn't have to call out the storm troopers. The General made some wise remark, and I drove on out."

"You see anything on the grounds?"

"Anything? What do you mean?"

"Anybody."

"No. No, it was dark, so I stayed on the paths and . . . Oh, I see. No, I didn't see any kidnappers or anything."

I said, "What time did you get back up here?"

"Don't know. Fuckin' truck broke down."

"Broke down? Where?"

"On the road, where do you think?"

"I mean, down there or up here?"

"What difference does it make?"

"Humor me."

"Just outside of Beacon Harbor. Timing belt went. Can't drive without it, so I just sat for a while, trying to decide if I wanted to be warm enough to go back to the estate. I decided I didn't care."

"So you stayed in your truck all night?"

Ethan shook his head. "After a couple of hours, guy comes along. Got the same kind of truck I do, has an extra."

"An extra timing belt?"

"Yeah. Lucky thing."

"And you guys replaced it right there?"

"Not that hard. Engine runs a little rough, but I'll get to that first chance I get."

"Let me get this straight. You're sitting on a road by Beacon Harbor for a couple of hours, broken down, and the cops don't cruise by and stop for you?"

"Didn't see any."

Ethan drained the last of his beer. I tried to decide if, all things being equal, I'd buy his story about the breakdown. If I bought his story about not caring for the General's money, I might.

196

"So it took you what, three hours longer to drive back here than it usually did?"

"No."

"No?"

"No, man. It took me three hours longer to get back here than it *should* have. I don't *usually* drive down there, and I hope to Christ I never do again."

"If I need to talk with you some more, is there a phone number I can use?"

"No. Like I said, we don't go in for most of that shit. Now, if it's okay with you, I've got to get back to work so I can keep Miss Moosehead in beer and Wonderbread. Have a nice trip back."

A hundred miles away, thinking of other things, I realized I'd forgotten to tell Ethan that his grandfather said he was sorry.

Chapter Seventeen

The relaxed air from Maine was long gone before Turgeon said, "Nothing from the kidnappers, but your partner wants you to call him back."

Turgeon walked away. Just wearing his sidearm, no M-16 today.

I knocked on the library door. No answer. I entered, closing it behind me. I dialed our office number on the line that didn't also ring in the living room.

"Langway and Dooley."

"Fred, Matt."

"Matt, I—"

"This line may not be clear, Fred."

"Oh, right, right. That's why I didn't leave you a message, just a callback."

"So what can you tell me?"

He lowered his voice, as though that would make a difference. "This Rivas, I found his house, on Cooney Street. Eyeballed it all last night, get me?"

"Go ahead."

"He's about a spit away from Upham's Corner, drug capital of the western world, but no activity at the house. Maybe he's on vacation."

"Not without travel money. I'll stop by later, try to see him. Anything else?"

"Yeah, about Van Horne, Allen, M.D."

"What is it?"

"Seems like he had to go to a place in the country."

"What kind of place?"

"For, like, meditation, solve his problems."

"A think tank?"

"Uh-uh. More like a shrink tank."

"Jesus. How long ago?"

"Seven, eight years. Couldn't see the actual paperwork."

I thought about what Ethan said about Allen and the cadaver, and I decided he must have meant it literally. "Okay. Anything else?"

"None of the service people, like the tree guy and all, look like possibles. All solid alibis for that night, and between you and me, no way anybody'd believe they had anything to do with this here."

I ground my teeth. "Fred, this may not just be between you and me, remember?"

"Oh, right, right. Sorry."

"That it?"

"One other thing, Matt."

"Go ahead."

"I went to that bar, 'Fellas'?"

"And?"

"Not much, but I got one of the bartenders to open up a little."

"About what?"

"This guy Binns."

"What'd he say?"

"Bartender says Binns is a regular, but not like an every-nighter. Remembered him because of the first name. Not so many 'Caspers'."

"Anything else?"

"Yeah. I asked him who old Casper's friends are."

"What'd he say to that?"

"Seems one of them sort of stuck out."

"How do you mean?"

"Guy maybe thirty-five or so. Odd duck, seemed nervous, shy. Bartender figured he maybe had just the one foot out of the closet, you know?"

"Get a name?"

"Nah, but I got a nickname."

"That Binns used on the guy or the guy used on Binns?"

"Neither. The one the bartender had in mind for the guy with Binns. Bartenders, they do that, you know? They make up names for the people on the other side of the bar, helps keep them straight on who ordered what, like that."

"What was this nickname?"

"I got here, 'Yul.' "

"Yul?"

"Yeah, seems this guy with Binns shaved his head like Yul Brynner."

So simple. "You did fine, Fred. Stay dry and follow through on the rest."

"Don't worry, Matt. I won't let you down."

As I came out of the library, Yale Underwin was standing awkwardly, like he'd been waiting for me. He was dressed in boat clothes, stylishly casual.

A girl popped up from a chair behind him. She was maybe fifteen and looked twenty-five, with terrific legs and baby-doll make-up. Her long, bushy hair was gathered on the right side of her head and cascaded down the side of her face, so that at first it looked as though a monkey were perched on her shoulder.

He said, "Uh, Mr. Langway?"

"Yes?"

"This is Dawn. She'd like to meet you, a real private eye and all."

Dawn gave me the twice-and-thrice over. I had the feeling I wasn't measuring up. "Hi, Dawn."

"Hi," she said, the way she would when she wasn't par-
ticularly interested in continuing a conversation but
couldn't just walk off.

I could. "Listen, I'd like to stay and talk, but I've got to
get going. Maybe I'll see you later."

Yale said, "Uh, sure. Thanks."

He seemed relieved. Was the boy running a con on
Dawn or on me?

I wasn't offended when Dawn didn't say good-bye.

The door to the security room was ajar. I could hear
deep, regular breathing.

I kicked the door inward. Turgeon was slumped in the
monitor chair, his eyes flaring open as he shuddered awake.

"For God's sake, Langway!"

"Snatching a few winks?"

He composed himself. "I could've shot you."

"Sunday night can take a long time to get to Monday
morning."

"What's that supposed to mean?"

"I'm thinking about you on the monitors again. Covering for O'Meara without enough sleep during the prior
seventy-two hours."

Turgeon had begun to rub the heel of a hand under his
eye, then caught himself as I finished. "I didn't fall asleep
on duty."

"Come on. You and I both know a man on any kind of
guard duty can drop off for five, ten minutes and not even
notice it. In the service, I even saw guys sleep standing up."

Turgeon changed his tone, probably hoping to change
the subject. "What do you want, anyway?"

"I want to know if your coming out of the closet is any
part of this."

His face ran a spectrum of expressions, settled on a grim smile. "My personal life has nothing to do with this."

"You and Binns. You lovers?"

"None of your business."

"Kenny's the General's business, remember?"

Turgeon inhaled and exhaled, dropping even the pretense of a smile.

I said, "Are you and Binns lovers?"

"No. I mean, yes. Yes, in the physical sense, but . . . He's really more . . . counseling me. That's not enough of a word, though. It's more . . ."

When his sentence died, I said, "Somebody made an effort to point a finger at Binns."

"What?"

"I don't see Binns taking the boy. He's too professional about wanting to help him. But somebody lifted a couple of the tapes Binns has of Kenny talking, and I think a tape is what the General heard over the phone."

"A tape . . . ?"

"Of Kenny, saying hello to him and all."

"God . . . I . . . God."

I let it sink in a little further. "Does the General know about you and Binns?"

"Know? About us being . . . No, no. I mean, I've heard him making bad jokes about Casper to Nusby, even to me. Calls Casper a 'Nancy-boy.' But . . . No, the General has no idea about me."

"I don't plan to tell him."

"You don't?"

"No. Like I said, I don't see Binns taking Kenny. And I don't see you being part of it without Binns."

Turgeon drew back a bit, like a turtle from a loud noise. "Why are you telling me all this?"

"Because I'm going to need a steady hand before long. Probably a hand with a gun in it."

Turgeon seemed to sit three inches taller in the chair, but all he did was nod.

"General?"

Van Horne was in one of the Adirondack chairs on the top of the cliff. He wore a thick-knit sweater that looked oiled against the wind. The pipe was in the mouth, but he seemed uninterested in lighting it. Or in me.

"General?"

He looked up. "Sorry, Langway. Didn't hear you coming. You saw Ethan?"

"Yessir."

"And?"

I took a chair, turning it to face both him and the ocean at the same angle. "He seemed surprised to hear about Kenny."

The General made no movement, no motion of head or eyes, nothing to reveal his thoughts. Finally, he said, "I can't believe Ethan would do this, and I certainly can't believe he'd do it for money."

"I feel the same about the money part."

Van Horne snapped to me. "Meaning?"

"Meaning could Ethan care enough about Kenny to want to spirit him away from all this. In good faith, I mean."

"You have any proof?"

"Ethan's car broke down, he says, just outside town here. I had him show me around his place up in Maine. No sign of Kenny directly, but he could have been hiding him somewhere I wouldn't think to look."

A snort, almost a laugh. "Langway, Ethan hates me,

hates my money, but even Ethan must realize Kenny is better off down here with attention and professional tutoring than learning how to bend sticks in the woods."

"Still, it might explain a lot of things, like why the note was written here instead of brought here. Ethan could have left it just as an afterthought."

"A red herring, you mean?"

"Yessir."

"I don't see that at all, Langway."

"It's a longshot, I know."

Van Horne grimaced, then shifted in his chair to ease something. "I've been thinking about our discussion last night."

"Our discussion?"

"About how and when Kenny was taken out."

"Yessir?"

"Could they have waited until *after* we discovered he was missing?"

"After?"

"Yes. Waited until we all were running around like chickens with our heads cut off, then taken him out of the house?"

Jesus, still the sharp mind, even through the pain. "Not likely."

"Why not?"

"All the commotion. Tends to make people alert, more likely to spot things."

"I thought you said that the commotion might make it easier for somebody hiding on the estate from the night before to slip back into the house?"

"Because it would be natural for that person, an insider, to be running around near the house. If you're trying to smuggle Kenny out, though, different question. Also, the kidnappers wait till Monday morning, they risk your calling the cops, who would seal off the estate entirely."

He passed a hand over his eyes. "I suppose you're right there. Anything else you've turned up?"

"No. I'm heading into Boston tonight, try to catch up on things from that end, then be back here by early tomorrow."

"To wait for the call."

"That's right."

"I think I'll do some of my waiting here."

Turning back to the sea, he looked so old.

"By the way, General?"

He looked at me.

"Ethan said to tell you he was sorry, too."

Van Horne nodded once, vigorously, then started fussing with his pipe. "Yes. Yes, I expect he is."

I got to Upham's Corner at about six p.m. Cars snarled and horns protested on Columbia Road, the main drag. Half the drivers were heading home, the other half buying drugs like you might buy a rose from a kid hawking at a traffic light. Smashed bottles, tumbleweed newspapers, trash scattered as though a garbage truck had exploded.

Finding Cooney Street on the far side of a burned out convenience store, I left the Blazer. I was wearing a Boston Edison baseball cap and a blue Eisenhower jacket. I pretended to read from a clipboard with some forms under the clip. If one of the few people still trying to live in the neighborhood worked for the utility, I wouldn't look just right. But most wouldn't notice.

Number 127 was a single-family house disintegrating into a hovel. I went through the motions of ringing the bell, flipping through my forms, and getting out from the overhang of the second floor to check something by the dim reflection of the streetlight. I knocked once, then knocked louder. Figuring I'd shown enough to be credible, I went around back.

The door I'd bet would lead into a kitchen was locked, but the curtains in the glass part were opaque. I entwined my two gloved hands on the knob and shrugged my shoulders in a torquing lurch. The rotting wood of the jamb gave way, and I pushed the door, bolt still engaged, into the kitchen.

I didn't hear anything except the ticking from the clock in the stove. Glancing around the kitchen, the clock looked like the only appliance that worked. Some Kentucky Fried and Burger King bags, roaches scurrying in that submarine zig-zag route, like they were avoiding depth charges from a pursuing destroyer. Plastic soda bottles, beer by the quart, pizza box torn in half.

Fred's kind of guy. I shook it off.

I edged farther through the kitchen until I could see into the living room. Nobody. Dark drapes blocking out even the streetlight, peeling wallpaper, most of the old plaster molding missing. A twelve-inch black-and-white on top of a lettuce crate, a couple of ancient arm chairs that made Ethan's couch in Maine look like an entry in the Home Show. Spanish-language newspaper, half empty bottle of Old Mr. Boston vodka, a Pepsi can that wasn't trying hard enough to be an ashtray.

Upstairs, a bath and two bedrooms. One used for sleeping, sheets rumpled, pillows without cases and stained from drool or other bodily fluids. The other bedroom used for storage. Some clothes in boxes or grocery bags, some nudie magazines, other personal stuff that looked like anybody's trash. The bathroom hadn't been cleaned for months. The tiles that weren't gone were cracked, sink dripping water the color of iodine.

Working my way back downstairs, I checked the closets. Nothing. There was a door off the kitchen that I thought might lead to the pantry but led to a set of steep, narrow basement steps instead. I climbed down, ducking my head under the beam at the midway point.

Except for evacuating himself, he hadn't started to smell yet.

A man lay on his stomach, head turned to the left, one arm up and out and the other back, a human semaphore. Two holes between the shoulder blades. Dark brown where the blood had caked, blackish around the frayed area of his shirt from the powder burns. Another stain in the seam of his pants from where the sphincter muscle would have let go, releasing the contents of his bowels.

Not relying on my memory from last April, I got close enough to the blue-skinned face to make out the stubby, Indian features and sparse eyebrows marking the Rivas gene pool. God writes in a plain hand.

I backed up the stairs, forgetting to duck the beam this time.

"How many is that?"

"Love your tone. Would you call it 'accusatory'?"

Dee hurled her shoulder bag onto the chair I wasn't sitting in and pointed at the glass I rested against my cheek. "How many, Matt?"

"What difference does it make?"

I took a bite of the Scotch. She paced in a blue wool suit and wide belt that matched the bag. Then she sat on the sofa, knees together, hands clasped.

"You don't really care about us. About what you . . ."

"Go ahead, Dee, say it. About what I'm doing to our relationship, right?"

She dropped her face, kneading her hands. "I went to church today."

I took another jolt from the glass.

"I haven't been to church since I was twenty-two, Matt, but I went today, middle of the afternoon between vendors coming to huck their lines. I found an old granite church. You know, the Gothic kind of place with the barrel vaults and the stained glass and the raised pulpit like a crow's nest. There was no Mass or anything going on, so I just went in a couple of pews and sat down. Figured maybe I could get back that feeling, that feeling you have when you're a little kid, and everything's pressing in on you that you can't do a thing about, but just sitting in the church, just sitting in with God, can make you breathe easier and feel better."

I stared at the blank TV screen and thought about my drive to Maine.

"So I'm sitting there, all alone except for a couple of old ladies near the front, by the candle box. Then this fat priest comes out of the side of the church. I forget what they call that."

"A fat priest?"

Dee affected her patient note. "The side of the church."

"The apse."

"Right, the apse. This fat priest with that hat that monsignors wear comes out from the side and down the aisle toward me. He looks lazy, waddling like a duck, when something catches his eye in a pew maybe four in front of me. He stops, frowns and starts edging sideways along the pew bench, like you had to move forward for communion when there are people still sitting between you and the aisle.

Anyway, he gets to the end of the pew and reaches down and shakes something with his hand. He says, 'Pal? Hey, pal? Come on. You have to leave now.' Well, his hand comes back up where I can see it, but it's resting on a shoulder, obviously a derelict. I mean, you didn't have to see more than the shoulder and the back of his head to know that. His hair was scrungy, his collar was torn halfway around his neck, holes sprung at the saddle of his shirt. Then the priest or the monsignor, he says 'Come on, come on, time to go,' and the bum says 'Father? Father, God's throwing me out? God's throwing me out of church?' And the fat priest doesn't answer him, only he does answer him, really, by handing the bum a hat from the bench somewhere and saying 'You've got to leave now, pal. Come on.' "

I said, "So what'd you do, come to the rescue?"

Dee shook her head, stood up and dragged on the strap of her bag till the bag itself swung free of the chair and bumped up against her leg. "No, Matt. I got up and left. Before God got around to me, too."

I could hear her go down the stairs and open the front door, then her voice. "Good-bye, Matt. I hope you can figure yourself out." The door closed behind her.

I got up, lifted the decanter of scotch by its neck, and brought it back to the chair with me.

Chapter Eighteen

I am in-country seven months. It is time for me to do my part to rid the villes *of official corruption. South Vietnamese officials are supposed to penetrate the hamlets that are controlled by Vietcong and "neutralize" the communist shadow infrastructure. Only problem is, the South Vietnamese officials are more concerned about bank accounts than body counts, bribery being rampant. I am supposed to go in with a team and make an example of a corrupt official who has taken over the main house of an abandoned rubber plantation. Neutralize one corrupt official, educate a hundred. The Americans will not tolerate corruption.*

It is late afternoon. My two-man team and I are huddled in ponchos over a can containing a heat tablet, cooking some C-rations. The rain keeps down the smoke and smell of the fire while we wait for dark. My team is a Georgian named Ike I've seen wearing three stripes and a rocker back at base camp and a Spec 4 with an unpronounceable Arabic name everybody calls Omar, after the actor or the tent-maker in the joke, I don't know which.

Ike, back against a teak tree, is rubbing his silencer. Not cleaning or polishing it with a rag, just rubbing it against his palm. He says to me, "L.T., you ever taken a life?"

"What difference does that make?"

"Begging your pardon, sir, but it makes all the fuck difference in the world, we're going out on this here mission with you."

I look from Ike to Omar, rain dribbling down my face every time I shift head. Omar just watches me, waiting for my answer.

"Animals. I've killed animals."

Ike seems to relax a little. "Same difference. Live thing, animal or human, it's going to move on you. Not be where it was when you decided to shoot. You gotta watch it, Lieutenant, watch and learn which way it moves. Into the wind, away from the light, whatever. Watch it and learn it. Then you'll be aiming at the right place. You'll pull the trigger and you'll be shooting where the guy moves to, bring him down no sweat."

Ike bobs his head, then puts away the silencer and picks up his M-16, moving off just a little, facing downhill.

Omar whispers to me. "Ike, he wrong, you know?"

"What do you mean?"

Black eyes in an emaciated face dance a little. "All the talk, about animals and people. Maybe the shooting the same, but the killing . . . no, the killing is different."

I don't say anything.

"Yeah, Lieutenant, killing people . . . I . . . I dunno, it's just . . . better."

Omar giggles, rolls over and closes his eyes. I notice he rolls away from the fire.

The music came on harsh and long, the dial still set on Dee's punk station, the end of some song the DJ credited to Echo and the Bunnymen. I yanked the radio off the bed table and tore the plug out of the wall. I tried digging the heels of my hands into my eyes, but it didn't do any good.

"It's them!"

I left my late breakfast, blowing by Nusby and running after Turgeon toward the library. Kerstein and the General were already there. When I'd arrived at the estate, Turgeon had told me Van Horne had been sitting next to the telephone since 5:30 a.m., waiting. I had quietly swept the room around him for bugs, the old man ignoring the ritual, staying deep inside himself.

I picked up the headset, hearing the metallic voice croak "—the money?"

The General said, "We have the money as you requested. All hundreds, used and not in sequence."

"Good. Separate the money into packages. One hundred bills in each package, bound by rubber bands. That will make one hundred packages. Put all the packages into a large green leaf bag. Seal the bag like it was trash, but with black electrician's tape instead of a twist tie. Twist the bag as far down as it will go with the packages of money inside it before using the tape to seal it. Understand?"

"I do."

"We can check for any homing devices. We find one, the boy's dead."

"There will be no such devices."

"Very good. Kenny's parents, Allen and Janine, will take the bag down to your boat."

"My boat?"

"Don't interrupt again. Allen and Janine will take the bag down to your big sailboat in the harbor. They'll put the bag on the rear transom just inboard of the lifeline, so the bag can be seen at all times. At exactly 2:00 a.m., they will motor out to Buoy Number 173 in the harbor and moor at that buoy."

"Please, I'm not trying to interrupt, but Allen is not . . . not very good around boats. He—"

"You want to see the kid again?"

Van Horne swallowed the rest of the sentence he'd intended to say. "Yes."

"Allen and Janine have to be alone on the boat. Once they're moored at the buoy, they stand at the bow of the boat and wait for us. Is that clear?"

"Clear."

"Just Allen and Janine on the boat. Is that clear?"

"Clear."

"You botch any of this, the boy gets killed."

The General didn't say that was clear. "When . . . when will you release Kenny?"

"When we have the money."

The sound of dead air filled my ears.

Van Horne said, "What about a seaplane?"

Turgeon and Kerstein looked at me. I had told the General I wanted Turgeon in on the council of war. All four of us were standing around the General's desk, a nautical chart of Beacon Harbor's waterfront spread before us.

I pointed with the eraser end of a pencil, tapping the chart around Buoy 173. "I don't see how they could land, all these buoys around. The pontoon catches one, it fouls the strut, plane flips over. No, it's got to be a boat, maybe a dinghy."

Van Horne said, "A rubber one, commando-style?"

I said, "Possibly. Or a Cigarette."

Kerstein said, "You mean like 'Miami Vice,' a drug runner's boat?"

"Right."

Kerstein said, "I've never seen one of those in the harbor."

"It's a long shoreline, counselor. They could bring the boat in from anywhere."

The General scratched his chin. "What's your plan, Langway?"

I moved the pencil from Buoy 173 to the barrier island at the mouth of the harbor. "Yale showed me the dinghy you use with the *Remagen*."

"Yes. For ferrying out to her and as a lifeboat."

"Would it look odd for the *Remagen* to go out without hers?"

Kerstein said, "Usually you trail the dinghy behind you under motor or sail. But the General told the kidnappers Allen wasn't much of a sailor, so they may not think it odd that he leaves it behind."

I waited till Kerstein looked up from the map. I said, "Counselor, doesn't it strike you that the kidnappers know Allen isn't much of a sailor?"

Kerstein looked confused.

I said, "They don't want Sinbad on that boat. Janine sail much?"

Van Horne said, "No. Doesn't care for the water."

Kerstein said, "My point is still a valid one. The kidnappers won't think it odd that Allen doesn't know enough to bring the dinghy. Why did you ask in the first place, Langway?"

I pointed again to the barrier island. "I say we put Zoubek and O'Meara in the dinghy snugged up against that island somewhere. Any boat that leaves the harbor has to pass close by. If something goes wrong at the pick-up, even a fast boat couldn't outrun a dinghy with a good outboard that's on a collision course."

Turgeon said, "Then you don't think Zoubek and O'Meara are in on it?"

I said, "I don't know, but I doubt both of them are. This is one way we get to find out whether either of them is."

Kerstein said, "With the General's money as the price of seeing their hands."

Van Horne said, "I don't give a tinker's damn about the money." Then, to me, "What about Kenny?"

I said as flatly as I could, "Everybody in this room who

214

thinks Kenny's going to be on the pick-up boat, raise your hand."

The General didn't have to look at any of us.

"Where . . . how will we get him back, then?"

"There's no guarantee you will. There never was. Without involving the Bureau and the kind of specialized manpower they can bring to something like this, there isn't even a good chance."

"Goddam it, Langway! Enough of the situation analysis. Tell it to me straight."

I said, "If I'm the kidnappers, I think I want insurance, insurance that Zoubek and O'Meara, or anybody else, doesn't stop my pick-up boat. They'll take your money and skate on out, then hopefully they'll call and tell you where you can find Kenny."

"Hopefully," said Van Horne, without that emotion in his voice.

I said, "There is another alternative, General."

He looked at me. "What, Langway?"

"We have Zoubek and O'Meara stop the boat as it leaves, then I interrogate the crew."

Kerstein glanced furtively at Van Horne, then at me. "General, I'll not be a party to—"

"Shut up, Sumner. Langway, you can force them to tell you the truth?"

"I can. If we get them alive, I can guarantee that."

Kerstein said, "I'm leaving."

"Sumner, stay where you are."

"For the love of God, General, he's talking about torturing somebody!"

"Sumner, you've never been to war." Van Horne looked at Turgeon. "Where do you stand on this?"

"I'll do whatever you say, General."

Kerstein said, "My God, I can't believe I'm hearing—"

"Sumner, I won't say it again. Shut up." The old man said to me, "That's a hell of a risk, isn't it?"

"General, given what you and I talked about before, it's no more risk than we're already running."

Van Horne went back to the map. "Why not put the dinghy with Zoubek and O'Meara closer to the *Remagen*?"

I said, "Have them moor up, too?"

"Yes." Van Horne moved his finger along the map. "We get them out there now, hours ahead. They moor to a buoy close to Number 173, then lie under a canvas or something. Be right there for it."

I said, "I thought about that, but there aren't many boats left in the harbor this time of year. My guess is that we'll find Buoy 173 has almost no other boats around it now. A dinghy would stick out like a sore thumb. They might even spray it coming in, just to be sure."

Kerstein said, "Spray it?"

I said, "With gunfire."

Van Horne said, "We'd be sacrificing Zoubek and O'Meara for nothing."

"That's right. Even if the pick-up boat didn't chop them, by the time they got the dinghy's engine up and running, the bad guys would be halfway to the harbor mouth, and with a fast enough boat, beyond the dinghy's ability to catch them from behind."

The General nodded, abandoning his idea for mine. "Then we put the dinghy at the island. All right, where will you be?"

"Up on the cliff, with Turgeon here."

"To do what?" said Van Horne.

"I'm going to be watching things with the best pair of

binoculars we've got. Turgeon's going to be zeroing a rifle with a starlight scope."

Turgeon smiled. Kerstein looked sick. The General studied the map.

After a moment, Van Horne said, "Anything else we should be doing?"

"Two things. First, get Yale to give Allen and Janine a crash course in handling the *Remagen*. We don't want any mistakes we can avoid."

"What's the second thing?"

I took a breath, held it. "You and Nusby should arm yourselves. With everybody else out at the harbor, I don't want our friends to be getting any ideas about stopping here first."

The old soldier looked back down at the map. "That won't be necessary, Langway."

I felt a little ping. "Why's that?"

He looked up, the eyes of the commander. "Zoubek and O'Meara will be here, guarding the house in each other's company."

I could see it. I could see it before he said it.

"General—"

"While you and Turgeon are up on that hill, Nusby and I will be out at the island, in the dinghy."

"General, I—"

"What's the matter, Langway? You don't respect my judgment on this?"

"I respect your instinct. I just don't trust your judgment where Kenny's concerned."

"The decision is made, Langway. Live with it."

Van Horne rubbed his hands together and almost smiled.

Chapter Nineteen

"Try one. Go ahead."

Lila had set the tray down in front of me. There were embroidered cloth napkins, some China dishes, and a casserole dish filled with dainty triangles of bread and filling.

She said, "I made them myself. Tuna was the only thing we had enough of to make so many sandwiches."

I took one of the triangular pieces and put it on a plate. "What happened to the Nusbys?"

Lila seemed impatient, more interested in my sampling her efforts than talking for a change. "Marcella's in bed. She can *sense* her husband's going to do something foolish, and she's scared shitless."

"Gloria Rivas?"

Lila shook her head, the impatience obvious now. "I wanted her to help me with these, but Zoubek said she went off somewhere on an errand."

"Where?"

"Don't know. She took the Nusbys' car, so I hope she went for food."

Lila cocked her head as I bit into the sandwich. I pronounced it "good," and she beamed.

"Never did much in the kitchen. Forgot it can be fun to make things." Her voice shifted, become more typical of her. "What the *hell* is going on, anyway?"

"Confidential."

"Who do you think you're kidding? The General has Yale down at the yacht club, supposedly teaching Allen and Janine, of all people, how to handle the *Remagen*. Marcella

218

is rolling her eyes like it's Judgment Day, and the security staff acts like we're on red alert."

"Maybe you should make some coffee, too."

She made a face instead. "Sumner took off, you know."

I stopped chewing.

"I *thought* that would get your attention."

"When?"

"He stopped to say good-bye to me about an hour ago."

"What'd he say?"

Lila stretched languorously over the leather couch, tugging at some of the brass studs, testing to see if any came out in her hand. "Confidential."

I figured I knew why he left. Or at least why he'd justify his leaving.

She said, "Something's really going to happen, isn't it?"

I finished the sandwich section, reached for another.

"The General's puttering around. I saw him like that when I was a little girl." She paused for effect. "Just before he went off to Korea."

I used a napkin to wipe my mouth and reached for the Diet Sprite I'd found in the refrigerator.

"He's an old man, Matthew."

"He's his own man, Lila."

"He's sick. I told you I came home here this time like always?"

"Like always?"

"Like always after a busted marriage. Well, that's not really true. I came home to be with him. For a little while to be his daughter, like I never felt I was growing up without him around."

"Kind of late for all that."

"Kind of, yes." Lila broke a lacquered nail on one of the studs, brought the finger to her mouth to chew on it. "And wasted effort, too. It wasn't just that he was away when I was growing up, Matt. It's that he didn't much care how I turned out. He cared about his male line. Quentin and Ethan and Allen and even . . . even Kenny. Kenny most of all, I came to realize."

"Why not take off, then?"

"You are a bastard, aren't you?"

"Just curious."

"I'm still his daughter, even if he's not much of a father. He's the last person left alive in this whole fucked-up family who's older than I am, Matthew. That gives you a sense of *mortality,* you know?"

"Good sandwich."

Lila got up and walked out, saying over her shoulder. "Just don't get him killed, all right?"

The time weighed heavily. Zoubek seemed glum at the front gate when I took a walk down there, half a tuna section still on the incongruously fancy plate in front of him. Lila Underwin, USO girl.

"Zoubek, how're you doing?"

"I am okay. You?"

"Fine. Where did Gloria Rivas go?"

"She did not say to me."

"She say anything?"

"Just that she go out for Mrs. Van Horne."

"For Janine Van Horne?"

"Gloria say that, yes."

I dropped my voice. "You realize we're trying to get Kenny back tonight?"

A nod.

"I'd appreciate it if you'd stay by this gate till we get back."

Another nod.

"It may be a while."

"Mr. Langway, in Czechoslovakia, I stay awake once two days and two nights at border so the guard to change so I can go across. I be here when you come."

"Another thing?"

He waited.

"O'Meara. Keep an eye on him, will you?"

A final nod. "This I do for four days already now."

As I moved back to the main house, I toyed with the idea of trying to persuade the General to replace Nusby with Zoubek in the dinghy. When I got to the fountain, I saw O'Meara outside the front door, leaning on the frame.

He said, "Got a minute?"

"Sure."

O'Meara glanced around, elaborately casual. "There anything you want me to do tonight?"

"Do?"

"Yeah. Like anything you want me to watch out for. Or anybody?"

I looked around the way he had. "Yes. Keep an eye on Zoubek."

O'Meara frowned. "Geez, not Ernie?"

"I'm not sure. That's why I need back-up here."

"Right, right."

I clapped him on the shoulder and kept a straight face through the door.

When I was halfway down the stairs to central station, Casper Binns came out of it. His face was flushed.

"Excuse me," he said, not waiting for me to get down the stairs.

"Sure," I said, letting him pass me in a hurried manner, his shoes tapping on the slats.

Inside the security room, Turgeon had his back to me,

221

staring at the blank wall instead of the video monitors.

Without turning, he said, "I told you, I've made up my mind."

"About what?"

He swiveled around in the chair, mouth moving, but no sounds coming out.

I said, "Are you all set for tonight?"

Turgeon searched my face, as though trying to figure out which question I was really asking him.

"I said, is everything ready for tonight?"

"Yeah . . . Yeah, I'm all set."

"Good."

I left him, thinking as I went upstairs to the library. I sat down to call the office. No answer. I left a message with the service and tried Fred at home.

Three rings, then a tentative "Yeah?"

"Fred, it's Matt. I'm calling from the General's house."

"Oh, right, right. What's up?"

"It's definitely tonight, Fred."

"Right."

"In the harbor."

He hesitated. "Where do you want me?"

"Where we talked about."

"You got it."

When I didn't say anything, Fred said, "Matt?"

"That's it for now, Fred. See you later."

"Right. See you."

"I, uh, thought it would be heavier."

We stood in the living room, a little after midnight. Allen was hefting the green leaf bag containing the ransom, wrapped one hundred bills to a package. Before dinner, the General watched Turgeon and me take the packages from the vault in the security room and stack them on the monitor desk. After I put the packages in the bag and taped it, they formed a multi-jointed block measuring approximately two feet long, one foot wide, and half a foot high.

I said, "I make it between twenty and twenty-five pounds."

He stared down at it, hefted it a few more times. "I agree."

Dinner had been a strained affair, everyone taking seconds on coffee against the lack of sleep we expected to suffer. Watching Janine, I had the impression pure adrenaline would have been enough.

Both Allen and Janine were now dressed in full foul weather gear, even though the marine forecast for the night was clear with less than a five-mile-per-hour variable wind. It gets cold on the water if you have to wait there long enough, and we decided it made more sense for them to be on the *Remagen* and in place at Buoy 173 earlier rather than later. Turgeon drove the General and Willie Nusby to the waterfront immediately after dinner, Van Horne feeling a need to be at the island for the ambush long before any one might be looking for suspicious boat activity.

Janine took a turn lifting the bag. She set it down, shaking her head.

I said, "Something the matter?"

She looked to her husband, then to me. "Not all that much for a child's life."

I shifted my eyes to the bag and said, "Gloria Rivas left the estate earlier. She told Zoubek at the gate that she was running an errand for you."

Janine's voice said, "Not for me."

I looked back up at her, then Allen. "No?"

Allen said, "Uh, not for me either."

223

Janine said, "Is it important?"

"I'm not sure. The security people say she hasn't come back yet."

"How peculiar," said Allen.

Janine, Allen, and I rode down together in the Blazer, the bag on the back seat next to Janine. Turgeon followed us in the Bronco. I reviewed the telephoned instructions with Allen and an increasingly edgy Janine. I made each of them repeat the instructions twice in his and her own words.

After the afternoon training session, Yale Underwin had left the *Remagen* tied to the dock so we could load more easily. At the wharf, Turgeon and I went through the sailboat just to make sure nobody was on board. I carried a Smith & Wesson Combat Masterpiece, Turgeon a Browning automatic. The *Remagen* was clean. I took the bag from the Blazer, nestling the money in place above the cockpit on the starboard side of the transom, snugly against one of the lifeline pickets.

Back on the wharf, I checked my wristwatch. 1:20 a.m. I looked up at Janine and Allen, following Yale's handwritten instructions on how to start up.

I said, "I left a walkie-talkie near the front hatch. It's not on, and don't try to use it unless you have to."

"Uh, right."

"And remember, don't look up at the hill. Turgeon and I will be keeping you in view."

"Right," snapped Janine.

"Good luck," I said.

Allen gave a half-wave while Janine berated him for skipping one of Yale's steps.

Turgeon and I got back into our vehicles and drove

about a quarter mile away. We parked at the bottom of the hill, each of us facing our cars a different way. He drew a long leather case from the back of the Bronco, and we climbed the hill. At the top, I hunkered down in the slick grass, uncapped the binoculars and swept the harbor. No activity, not even any noise except for the increasingly smoother sound of the *Remagen*'s engine.

I used my communicator to check with the dinghy at the island. Nusby's voice crackled back, "All set. Nothing yet."

When I clicked off, Turgeon said, "Should have brought a blanket."

"Can't think of everything." I felt the dampness soaking through at my elbows, stomach, and knees, chilling me. "The starlight working?"

He adjusted a knob, sighted, adjusted again, sighted again. "Which is 173?"

I pointed, holding out my binoculars for him.

His eyes to the lenses, he said, "Can't read anything but one-seven. Not enough chop to move the buoy around."

"Good."

He gauged the position of the buoy and handed me back the binoculars. "Why good?"

I gestured toward the island, which seemed to balance like a ballerina on the reflected moonlight at the entrance to the harbor. "The dinghy. The less the chop, the more even its chances are of catching a bigger boat."

"Right."

A shift in noise from the *Remagen* attracted our attention. Janine was casting off lines, Allen inching the wheel to starboard, then inching it back. As the big boat pulled slowly away from the wharf, Turgeon said, "Here we go."

There was no need for the glasses to follow the *Remagen*'s movement through the harbor. Allen circled slowly, agonizingly, around markers for lobster pots and other mooring buoys, Janine's body language motioning him impatiently to the left or right, him always out of phase with her motions. They managed to negotiate the route to number 173 without fouling any of the ropes beneath the markers and buoys. However, it took three passes by Allen and an apparent threat from Janine to let her take the wheel before he was able to put the bow close enough to 173 for Janine to reach it with a boathook and lash the *Remagen* to it.

I said into the communicator, "Moored at the buoy."

Nusby said, "Understood."

Allen started forward toward Janine, who waved him back. He stumbled back into the cockpit to kill the engine. Allen then came forward again, joining Janine, who sat at the front of the boat. He tried to put his arm around her shoulder once, but she shrugged him off.

I checked my watch. 1:48 a.m.

1:54 a.m. The *Remagen* settled into a steady position off the mooring, maybe a hundred yards from shore, her starboard side to the sea.

2:00 on the button.

2:03. The only sounds were the singsong of the halyards against the masts of the *Remagen* and the other boats still in the harbor. I watched Janine and Allen through the glasses. They weren't talking, Allen checking his watch more often than I was mine.

2:09.

Turgeon said, "I don't like this."

"Patience."

"They've been right on about everything else."

"It's tough to measure time across water. It's probably—"

I stopped as Turgeon tensed, because I heard it too. A distant rattle and hum.

Nusby's voice came over the communicator. "Boat."

Turgeon said, "I can't see him . . . there!"

An irregularity in the moonlight just north of the barrier island. Through the binoculars, the irregularity became a boat, displayed lengthwise to us half a mile away as it turned to enter the harbor. Dinky cabin disproportionately forward of midships.

"Lobsterman."

Turgeon said, "Awful late to be checking his traps."

The boat came on, slow speed, the rattle and hum clarifying to a whomp-whomp-whomp sound. I stole a look at Janine and Allen, standing now, she pointing, him craning his head forward.

Turgeon wrapped the sling of the rifle around his front arm and began sighting toward the lobsterman.

I said, "You'd better just be practicing."

"I am, I am."

Only about fifty yards now separated the two boats. Suddenly the lobsterman slewed to port, increasing speed on a parallel with the shoreline like a plane deciding to try another approach to the runway.

I felt Turgeon tensing again. I said, "Easy. He's just checking it out."

The lobsterman threw a high wake that rolled toward the *Remagen* as the pilot swung back, throttled down, and approached the bow of the sailboat. The lobsterman was taking its time. I watched the dinky cabin through the binoculars, Turgeon through his scope.

I said, "Can you see the pilot?"

"No. You?"

"No. Keep the cabin in your sights."

The wake now rocked the *Remagen*, Janine toppling into Allen, both of them hugging each other and the halyards to keep from being tossed off in the exaggerated pitch and yaw at the narrow bow. The lobsterman shilly-shallyed to and fro, not quite wanting to kiss boat to boat.

Turgeon said, "What do we do?"

"Nothing from up here. Wait it out."

I shivered, clamping my teeth shut to keep them from chattering. Turgeon had been right about the blanket.

Finally, the lobsterman seemed satisfied. The pilot pulled alongside and came out from the cabin. All-weather gear, the floppy hat covering facial features from our high vantage point. The arm motions seemed masculine as the pilot hurled a hawser to Allen, who missed it the first time. The guy gave Allen the finger.

I said, "Recognize him now?"

"No, goddammit! Do you?"

"No."

The pilot recovered the line and threw it again. This time Allen caught it and went to wrap it around a cleat. The pilot yelled something to him, and Allen then just seemed to stand stauncher, taking a double grip on the rope.

I said, "He doesn't want Allen to tie up. Keep your sight on the guy."

"I know, I know."

The pilot watched Allen as the lobsterman slid further and further along the starboard side of the *Remagen*. Turgeon and I shifted our attention to the stern as did Janine, who stood with her hands on her hips, watching the pilot produce a boathook of his own. He caught the sailboat on a jib cleat just forward of the wheel. Pulling the lobsterman man close onto the *Remagen*, the pilot nimbly hopped out of his boat and onto the transom, grabbed the green bag, and hopped back.

The pilot yelled something at Allen, who yelled back.

The pilot yelled again, and Allen let go of the rope. The pilot ran back into the cabin and gunned his engine, coming back out of the cabin only to gather in the line Allen had been holding.

I said, "Don't shoot."

Turgeon said, "I wasn't going to. Be easy, though."

Into the communicator I said, "The boat picked up the bag. One pilot visible. No sign of Kenny."

Nusby said, "Understood."

I glanced at Janine, who was obviously screaming at Allen. Then I focused the binoculars on the retreating lobsterman.

I said, "Stern reads 'The Widow/Colesport.' "

Turgeon said, "Colesport is north of here, maybe ten miles up the coast."

The lobsterman was going hard, but not that fast. I could hear the dinghy's engine start, but with the racket from his own, the pilot probably couldn't. The dinghy appeared on time, pancaking across the calm ocean like a flying fish on what looked to be a collision course with the lobsterman. I could hear a higher, reluctant whine from the lobsterman's engine, then two bursts of noise like someone blowing air through their lips. The pilot seemed not to like the General's M-16. The lobsterman throttled down and heaved to, the dinghy coming longside.

Nusby's voice said, "We have him. We're coming in."

"I got rights."

Turgeon showed him the butt of his rifle. "Shut up or I'll knock every tooth down your throat."

The pilot shut up, stared down at the dock. Early thirties, pot-bellied outside the all-weather gear, the look of a poor loser in his eyes.

I held his driver's license to the light. " 'Patrick J. Craven, 34 Back Street, Colesport, Massachusetts.' "

Van Horne said, "Shouldn't we be doing this somewhere else?"

"Just who the fuck are—"

Turgeon shoved the butt of his rifle into Craven's shoulder. Craven fell silently, rubbing his collarbone and studying the dock again.

I said, "You're right, General. Turgeon, get our stuff from this guy's boat."

Nusby had brought the dinghy in behind Craven's boat as the General in the lobsterman held a gun on Craven. Now Nusby was running the dinghy out to the *Remagen* to retrieve Janine and Allen, figuring Yale could bring the sailboat back to the dock in a few hours.

Turgeon swung his leg over the side of the lobsterman and grabbed the green bag. As I motioned Craven to his feet, Turgeon said, "Shit, this water is cold."

I stopped dead. "What did you say?"

Turgeon looked up at me, the bag in his hand, dripping water on the otherwise dry deck. "I said this water on the bag is cold. I should've worn—"

I cut him off. "How the hell did the bag get wet?"

Craven sought to redeem himself. "It was wet when I picked it up."

I turned and glared at him. "What?"

He shrunk a little. "When I got it off the transom on the sailboat there. It was already soaked."

I looked at Van Horne, who was gesturing to Turgeon. "Open the bag."

Turgeon tried to work his fingers on the tape. "I can't. Langway wound the tape too tight."

"Tear it open!"

"Yessir." Turgeon dug his fingers into the side of the bag and tore away at it. "Okay?"

I said, "Reach inside and pull out some of the packages."

He did. "Holy shit!"

Even in the moonlight, you could see it was newspaper, cut and bound into stacks the size of hundred dollar bills.

I said, "General, take Craven back to the estate. Turgeon, get to your car and drive north toward Colesport along the water. I'll go south. Fast as you can!"

Running, I heard Turgeon yell behind me. "What am I looking for?"

"Anybody you recognize," I said, and kept on running.

Chapter Twenty

I got back to the main gate at 4:30 a.m. Turgeon was waiting for me. Rolling down my window, I sneezed twice before he could speak.

Turgeon said, "You look like shit."

"Thanks. Anything?"

"I drove north to Colesport, then two miles past, then crawled it south again to here. Got stopped by two cops who thought I looked suspicious. I didn't see anything. What the hell was I supposed to be looking for, anyway?"

I shook my head. "I didn't see anything either. Where's Craven?"

Turgeon jerked his head toward the house. "Zoubek is keeping him on ice in central station. Nothing happened here while we were gone, but the General isn't too good."

"What do you mean?"

"Took O'Meara twenty minutes to get down to the dock with another car."

"What?"

"You and me took the two that were there, remember?"

"Right."

"Well, I guess when they got inside the gate here, the General seemed to run down, like the dinghy and all took it out of him. He's up in his bedroom."

"Let's talk to Craven first."

Turgeon came around and got in beside me. We drove up to the fountain, passing O'Meara at the door, who said, "Nothing happened while you were gone," to my back as I went by him and down to the security room with Turgeon.

* * * * *

"You guys CIA or what?"

Turgeon stared at him while I blew my nose. Craven sat in the swivel chair, forearms belted to the arms of the chair, bootlaces tied together. Zoubek had been sent upstairs to relieve O'Meara at the front door.

"Because if you are, I'm here to tell you, I won't say a word about this to anybody. Not a word. Honest, I'm telling you."

I said to Turgeon, "You got a cigarette lighter?"

"In the desk. Center drawer."

"Get it."

He crossed behind Craven and rummaged through the drawer. Craven did his best to see what Turgeon was doing without seeming to twist too much doing it.

Turgeon came back. "Here."

I weighed the lighter in my palm, tossing and catching it a few times. A Bic.

I said, "When I was in the Nam, I once broke a North Vietnamese colonel in five minutes with one of these."

Craven's face took on a doughy look, his tongue wetting his lips. "I don't . . . I don't know nothing, honest."

I flicked the lighter to flame. "You're going to tell us what you know. In your own words. Then I'm going to ask you some questions about it. Get started."

Craven said, "All I know is this guy comes up to me on the wharf. Two days ago."

"In Colesport."

"Right, yeah. In Colesport there. He says to me he needs a harbor pick-up, no questions asked. He wants to know, am I interested? I says sure, long as no drugs. He says don't worry, no drugs. I says what's the delivery charge. He says $1,000 up front, $1,000 on delivery to him."

"Delivery where?"

"Up in Colesport. I'm supposed to go back to base, he's gonna meet me there."

"What else?"

"He says to me, come down to Beacon Harbor, Thursday night. Come along the shore, fool around with some traps, look like you know what you're doing. Only, you gotta be inside the harbor by 1:55 a.m."

I sneezed. "He said that? 1:55 a.m. precisely?"

"Yeah, yeah. He said I had to be there on time. Only running at night like that, and me not being all that familiar-like with the harbor here, I got fouled on some lines. Stupid fuck left them there oughta be shot, you know?"

Craven cringed, suddenly aware of his poor choice of words.

I said, "Go on."

"Anyway, like I said, this guy tells me, be in the harbor by 1:55, so I get there instead like by two, little after maybe, and I come in like he says. Then—"

"What's 'like he says'?"

"Huh? Oh, he told me, come in slow, there's gonna be this big sailer in the harbor. Way he talked, I didn't get the idea he knew a lot about boats, you know? Least not plea-sure boats, because I asked what kinda boat we're talking about, and he didn't know, just said there'd be two people on the bow of a sailboat in a near empty harbor in fuckin' October at two in the morning, how fuckin' hard would it be to spot them? So I says to him, what do I do when I spot this boat? And he says, just come up within fifty yards or so and gun the engine, roll a big wake at them. Then I'm—"

"Hold it. He told you to roll a big wake at the sailboat?"

"Yeah."

"He tell you why?"

"No. Just to do that, then come up on the sailboat from the bow end, which was supposed to be at a mooring, but not to come alongside till the wake passed."

"Just a minute." I looked at Turgeon. "That the way you saw it?"

Turgeon said, "Yeah."

Craven said, "I did it just like he said. I was just a little late because of the line I fouled, like I said there."

"Go on."

"So I do the wake, and come around and approach bow up, like he says, and I come alongside and throw this geek on the bow a line to hold to. But the geek, he starts trying to lash me down to a cleat, so I yell at him, but he don't seem to be too bright, so I yell again. Then I see the bag, like the guy tells me will be there, right on the transom, so I use the boathook to pull close enough. I jump onboard, get the bag, and jump back. Then the geek starts yelling something about his son, I yell back I don't know what the fuck he's talking about, he yells some more and I hear the woman, real looker, what I could see of her, start yelling and finally he gets the idea and casts me off. Then I take off and some nig—some old guys in a dinghy come after me from the island there and just fuckin' start shooting. First they don't hit nothing, then I hear some bad noises up forward, and I figure I'm next if I don't heave to, so I do."

He looked from me to Turgeon to me. For approval, I guess.

"You ever see this guy before?"

"The geek or—"

"The guy who paid you."

"No, never seen him before."

"Describe him."

"I don't know, average-looking guy. Maybe fifty, sixty,

not in such good shape. Suit, tie. Limped a little."

I coughed, but not from my cold. "What?"

"He was gimpy. Didn't notice it when I first talked to him, cause he hailed me from this wharf post he's leaning against and I come over to him. But after he talks to me, he waits till I get back to my boat to leave, and I notice him going up the walk, favoring his leg."

"Which leg?"

"Which?"

"Yes. Which leg did he favor?"

"I don't know. I mean, I didn't pay that kind of attention, you know? I was just figuring on seeing the guy one more time, to give him the goods and get the other thousand, and I figure I can recognize him good enough for that."

Turgeon was watching me now. I said, "Keep him here till I say otherwise."

As I opened the door, Craven said, "Look, you guys want, I'll give you the thousand."

"What?"

"The thousand I got up front. Let me loose, I'll bring it here."

I said, "You'd be a mite short."

"You did well, Nusby."

He didn't smile, the forty-five laid in his lap like a little kitten whose weight he didn't mind. Either his body required him to sit stretched out in the chair outside the General's bedroom as though it were a chaise lounge, or the cramped quarters at the island made him want to sit that way.

Nusby said, "I was in the dinghy because the General wanted to be there. The cold air, the long wait, it might have killed him."

"Is he awake?"

"Only because he can't sleep without knowing what happened to Kenny."

"I wish I could tell him. How are Allen and Janine?"

"She was upset when I picked them up in the dinghy. When she realized at the dock what had happened, she tried to attack the lobsterman. I am told she became hysterical during the ride back here with O'Meara."

"You didn't come back with them?"

"I stayed at the dock to secure things. O'Meara came back for me after he dropped the General and the others here."

"Where is Janine now?"

"With her husband. Dr. Allen gave her a sedative and put her to bed."

"You must be pretty tired yourself."

"I'll manage. Do you need to see the General now?"

"I'm afraid so."

Rising, Nusby held the forty-five like a soldier would, index finger outside the trigger guard. He opened the door for me. "Please use your judgment on how long to stay."

Inside, I could see the General in shadow, his face looking five years closer to the grave than it had when he'd left the dinghy only hours earlier.

"General?"

"Langway." His voice was hoarse. "Come closer, please."

I drew even with the bed and turned away from him to sneeze.

"Sit."

"I'm all right."

"So I can . . . see you more easily."

I sat on the edge of the bed. His eyes lay low under the

brows, the last remnants of Japanese defenders in a cave.

"Report, please."

"I blew it."

"Please keep talking . . . Hard for me . . . to ask questions."

"The lobsterman, Craven, was just a decoy. I think I know how the kidnappers pulled the switch on the bag, but Turgeon and I didn't see anything along the coast twelve miles in either direction. The money's gone, and I don't know where Kenny is."

"Do you know who . . . took him?"

"I think so."

"Will you honor . . . our agreement?"

I shook my head. "I have to bring in the authorities, now, General. We have no leverage for getting Kenny back ourselves anymore."

"No . . . no . . ."

"General, there's been a killing."

The eyes flared briefly. "Craven?"

"No. Jaime Rivas."

"He was . . . involved then?"

"Probably. I found him dead on Wednesday. Once the cops find him—and they will, as soon as some neighbor starts complaining about a stink from his basement—they'll start nosing around here as his last place of employment."

"I can . . . protect us . . . from that."

"I don't think so. Besides, if we leave it as is, there'll be no way of finding . . . of finding Kenny."

His eyes closed, but his lips kept moving. "Do what . . . you must."

I stood up, walked out the door past Nusby and downstairs to the library to call Paul Iannelli.

Chapter Twenty-one

Iannelli pressed the transmit button on the radio and said, "Right. Team Alpha, out." To me, he said, "They're at the back entrance." To Detective Lieutenant Quinn from the Saugus Police Department, he said, "Okay with you if we kick in?"

Quinn, a barrel-chested man of forty or so, looked at the four special agents from the FBI wearing white on blue windbreakers, his own three uniforms with shotguns, and the EMT's behind their ambulances. "Your party."

"Thanks. All right if Langway here goes in with us?"

"Yeah, but not in the first wave, okay?"

I said, "Fine with me." Sneezing twice, I wiped my nose on my sleeve. "Remember, Fred used to be a cop."

Without inflection, Quinn said, "Used to be."

Iannelli nodded to his people, Quinn to his. Weapons were drawn, Kevlar vests readjusted, a female agent and a male cop spit, almost in unison. I just watched the old brown house, the Nusbys' Cavalier parked next to Fred's Plymouth in the driveway.

Iannelli clicked the radio and said, "Team Bravo, on the count of ten."

Iannelli then moved forward, remarkably graceful for his size, the other FBI and police forming a vee-wedge. The first agent hit the front door with a sledgehammer, Paul diving in low as the next agent behind him went in high. I could hear the back door give way.

Two more agents and two cops entered the front. The clumping of booted feet on the stairs.

From inside, a voice I didn't recognize. "All clear."

Then Iannelli's voice. "All clear. I say again, all clear. The house is secure."

I followed Quinn's broad back over the threshold.

Iannelli was holstering his weapon, bending over Fred on the floor, two fingers perfunctorily pressing on the side of Fred's throat. The female agent was doing the same for Gloria Rivas, slumped forward at a table.

Iannelli said to the other agent, "Get the EMT's anyway." In a louder voice, he called out, "Anybody see the kid?"

The agent next to Gloria said, "Might want to read this, Paul."

The Essex County Assistant District Attorney tented her fingers and said, "Why don't you tell me all about it, too?"

I blew my nose for the tenth time in the last hour. We were sitting at Fred's kitchen table, a male State Police investigator taking down what she had said and what I was about to answer, despite the tape machine rolling next to the salt and pepper. Iannelli and Quinn hung back against the refrigerator, the technical personnel having their usual track meet in the front room around the bodies.

I kept the handkerchief in my hand. The prosecutor's name was Anna Biagi. She had frizzy hair and the kind of eyes you expect to see on a creature that has to kill every day in order to eat.

"I was contacted by General Alexander Van Horne to look into the disappearance of his great-grandson, Kenny. I apprised Special Agent Iannelli of my feeling that the disappearance might be a kidnapping."

She turned to Iannelli. "When was this?"

"Monday evening, about 7:00. At my home."

Biagi came back to me. "Go on."

I took her through my interrogations, the ransom calls, the harbor scene.

"When Turgeon mentioned the bag was wet, I got suspicious. There wasn't enough chop to soak it, that high on the transom and all. When it turned out the bag had been switched, and especially after Craven told us about having created the wake on instruction, I realized what happened. While we were all watching Craven on the lobsterman approach the bow of the sailboat, a scuba diver must have surfaced behind the *Remagen*, reached up to the picket on the lifeline, switched bags, and submerged again."

"Taking the real money to shore and leaving you with the newspaper."

"Right."

She said, "You figure that's why the instructions on denomination were so specific?"

"Yes. I figure they needed to switch a bag that was pretty generic but with the right shape and weight to its contents. With tens, twenties and fifties, the switched bag might be too heavy or too light compared to the real one."

"So the kidnappers expected it would be a while before you noticed the switch?"

"I don't know. I don't see how Fred and Gloria could have known that we were going to intercept the lobsterman. I sure as hell didn't tell them. I figure that they were just leaving themselves options if we did try something and got our hands on the bag earlier rather than later."

"Earlier?"

"Early enough, I mean, for us to tip to what they were doing and go beating the reeds for the scuba angle."

Biagi sat back, plainly dissatisfied. "But you and Turgeon tried beating the weeds anyway."

"Yeah, but we really didn't know what to look for, other than somebody along the shore doing something wrong. There are dozens of private roads north and south of the harbor. Fred could have left his car and clothes anywhere within kicking distance of the *Remagen*."

She arched her head back toward the living room. "He doesn't look to me like he was in such great shape for diving."

I shrugged. "He was a frogman in the Navy. Long time ago, but maybe you don't forget."

"What, like riding a bike?"

Iannelli said, "We found a wet suit downstairs. Tanks, weight belt, the whole nine yards. Still dripping salt water. The trunk of his car's the same way. Also found the voice scrambler he probably used to make the ransom calls."

Biagi still didn't like it. "How does Fred Dooley connect up with Rivas?"

"Which one?"

"Start with Jaime. He's the one that Boston's gagging over now, right?"

"Jaime Rivas was working security at the estate when Fred and I checked out their system last spring. We both met him then."

"And Gloria?"

I gestured around the room, but meaning to take in the whole house. "After Fred's wife left him, things went kind of downhill. Fast. I noticed him talking to Gloria, kind of joking with her at the estate back in April. I didn't think anything of it, I was glad to see him getting back a little into the swing of things. After he started dipping into our partnership for more than his share, I figured he was dropping it on gambling and booze. If Gloria entered into it, I never knew."

I sneezed three times. Biagi waited with an expression she probably thought was sympathetic.

Finally, the prosecutor said, "So you figure Fred comes up with the idea of kidnapping the boy, brings in Jaime and Gloria as accomplices."

"That's what I figure."

"Then why does this Jaime quit his estate job two weeks before the thing goes down?"

"Maybe just to throw people off him. Plus, with Gloria still on the inside, both for the security system and calming Kenny at the important points, I'm guessing Fred didn't need him so much anymore."

"Except for the actual kidnapping."

"Right. I figure Gloria gets Kenny from his bed, some story about a game, maybe a treasure hunt, you fill it in. They leave the house on one of Turgeon's trips to the main gate. They get out by the fence somewhere and Jaime's on the other side with his car. Then it's up and over the fence with Kenny, and Jaime brings him down here. Gloria goes back to bed, and Jaime goes back to Dorchester. With Fred and me being called in on the investigation, they get a bonus: Fred can keep up with the progress on the case."

"Then why kill Jaime?"

"I don't know. Maybe Jaime gets nervous. I have to figure Jaime's house or here is where they're keeping the boy, with here the better bet."

"Why not some place else?"

"Because this is as isolated as they're likely to find, plus Fred can stay in touch with me by phone. Probably Jaime's the main day-care provider, though, since Fred is out running around for me. Kenny would know him, maybe think it was part of the game to have one of the guards from the estate around."

Biagi paused. "Maybe that's why Jaime left before the night of the snatch. To be available to watch over the boy."

"Maybe."

"But then what happens to the boy after Fred kills Jaime?"

I exhaled, loudly. "I don't know."

She reached over to the right of the trooper, who seemed to welcome the pause by shaking out his writing hand. She came back to me, dangling an evidence baggie with a note scratched on scrap paper inside it.

"You ever see this before?"

"Something like it was next to Gloria out there as I walked by her."

"By her body."

I said, "Right. The one with the black hole by one ear and no ear on the other side."

Biagi said, "Read what this says."

I took it from her with my left hand and angled it for the best light, putting my right hand behind it for contrast. " '*Dios mio,* I kill him. He hide the money, hide Kenny but no tell me when'—no, sorry, I think she says 'where' here. 'If he kill him? *?Dios mio, Dios mio, porque me has abandonado?* What can—'." I turned the note over. Nothing on the other side. "That's it."

The prosecutor watched me for a minute. "You read the Spanish part like you can speak Spanish."

"A little. I did two years in San Antonio."

"What does the Spanish sentence mean?"

"It's from the Catholic Mass, I think. It's 'My God, my God, why have you forsaken me?' "

"You recognize this as her handwriting?"

"I can't be sure, but I took exemplars from everybody at the estate on Monday. It looks like hers, but I can give you her exemplar for lab comparison."

"Do that."

She returned the bagged note to the trooper. I coughed and closed my eyes.

I heard Iannelli say, "It's almost noon. Langway here has been up for a day and a half. Anything else you need right now?"

I opened my eyes. Biagi looked at the trooper, who shook his head.

Biagi said, "Not from the homicide end." She looked back to me. "You going home?"

"Eventually. I'd like to stop back in Beacon Harbor first."

"Why?

"Tell my client how all this worked out."

Lieutenant Quinn spoke for the first time in an hour. "Good luck on that one."

Chapter Twenty-two

"Langway!"

Kerstein's voice came from the bottom of the central staircase. Halfway up, I stopped and turned.

"I understand things grew a little dicey last night." He had a drink in his hand, the other curled around the last post of the banister.

"You've had a long time to think of an opening line, counselor. You should have done better."

A superior smile, glass raised in toast. "E for Effort, then?"

I sneezed. "Tell you what, Kerstein. You didn't want to play in the game, you don't belong in the locker room."

As I resumed the climb, he said, "Even the loser's locker room?"

Lila was at the branch of corridor heading to the north wing. "Matthew?"

I sneezed and coughed.

She bit her lip. "Are you sick?"

"Not now, all right?"

"I just wanted to say—"

"Lila, not now."

"I'm sorry," she said and headed toward her room.

I moved into the south wing. Nusby wasn't in the chair, and the chair wasn't by the General's bedroom door anymore. I knocked instead at the screening room entrance.

The door cracked open, half of Nusby's face peering around the edge. Over his shoulder he said, "General, it's Mr. Langway."

I heard something, barely a croak. Nusby opened the door for me, then left the room, closing it behind him.

The image of Kenny flashed and flickered across the screen in the darkened room. There was no sound this time, just the pantomime of a boy, forever young and unspoiled, cavorting around the yard, tagging and being tagged by Gloria Rivas in a game with flexible rules.

"Langway?"

He was propped up in a chair with hassock, a blanket over most of his body. As I drew even with him, I could see a plug stuffed into his left ear.

He made a motion with his hand that could have meant anything. "The headphones . . . too much . . . pressure."

I pulled over a chair, sat heavily into it.

"Report."

"I told you Jaime Rivas was killed. It looks like Fred Dooley, my partner, and Gloria Rivas were in on the kidnapping. Gloria killed Fred, then herself, sometime last night. No indication of where Kenny is. Or the money."

"Don't care . . . about money."

"I do. I never should have agreed to such a complicated pick-up."

"Kenny . . . any hope?"

It was like listening to a voice over very long distance with a bad connection. I coughed hard.

"There's always hope, General. But, even with the Bureau and the local departments in it now, it gets less likely the more time that goes by."

He blinked rapidly. "My son . . ."

I hunched a little closer. "Yes, General?"

He moved his head, left to right on the pillow. "No . . . my son . . ."

It was hard to follow him. "You in pain? You want me to call Allen?"

"God . . . dammit. Kenny . . . is . . . my son."

I'm not sure I breathed. I know I didn't speak.

"Janine . . . eight years ago . . . Helluva woman . . . irresistible . . . Made me feel . . . first time, years . . . worth it, but . . . too old . . . seed too old . . . retarded."

The last word seemed wrenched from his throat.

"Money . . ."

I said, "General, we don't know where it is."

Van Horne moved his head a fraction this time. To his right. "Your money . . . here . . ."

I rose high enough to see a hard-sided Samsonite next to him on the other side of his chair.

"General, I didn't . . . I didn't keep our bargain."

The head turned to me, a gargoyle's smile, a small rally. "Police . . . stupid . . . You got them . . . Turnabout . . . yours."

His hand flopped toward the case.

"General, I can't."

"Take it . . . or the others . . . will . . ."

I stood, steadying myself by holding the back of his chair. I stooped, lifted the case by the handle. Heavy, but not like the green bag with the hundreds in it.

As I moved toward the door and past the rack of video equipment behind him, I heard, "Sound . . . louder . . . louder . . ."

I found the volume dial and advanced it half again as high as it had been.

Outside the door, Nusby examined my face.

I said, "Maybe you'd best alert the rest of the family."

He thanked me for my concern and went back inside to the General, alone.

★ ★ ★ ★ ★

I am inside the plantation house, a decrepit cross between a French chateau and a Mississippi mansion. Behind me in the upstairs corridor, Ike is dragging the village headman, doped up and bound and gagged. Omar is at a listening post, thirty meters up the road, just in case the rest of the headman's cronies come back at the wrong time.

We step over the guard Ike killed at the head of the stairs. We left another in a closet next to the front door and two more in the bushes at the beginning of the elliptical drive. All dead by knife. One of the drive sentries I killed, my blade shoved into the side of his neck and wiggled around, like cleaning out a walnut. My hand over the sentry's mouth, his uneven teeth rough against my palm, reflexively trying to bite me.

Through an open window, I hear a voice, Vietnamese, then two, three more. Gregarious, joking and singing. I stare at my PRC-6 handheld radio, astonished that Omar has not warned us from the listening post. Then I realize, he must be dead.

I turn around. Ike has already cut the throat of the headman and put out his eyes, I don't know in what order.

He says, "Fuckin' Omar. He fuckin' fell asleep and then decided they were too fuckin' close to him to warn us. Fuck, fuck, fuck!"

"Maybe they killed him."

"No fuckin' way. They ace him, they come in like ghosts, not fuckin' New Year's Eve. L.T., we gotta get out of here."

I stare down at the PRC-6, my thumb just off the squelch button. If I hit it, a noise like static will jump out, a way to signal someone. A noise just like it will jump out of Omar's radio at the listening post, barely into the trees off the road.

Ike grabs my arm, yanking. "C'mon, L.T. Out the back."

I say, "Let's buy some time first." I hit squelch three times, then a fourth.

I can't hear the Vietnamese singing anymore. I can hear running, through the bush, and shouting. Then small arms fire.
I rush past Ike toward the back of the house.

My hand was on the phone before I was aware it was ringing. I raised my head off the desk in my office, reminding me of Gloria Rivas, slumped over the table at Fred's house, the wrong side of her head up. I swallowed what was rising in my throat and lifted the receiver.

"Langway."

"Matthew, it's Paul."

"Paul?"

"Paul Iannelli."

"Right, Paul."

"Are you all right, Matthew?"

I pressed on my blocked sinus passages and looked at the clock. "Must have fallen asleep for a couple of hours."

"No problem. I've got agents up at the General's house and running down your list of the people Rivas knew down in Boston." A slight change in tone. "Some of them are looking into Fred and you, too. Sorry."

"Can't be helped now."

"Gloria's friends are scared to talk with us, but what else is new? We did find some shit in her room at the estate. Some kind of oil, but the agent can't place it so we're sending it on to the lab."

I sneezed and coughed. "Gloria told me it was some kind of home remedy from the old country."

"We'll check it out. Preliminary from ballistics says the gun that did Fred and Gloria was the same one used on Jaime over in Upham's Corner. Imagine, Fred holding onto a hot piece like that."

"Should have had better sense."

"About a lot of things. He even had Gloria call him from the estate."

"What?"

"Yeah. On Sunday night. We pulled it off the phone company's computer. Starting at 7:52 p.m., we got eight minutes, fourteen seconds of elapsed time to your office number."

"Jesus. I should have checked that."

"Don't beat yourself over this one, Matthew. Nobody could have predicted Fred'd turn like this."

I took a breath. "Thanks, Paul. Any sign of the boy?"

"No. Can't find the money, either. We've got people going every which way on this now, but it's kind of late."

"You need me for anything else?"

A pause. "Why?"

"After I clean up some things here at the office, I'm closing it down."

"Going out of business, you mean?"

I rested my forehead on my upturned palm. "No, but maybe after a while. First I'm going up to Maine."

"Maine?"

"Yeah, Paul, Maine. State of."

"Why are you going up there, Matthew?"

"Because I'm sick to death of this whole mess, and I drove up there a couple days ago and felt as good as I've felt in a while. I've just got to blow off some time, get myself back on track. Okay?"

"Okay with me. With the Bureau's end of all this. Anything you got that's not in the file you gave me?"

"No. You send off the note from Fred's house and Gloria's exemplar?"

"Hour ago. We're all set there."

"Paul, I appreciate your understanding. Really."

"Hey, it's been a tough time all around. How's the General doing?"

"Slipping away. Seems like short time to me, but I'm no doctor."

"Well, enjoy your trip, Matthew. Call me when you get back, huh?"

"Sure."

Carrying the General's Samsonite downstairs, I sneezed, then checked my watch. Too late to make the bank's safe deposit hours. Fuck it.

As I came out of the building, a girl approached me. She looked only vaguely familiar until she smiled. Crooked teeth.

"Excuse me, sir. I'm sorry to bother you, but I'm really up against it. I was riding down from Burlington, Vermont, and somebody slashed my purse and—"

"—stole all your money and now all you need is ten bucks for a ticket home."

The smile backed off a little, the girl trying to place me.

I said, "You know what the penalty is for Obtaining Money Under False Pretenses?"

She closed her coat, hugging herself. "I'm just panhandling here—"

"No! No, you're not. You're telling lies, lies to get people to give money to you." I grabbed her wrist with my free hand. "That's against the law, honey. That's wrong! That's very, very wrong!"

She was twisting away from me. Then she cried out, and I realized I had been doing the twisting. I let go.

She turned and ran from me. Stumbling on a broken cement block in the sidewalk, she caught her balance and kept on going.

Shivering, I got in the Blazer, started up, and drove home.

Chapter Twenty-three

Too tired to deal with the garage doors, I left the Blazer in the driveway. I went in the kitchen door, juggling the Samsonite and thinking about a beer at the refrigerator. Sneezing, I decided a couple of scotches might make better bedmates. I climbed the stairs to the living room, almost crossing to the decanter before I saw her.

Lounging in one of the easy chairs. White, clingy wool dress, right leg crossed over left, black stockings. A thirty-eight Chief's Special in her right hand, probably the one from next to my bed. The muzzle was pointed casually at me, a look in her eyes like the one Biagi the assistant DA had.

I said, "The General told me, Janine."

"About what?"

"About Kenny being his son."

A dismissive flip of the head. "I thought it would be a good hold on him, get me the biggest chunk of the estate. Who knew he'd live so long or that the kid would come out retarded?"

"Just bad luck, huh?"

"That's what I thought." She gestured with her gun hand. "What's in the case?"

"Blood money."

"There's a lot of that around these days."

I clicked the catches, holding the case open as though I were prying apart the jaws of a crocodile. "A hundred grand, Janine. For killing the kidnappers."

"Fred and Gloria."

"That's right."

The features softened. "Oh, Matt, I'm so sorry."

I closed the Samsonite and stuck it behind the door. "Just put the gun down, all right?"

"I was only trying to surprise you." She set it on the coffee table, the butt clattering loud enough to jeopardize the glass.

Coughing, I took the top off the booze, but turned to her before pouring it. "Do you have any idea how stupid it is for you to even be here?"

"I wasn't followed."

"What if I'm being watched? Did you think of that?"

"There's no reason for you to be watched. Besides, everyone understood when I said I had to get away for a while. I drove my car to Union Square, then took a cab. I even cut through a back yard and used my back door key to get in."

"I had this whole place cleaned down to the paint, so there wouldn't be even a suspicion of us having been together since last April. Then you fuck that up by coming down here now."

"I couldn't help it, Matt. I want you, I had to see you."

Turning back to the scotch, I lifted the decanter to pour. She said, "Wait! I really do have a surprise for you."

"Another surprise from you, I don't think I need right now."

She was up behind me, pressing a breast against each of my shoulder blades, then rolling her torso and pelvis in a syncopated manner. "I'm awfully hot for you. And wet."

I felt myself stirring.

She coaxed the decanter from my hand, settling it gently back on the counter. "My surprise is better than this." I felt her break contact and myself leaning back, stepping back to re-establish it.

Janine moved to the armchair, bending over so I could see what she really wanted to show me. Then she straightened, holding a wine bottle by the corkscrew already driven down into the cork. "I wanted to open this myself, to let it breathe, but I couldn't get the damned cork out."

I walked to her, taking the bottle and reading the label. "Chateau LaTour, 1970."

"Only the best for you, Matt. For us."

"With my cold, I'm not sure I'll enjoy it."

"Just the first of many. Go ahead, we can afford to waste it."

The way the General looked that morning, I couldn't see him missing it from the wine cellar. I wedged the bottle between my thighs, squeezing it as I put my left hand on the neck of the bottle and exerting increasing pull with my right till the cork popped free.

She went down behind the armchair again, retrieving two goblets this time. She poured us each half a glass, swirled hers, and inhaled. Clinking her glass to mine, she said, "To our life together."

I skipped the bouquet, swallowing one, two, three mouthfuls. Even with my nose clogged, the wine, without being permitted to aerate, was musty and harsh. It felt appropriate, somehow, to treat with contempt a bottle of wine that cost as much as I used to make in a week.

I poured some more, drank it, then settled into the chair. Janine put down her glass, gliding her hand over the front of her dress to prove she had on nothing underneath. "I've been thinking about you. Only about you for so long now."

"But not at all about Kenny?"

She dropped her hands and the bedroom expression at the same time. "I told you it was an accident. I was giving him his bath, and he swiped at me with the brush. Almost put my eye out. You didn't know him, what a pest he could be. I just meant to slap him, but I caught him as he was getting up from the tub, and he slipped and fell back on that horrible faucet. His head . . . My God, what more can I do to prove it to you?"

"You mean, to prove it was an accident?"

"I told you! I didn't mean to hurt him, much less kill him." She came over to me. Small, uncertain steps, the naughty little girl now, craving forgiveness. She dropped to her knees. "If I intended to kill him, I wouldn't have done it with twenty people in the house. My God, Matt, I wouldn't even have killed *Kenny*. I'd have killed the General and been done with it."

I gestured with the wine glass. "You're right there. Your cut of the inheritance is a lot bigger if the General dies before Kenny."

Janine cradled her chin on my knee, rocking her head back and forth. "The money doesn't matter to me, Matt. We faked the kidnapping to keep me from a manslaughter charge, not to make me rich. What matters is you, and what you think."

What I thought. When I didn't respond, she said, "Where's Kenny now?"

"Downstairs. Still in my carry-box." I thought back to Monday, folding Kenny's body so he would fit in the carry-box. Breaking his arms and legs, really, then lugging him past Turgeon and Zoubek to the Blazer. "By the way, you did a good job of sewing him into that ski suit. He wasn't even smelling when I took him out of the zipper bag hanging in your closet."

Janine thrust her face hard toward mine. "All right. You helped me when I needed you. If you need to tell me the

. . . details now, you go ahead. Tell me everything you had to do to save me."

Was that the thing about her that made me feel ten feet tall? Her willingness to take the risk but share the responsibility? "Fred was happy to go along with faking the kidnapping to cover the killing. Hell, he was so desperate after what he'd done to the business, he'd have agreed to buggering the Pope to get off the hook. It looked as though he killed Jaime quick and clean, by the way. No muss, no bother."

"I'm glad. Jaime wasn't a bad guy."

I felt it flowing, tumbling out of me. "Without Jaime, the cops will never think that Gloria wasn't having an affair with Fred. Her people are clamming up, just like I thought they would. My telling her to drive to Fred's house on an 'errand' for you worked perfectly, and set up the security staff to corroborate it. Fred even figured we were going to take her to Jaime's before we killed her."

The wine seemed to be easing the cold symptoms, so I took another swallow of it. I settled in, getting to share how clever I'd had to be to bail her out. It even felt good to rub her nose in it a little. "The look on Fred's face when I asked him to turn around. Like he really thought I'd let him off the hook after what he'd done to me, the way he'd cheated on our partnership, our friendship. Of course, that was nothing compared to the look on Gloria's face when I turned back to her. She wasn't really getting it yet. She didn't know Jaime was dead. She remembered Fred as working with me, so she'd even waited for him at his house while he went off with the scuba gear to Beacon Harbor. But then she saw me shoot him."

"Gloria was almost a friend to me, Matt."

"She started to stand up, so I said 'Sit down,' first in

257

English, then in Spanish. I told her that Fred was the kidnapper, the bad one, and that I needed her as a witness. She didn't buy it, she just soiled herself, and started to cry. Which wasn't half-bad, actually. Lent just the right chemical touch to the scene. After I shot her, I pressed the weapon into her hand and fired a few rounds with her into the wall past Fred's body, so it would seem she used the last one on herself. Then I put down the note, copying her handwriting close enough, given I'd already replaced her true exemplar in the file with my version of it."

"So when the FBI checks her handwriting against the suicide note . . ."

"They'll both look like her handwriting, because both are my copies of her handwriting."

"The government trained you well for this sort of thing, Matt."

"I may have been trained for it, Janine, but you were born to it."

"I'm truly sorry about Fred. I know—"

"Fred was a piece of shit!" I took another swig of the wine. "Fred was somebody I stood up for, carried. Then he screwed me, Janine. Besides, once you called me at the office on Sunday night, it had to be Fred."

"I told you. I was so scared. Kenny was dead, I'd killed him. Who was going to believe it was an accident?"

"Doesn't matter. The Bureau or the cops would have come into it eventually and found out about the call to our office from the estate on Sunday night." I tilted my head forward, a little further than I intended. "Once you made that call to me, Janine, it had to be Fred. Without him in the frame with Gloria, the cops would never buy that call being made ten hours before you discover Kenny 'missing.' "

"The tub. Did I—"

"You washed the blood away from the faucet enough to fool the eye, but you nearly fucked us good with the window stuff."

"Matt, I—"

"His window didn't have to be opened, and if it was, Turgeon sees a panel light come on in central station."

"But I didn't know that, Matt. They told us months ago that they disconnected the windows."

"Just from the Klaxon alarm, not from the panel lights."

"Matt, I'm sorry, okay? You told me on the phone to leave the note on Kenny's pillow so the General would call you on the security system. After we hung up, I figured our 'kidnappers' would need some way to take Kenny out."

"Yes, but—"

"You said we couldn't see each other alone if you did come to the estate. If we couldn't plan things, what was I supposed to do?"

"Forget it. Nobody's going to unravel the window business now."

"Good." Relieved. Then she shook her head. "So many people dead . . ."

"Don't even think about it." I drained my glass. "I don't."

Janine had started undoing my belt. "I want you so much . . . so much . . ."

"You know, you've ruined me for other women."

"I want you to melt in my mouth, Matt. In the bedroom."

I got up, staggered and reeled a little. "Jesus, between no sleep and the wine . . ."

"Don't worry," she said, clutching me by the waist the way a trainer helps a sacked, woozy quarterback off the field. "I'm going to do all the work."

I opened my eyes, feeling incredibly relaxed. Almost at peace, except for the cold and a little nausea. Too much wine on an empty stomach.

Lying in bed, I was propped up from behind by my pillows. The radio was on, still the easy listening station Janine had tuned in for mood music. Even without the music, she would have been . . .

Janine was in front of my bureau, her back to me. Naked, as I was, but using a handkerchief to open the drawers and using a ruler to lift up my sweaters and such.

I said, "Hey?" but it came out softly, like a whisper.

She turned, startled, then smiling. "Matt, you're awake." She set the hankie and the ruler on top of the dresser, then came back to me, casting a sideways glance at my groin.

"You don't look like you're ready again."

"What the hell . . ." For a second, I forgot what I was going to say.

" . . . am I doing? Darling, I'm looking for the million, the ransom."

Janine went back to the dresser. I could save her the trouble, tell her it was buried near a park in Saugus, still in the green trash bag I'd taken off Fred. But it seemed easier just to get up. I tried, but only grunted. I wanted to bend forward, see what was the matter. I couldn't.

"What's . . . what's going on?"

She spoke over her shoulder, almost absently. "Oh, now, don't think me too greedy, all right? I should have asked you about it downstairs, but I didn't want to push my luck. I'm not really looking for the ransom to take it with me. I love money, darling, but I wouldn't be caught dead with that green bag." She turned to me again, smiling. "And neither should you."

I couldn't think of what to say, what she was doing. "Why?"

"Why? Because I need to have the authorities still think that Fred and Gloria and Jaime were the kidnap team, Matt. I can't have anyone start to think you were in on it."

It didn't make any sense. I couldn't move, and Janine didn't make any sense.

"Please . . ."

"Oh, Matt," finishing with the dresser, going to the closet next, "I've tried to make you as comfortable as I can, but you see, I really couldn't go on seeing you, not after the way you and I were at each other's throats at the estate this week. It wouldn't look right. And we couldn't go away together for the same reason."

She mooned me from the closet floor, poking and prodding with the ruler, her voice muffled. "And I obviously can't leave you loose without our little love sessions to keep you in line on what you did and why you did it for me."

"What . . ." It sounded like I was bleating. "What's wrong . . ."

"With me, nothing. With you, a whole lot, I'm afraid. That Gloria Rivas, she wasn't just a kidnapper, she was a real psycho. I bet it'll turn out that she had poison in her room, a little concoction she called La Flor Blanca, but we'd know better as 'hemlock.' I bet it would even turn out that Kenny had traces of it in his system, if he was ever found and autopsied. Yes, that Gloria, she probably fed it to him as a folk remedy for hyper-active kids, though I don't remember her phrasing it that way."

Janine seemed satisfied with the closet and moved back toward me. "And the psycho part? Well, after the police

261

find you, and check that wine bottle in the living room, why I just bet they'll go back to the estate and find four more bottles doctored the same way, with a tiny little hypodermic mark through the foil wrapping and cork on top. Hemlock, injected into the General's wine to kill him, the same way she killed you. By accident of course, and kind of ironic, too. You shoplifting that bottle when you were checking the cellar on Monday for any security breaches, then not noticing the smell through the cold Lila and Turgeon told us all you had."

Jesus. Jesus Mary, somebody help me. I was salivating, but my throat felt full, thick, like I had food there I ought to be washing down with drink. "Why . . . why . . . ?"

She laid her hand on my cheek, caressing it. "Because it had to be someone, darling, and it wasn't going to be me. Sorry I had to turn on you."

Turn . . . Turnabout.

Janine began to dress, pantyhose first. "I've gone through your whole house except for the basement. I've been putting that off till the end, so I could take Kenny out on the lift to your Blazer. Remember when we made love on that lift? Those were the days, huh Matt? After I put Kenny somewhere safe, I'll return your car, put it in the garage, and go back to the estate, refreshed but still grieving. Tell you what, though."

She leaned over me, breasts teasing my chest, tongue working its way over my lips. "If you'll tell me where you put the ransom, I'll stay here with you so you don't die alone."

I tried to bite her tongue, but couldn't make my mouth work quick or hard enough. It reminded me of something, someone trying to bite me, but I couldn't remember, I couldn't quite . . .

"No sale, Matt? Guess I can't exactly blame you. By the way, the poison works on the extremities first, slowly building its way to your throat. When you feel the gorge rise, it won't be too much longer."

Janine shimmied into her dress. "I don't really need to find the ransom, by the way. I just need to be sure they won't find it here when they find you. I don't even need the money you flashed downstairs. Imagine anyone leaving so many thousands behind anywhere? That ought to eliminate everybody but Gloria right there."

Smoothing the material at her hips, Janine said, "You want to know why I don't need the money, darling? Because the General died this afternoon, the old warhorse. No one will ever find Kenny to prove that the retarded son died before his aged, natural father. That makes Allen and me the proud parents of one . . . hundred . . . million . . . dollars."

She leaned back over my face, another sloppy kiss. "I'm afraid this will have to be good-bye, Matt. I hate to say it, but I was really quite fond of you. On the other hand, for all his liver spots and wrinkles, the General was twice the man you were in bed doing the worst stud work of his life, which was how all this mess really started anyway."

As Janine passed the dresser, she picked up the hankie and the ruler. Moving through the doorway, she said, "Don't worry about my wineglass. I'll rinse it and put it away."

I tried to call to her, but my voice sounded like Kenny's, so I stopped.

I think I just closed my eyes, but when I opened them again, at least, when I think I opened them, I couldn't see anything, not even a streetlight. I still can't. I do remember hearing Janine working the lift in the basement and starting the Blazer.

It's a different disk jockey on the radio. Less music, more talk. He just said something about the time, but it's not making much sense to me anymore.

I wet myself, then evacuated. The stink alone should keep me awake.

I can feel it in my chest, that squeezing-hand sensation. It's so hard to swallow, I stopped trying, but the saliva from my mouth and the mucus from my nose keep running back down my throat, and I'm not gagging. I think I should be gagging.

My lungs don't want to work right, like they're closing up shop for the night. Dizzy. Not enough . . . oxygen, I guess.

Now the new . . . disk jockey's . . . signing off . . . Jesus Mary, help me . . . Jesus Mary, pray for